THE GHOST OF JOHNNY NICHOLS

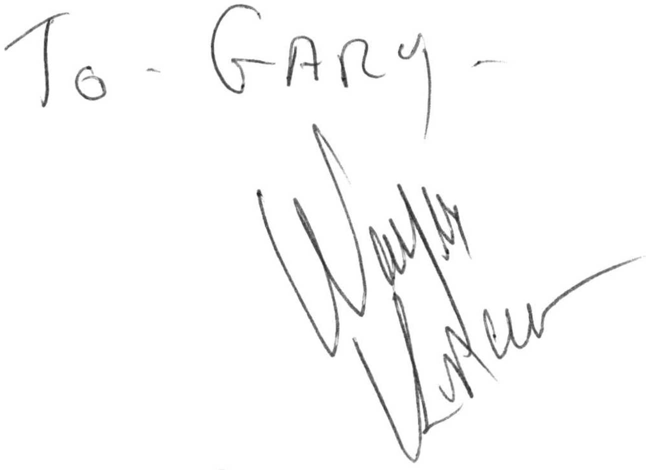

Wayne Hancock

Hancock Press, Fort Smith, AR

THE GHOST OF JOHNNY NICHOLS

Wayne Hancock

Hancock Press, Fort Smith, AR

The Ghost of Johnny Nichols

To order additional copies of this book, contact:
www.hancockpress.com
www.amazon.com
www.barnesandnoble.com

Published in the United States of America

ISBN *hardcover: 9781938366727*
ISBN *softcover*: 9781938366734

THE GHOST OF JOHNNY NICHOLS

A novel based on the true story of

John S. Nichols, a Rebel Soldier

mistakenly hung as a bushwhacker

during the Civil War

October 28th, 1863: We had a most affecting scene in prison yesterday. A young man named Nichols is sentenced to be hung next Friday. His sister came to see him, the interview was heart rending. The poor fellow had ministers with him all evening. It is to be hoped they were faithful and fed him with the pure bread of life. There are none but they need the aid of spiritual comfort at such a time, and woe unto the hand that should offer them husks. Nichols, no doubt, is a sinner, like the rest of us, but he thought he was right in fighting the enemy in his own way. Bushwhacking is the mode of warfare practiced in Missouri by both parties, but any candid man must acknowledge that the Federals have been the worst and the most destructive. Look at the long list of men butchered in cold blood: Jim Lasly and two others, as they were coming home one Sunday from church—Lasly dying in his wife's arms; Col. Owens, Frisby McCullough, and hundreds of others, shot down like dogs, when they were helpless prisoners, many of them, as Lasly and his fellow victims, having taken no part in the war. These things will come up when we see the hand so red with innocent blood, daring to pretend to lift itself in vengeance...**From the journal of Captain Griffin Frost while a prisoner at the Gratiot Street Federal Prison (pronounced-'grass-shut') in St. Louis, Missouri.**

Chapter 1

October 16th, 2012:

Sedalia, Missouri – The football game between the Smith Cotton High School Tigers and the Raytown High School Blue Jays of Raytown, Missouri, had ended in 21 to 20 victory for the Tigers and the local fans whooped and yelled as they came pouring out of their nearly new stadium southwest of Sedalia. It was a sweet victory because the Blue Jays were picked to finish high in their conference this year and usually beat the Tigers handily.

Johnny Clayton and his girlfriend, Mary Schroeder, were celebrating with the rest of the crowd as they made their way to Johnny's 2008 Mustang in the parking lot. John William Clayton Jr., or J.W. as his parents called him, had been given the Mustang by them as a gift when he graduated from Smith Cotton in 2011, third in his class. He had been awarded a two year scholarship to the University of Missouri at the Columbia campus and, with the Mustang, he could come home to visit on his free week-ends.

Mary was a senior at Smith Cotton and she had been dating Johnny for nearly two years. She lived with her parents on a farm a short distance southwest of Sedalia and rode the bus to school almost every day. Sometimes, if her mother had something to do in town, she would drop Mary off at school on her way. Her dad worked in the Maintenance Department at the Whiteman Air Force base at Knobnoster, Missouri which was about eight miles west from where they lived. The house they lived in and, the 116 acres of land that came with it, had been inherited from Mary's grandparents on her mother's side. Mary's dad didn't want to farm for a living so they rented the land out to a neighbor who pastured his cattle on it. They lived on the salary he made at Whiteman plus the rent from the land. Mary had an older brother who was currently serving in the Marine Corps.

They were almost to Johnny's car when someone yelled, "Hey guys, where are you going?"

It was Brad Compton and his girl Jeanie Crabtree. Johnny and Mary stopped and waited for them to catch up.

"We were going downtown to Eddie's for a Coke," Johnny yelled back, "and then maybe just cruise around a little bit. Do you want to come along, or do you have your car here?"

"I've been grounded for a week, so the Monte Carlo is home in the driveway," Brad said as they joined up. They continued on to Johnny's Mustang, "I got a ticket for speeding, so my dad grounded me for a week. He dropped Jeanie and me off at the game, and told us to get home the best way we could. He's pretty sore at me for getting the ticket."

Johnny looked over at Mary to get her thoughts and she nodded slightly. "Well," he said, "if you and Jeanie can squeeze into the back seat of the Mustang you can go with us. I'll take you guys home later."

It was 11:05 p.m. when Johnny guided the Mustang into the parking lot at Eddie's drive-in on Broadway and pulled into a slot close to the building. He pushed the buttons that rolled the windows down, and the mouthwatering odor of frying hamburgers wafted in on the slight breeze blowing from the west.

"Anybody hungry?" he asked, "Mary and I had hot dogs and popcorn at the game, so I'm just going to order drinks for us. How about you guys?" he asked over his shoulder.

Brad turned to Jeanie, "Are you hungry?" he asked. She shook her head. "We'll just get drinks, too," he said.

The young girl car-hop came to the driver's side window with pad in hand to take their order. "What can I get for you?" she asked.

"Mary and I will each have a medium Pepsi," Johnny said, and then turning to look over his shoulder and said to Brad, "how about you and Jeanie?"

"Make that four Pepsis," Brad said, "and just for the heck of it, bring us a large order of fries and we can pass them around."

"Did you get that?" Johnny asked the car-hop.

"I sure did," she said, "I'll bring your order right out." She turned and went back into the building.

Johnny felt a tap on his shoulder and turned to see Brad's hand holding a five dollar bill. "This should cover Jeanie and my drinks and the fries," he said.

"Thanks," Johnny said. He added another five to it as they waited for the car-hop to bring their order.

It wasn't long before they were cruising west on Broadway, sipping their drinks, listening to a soft rock FM station on the radio, and talking about the exciting football game they had just seen. When they came to Limit Street, Johnny turned left and drove south to 16th street. Going nowhere in particular, he turned right on 16th and headed west out of town. Next, he turned south on Quisenberry Road and somehow wound up heading south on County Road AA.

They were about three miles north of Green Ridge when Mary tapped Johnny's arm and whispered, "I have to go the bathroom, can you stop someplace?"

"Where?" he asked, "we're out in the country."

"I don't know," she said, "but I have to do something soon."

Johnny spotted a lane some farmer had built to get his machinery into and out of his field. It went in about 20 feet from the road and stopped at a gate in the fence. He backed into it, turned the motor off and said, "Jump out and go behind the car a few feet, you can do your business there."

Mary was desperate, "Okay," she said, "but don't you dare put your foot on the brake while I'm back there." She opened the car door, grabbed her little handbag from the console between them and slid out onto the hard ground.

"Me, too," Jeanie said as she squeezed out of the back seat right behind her.

In just a few minutes, the girls were climbing back into the car.

"Do you hear that?" Mary asked excitedly. She seemed frightened.

"What?" Johnny asked.

"Turn the radio off and listen," she said.

Johnny turned the radio off and the four of them sat silently with the windows down and strained to hear what had frightened Mary so. They soon heard a 'clumpity clump-clumpity clump' sound coming from the field behind them.

"That sounds like a horse running through that field," Brad said.

"It sure does," Johnny replied, "but why would a horse be running through a field at night? They just don't do that."

"I'm scared," Mary said, "let's get out of here!"

Just as Johnny reached up to turn the ignition on, a big reddish-colored stallion jumped over the fence about 10 feet from the car. The moon came out from behind a cloud just as the horse soared over the fence and landed on the shoulder of the road. It pranced out onto the blacktop road and stood for a moment. That's when they got a look at the rider. He was tall and slender, especially when he stood up in the stirrups. He wore a cavalry man's hat with the brim pinned up on one side and a feather plume stuck in the band. He had on cavalry boots and brandished a saber in his right hand. He was young and handsome and cut quite a figure as the horse reared up on its hind legs and then galloped past them towards Green Ridge.

"Who in the world was that?" Johnny gasped.

"He looked like a ghost," a nearly hysterical Mary blurted.

"Shush," Johnny said, "he's coming back."

The horse stopped about 100 yards down the road and reared up again. Then they saw the rider slap him on the rump with the broad side of the saber. He lurched and came running at a gallop towards them. The girls ducked down on the floor of the car to hide while Johnny and Brad sat staring as the horse galloped past. When it got a few feet past the car, the rider raised up in his stirrups and shouted, "Mary! Where are you?"

Mary Schroeder gasped, "He called my name!" she said.

The horse galloped down the road a ways, and the hoof beats started fading out. The four of them sat up in the car and watched as the rider guided the horse down an obscure lane that ran east from the road. There was a collective sigh of relief when the hoof beats faded out completely.

"I'll bet that was the Ghost of Johnny Nichols," Johnny Clayton said, more to himself than to the other three in the car.

"Who was it?" Mary asked.

"Johnny Nichols, he was a local man who was tried and hung as a bushwhacker back during the Civil War. He contended that he was in the Confederate Army and should have been treated as prisoner of war and not as a bushwhacker, but they hung him anyway."

"How do you know all this?" Mary asked.

"My dad told me about him. I think he's buried around here someplace. My dad said he thinks that we're related to him."

"That's spooky," she said, "I've never seen a ghost before. It scares me, but I have to admit that it's interesting. If that's his ghost, I'd like to know more about him."

"I think we have some information about him at home" he said. "You've got me curious about him now. I've got to do a story for my history class at the university, and he would make a good subject for that. I tell you what, I'll dig up some information on him at the State Historical Society when I get back to Columbia, and bring it with me the next time I come home for a weekend."

"That sounds like fun to me," Mary said. "Have other people seen his ghost?"

"My dad said he saw it when he was a boy, he said he heard it had been galloping up and down this road ever since the Civil War ended."

CHAPTER 2

Mercer County, Kentucky, early December, 1841.

Wilson Nichols sold the farm he inherited from his parents at a good price and had the money converted into gold at the bank in Lexington so he could carry it with him to Missouri. The buyer of his farm had come west from Virginia with his family in a big Conestoga covered wagon pulled by two yokes of oxen. Wilson didn't want the oxen, but he liked the idea of going to Missouri in a wagon big enough to carry him and his wife Sarah, plus their daughter Martha who was almost 2, and their son John who was 4 months old. It would also have to serve as living quarters for the family while Wilson built them a log cabin for a more permanent residence. He made the man a fair offer for the wagon and bought it.

Just 21 years old at the time Wilson was a tall slender man, standing 6 feet 3 inches tall, and weighing about 190 pounds. He was a head taller than most men of that era who averaged a mere 5 feet 5 inches tall. He was muscular, having farmed and worked with his hands all of his young life. He was also very adept at blacksmithing and carpentry. These trades he had learned from his deceased father, who had died from being kicked in the head by a horse he was shoeing in January of that year. Wilson's mother had died from scarlet fever a year earlier.

Wilson had married a neighbor girl, Sarah Todd, in March of 1839, when they were both just 19. Their daughter Martha was born a year later in June of 1840, and in August of 1841, their son John was born. Wilson had big ideas about farming, and his plans called for more land than was available for him to buy in Mercer County, so he began to dream of moving further west, possibly to Missouri or to Kansas Territory, where land was cheaper and more plentiful.

In November of 1841, Wilson moved his family into the big wagon he had just bought, and he rode into Lexington, one sunny day, to buy some horses to pull it. He started at seven that morning and it took him until almost noon to make the 30 mile trip to the sale barn where he figured he could find the horses he wanted. He wasn't looking for thoroughbred horses. He wanted big sturdy draft horses to pull his covered wagon, and as he rode up to the sale barn near Lexington, he spotted just what he was looking for. A breeder was driving a small herd of draft horses out of one of the pens near the barn with a disgusted look on his face.

"Hey, there," Wilson greeted him, "are those horses for sale?"

"Yup, they sure are," the breeder replied as he rode up to the front of the herd to stop them.

"You lookin' for draft horses?"

"Yes," Wilson said, "but those look a little scrawny to me." He was trying to feel the man out.

"Scrawny?" the man said indignantly, "Theys half a hand taller than anything is this county, and a lot stouter too."

"Mind if I look them over?" Wilson asked.

"Help yourself," the man said, "but bear in mind that these ain't purebreds. If they had been purebred Clydesdales, or Percherons, I could have sold them easily at the auction this morning."

Wilson dismounted and looked the horses over carefully. His heart was pounding in his chest. These horses were exactly what he was looking for. He strolled among them trying to look disinterested. Finally, he picked out four that suited his purpose to a tee. They were big and stout and looked like they could pull his wagon, fully loaded, without much effort. "How much for these four?" he asked.

"You know them four horses are mostly Percheron stock, the stoutest horses in the world," the man boasted. Percherons came from France originally and hold all kinds of world records for pullin' stuff. I'd have to have $200.00 for those four."

Wilson whistled through his teeth and shook his head. "That's a lot of money for four horses," he said, "I'll bet two bits that I can buy all kinds of draft horses in this county for $30.00 a head."

"Not like them horses, you can't."

"Are they related?" Wilson asked.

The breeder took his felt hat off and scratched his head while he thought. "Well, let's see, there's three mares and a stallion. Two of the mares are sisters, but the stallion ain't related to any of the mares, so you could breed all three of them to him, if that's what you're thinkin'."

"That's what I was thinking," Wilson said. When these horses get to be about 10 years old, I'd like to have some younger ones coming on."

"That's good plannin'," the man said. He paused for a few seconds and then continued, "But I'll still have to have $200.00 for the four?"

"I'll give you $150.00," Wilson countered.

"No," he said, "but I'll tell you what I will do. I've got four sets of, nearly new, handmade leather harnesses with collars to fit those guys, and I'll throw them in for the $200.00. How about it, you'll need the harnesses anyways, regular harness is too small for these animals."

Wilson scratched his head and thought.

"The harness has solid brass buckles and snaps," the man added.

"Done," Wilson said and reached out to shake the man's hand.

After they shook hands, and while Wilson was counting the $200.00 out of the handful of gold coins he had brought with him (he had left the bulk of their money from the sale of their farm with Sarah in a leather pouch) he said, "How am I going to get the harness to my place?"

"Where do you live?" the man asked.

"Over in Mercer County," Wilson said, "about 30 miles from here. I made it over here in just under four hours today."

"Wait here," the breeder said. He cut the four horses Wilson had bought out of his herd and passed a rope through their bridles. He handed the end of the rope to Wilson and then proceeded to drive the rest of his herd into one of the empty pens. He yelled at one of the employees of the sale barn and pointed to his herd, "Feed these horses some hay tonight," he yelled, "and I'll pick them up tomorrow." The sale barn employee nodded and headed for the herd.

The breeder rode back to Wilson and said, "Tell you what I'll do, my place is three miles west of here, you probably passed it on the way up here from Mercer County. Why don't you go home with me and I'll throw the harness in the back of one of my wagons. Then I'll hitch my team up and follow you and the horses to your place. Would that be alright?"

"That would be fine," Wilson said, looking at his pocket watch, "but we'd better get started because it's 1:30 now. You're not planning on coming back home this evening are you? It would be awful late before you got back."

"No," the breeder said, "I'll throw a bed roll in my wagon and sleep on the ground tonight. Is that alright with you?"

"It's fine with me," Wilson said. He spurred his horse and started down the trail in the direction of Mercer County pulling his horses after him.

"By the way," the breeder yelled after him, "my name is Fred Bradbury, what's yours?"

"It's Wilson Nichols," he yelled over his shoulder, "and you can have supper with Sarah and me when we get back to my wagon."

It was 5:00 p.m., and almost dark, when the little caravan got to the glade where Wilson's wagon was parked. Sarah had kept the fire going and had a pan of beans and a coffee pot near it to keep them warm. She stood up with their old shotgun in her arms when she heard more than one horse coming.

"Hello, Sarah! It's me, Wilson," he shouted when he saw her standing next to the fire with the shotgun cradled in her arms. He led the draft horses up to the wagon and dismounted. Fred pulled up in his wagon, wrapped the reins around the brake lever and jumped down to the ground. Wilson introduced him to Sarah and told her that he had brought the harness for the draft horses he had bought.

"Sit down, Mr. Bradbury," she said, motioning to some sections of a big log next to the fire that Wilson had sawed off to use as chairs. "Would you like a plate of beans and a piece of cornbread?"

Fred took his hat off and tossed in on the ground next to his seat. "Yes ma-am, I sure would," he said, "I'm about starved."

Sarah dished up two tin plates of beans and put a square of cornbread on each of them. She handed a plate and a spoon to each of the men, and then poured them a steaming mug of coffee from the big pot near the fire.

Chapter 3

Fred looked around the camp site as he shoveled big spoons full of beans into his mouth, pausing only long enough to take a bite of cornbread and a sip of the coffee. "Where are your children, Mrs. Wilson," he finally asked.

"I fed them early and put them down for a nap in the wagon," Sarah said as she studied Fred's face. "I'll get Martha up about 7:00 and feed her again, then I'll put her down for the night. Of course, I have to nurse the baby whenever he's hungry."

"I know how that goes," Fred said, "we've got three young'uns at our house. The baby's not quite a year old, so Sally, that's my wife, still has to nurse him during the night."

"So your baby is a boy, too?" Sarah asked.

"They're all three boys, ma-am," Fred mumbled, his mouth full of beans, "and, hopefully, they'll all be horse breeders someday like their daddy."

Fred Bradbury was already up the next morning when Wilson climbed out of the big wagon at the first sign of daylight. He had pulled his boots on, stirred the bed of coals from last night's fire, and added some wood to get it going again.

"If you'll wait a few minutes," Wilson said, "I'll put a pot of coffee on and fix us some pancakes."

"That would be good of ya," Fred said, "it got a mite frosty last night, and I could use some warm food in my belly."

While Wilson made a pot of coffee and stirred up a batch of batter for the pancakes, Fred made him a proposition that interested him.

"I got no use for that wagon I drove over here in yesterday," he said, "I got two more like it out by my barn. Would you be interested in buying it from me?"

Wilson knew what he was leading up to, and was anxious to hear his proposition. "Maybe," he said, "what are you asking for it?"

"Well," Fred said, "I'll take $50.00 for it…

"Too high!" Wilson interjected.

"Let me finish," Fred said. "For another $20 I'll throw in one of those two mares that pulled it over here. That's $70 for the wagon and a very fine horse."

Wilson stirred the pancake batter for a moment while he thought the deal over. Finally, he looked up and said "throw in both horses and you've got a deal."

"I can't do that," Fred said disgustedly, "how would I get home?"

"I could take you home in the wagon and drive it back here myself," Wilson answered.

Fred stood up and stretched and yawned. "Naw," he said, "I can't do that. I'm not givin' a horse away today." He reached down and picked his hat up off of one of the stumps and made like he was going to leave.

"I'll give $60 for the wagon and my pick of the horses.

Fred walked to where his two horses were tied and untied them. "Naw," he said, as he led them to the wagon, "I'd better be gittin' on home."

"$65," Wilson said.

Fred stopped, "Done," he said as he tied the horses back up and sat down by the fire. Wilson put a big tin skillet on the fire for the pancakes. Sarah climbed out of their wagon with a half dozen fresh eggs wrapped up in her apron. She had kept six of her best laying hens for fresh eggs when they sold their farm, but she had worried about how she could take the cage that Wilson had made for them to Missouri. It was too big to go in the Conestoga wagon, along with everything else they had to take.

She walked over and carefully laid the eggs on the ground beside the fire. "Why don't you fry these for you and Mr. Bradbury to eat with your pan cakes?" she said.

Fred looked up from watching Wilson pour the pancake batter into the skillet in small globs that flattened out into round cakes about the size of a saucer as they cooked. "I'll only eat two eggs myself Miss Sarah, why don't sit down and eat with us, which would be two eggs for each of us?"

She smoothed her apron out and sat down on one of the stumps, "That's mighty kind of you Mr. Bradbury," she said. She had just gotten seated when she jumped up again, "I forgot the sorghum molasses for the pancakes," she said "I've got a quart jar of it in the wagon."

"Shall I fix a couple of cakes for Martha"? Wilson asked.

"Yes, she said, and I'll get another egg too. That will be a good breakfast for her."

"Is she up?"

"Yes, but I'll feed her in the wagon, it's too chilly for the children to be out yet."

While they ate, Wilson thought about the deal he had just made for the extra wagon and the horse. He was more than pleased, and grateful. He would hitch Sarah's riding mare up with the mare he got with the wagon and that would make a great team to pull the wagon to Missouri. He could put the chicken coup in the wagon and there would still be room for some more things. The harness would be gone because he would use it to harness the big Percherons to the Conestoga. That would make more room in the big wagon for the children too. He smiled as he thought about the caravan they would make as they traveled across Kentucky and Missouri to their new home in Pettis County.

He would drive the big wagon and Sarah could easily handle the smaller one. He could tie his red stallion behind the big wagon and the cow behind the smaller one. They could travel about five miles an hour, with stops enough along the way to rest horses and the cow, and still make at least 25 miles a day. They could be in Pettis County by the middle of January, depending on the weather, and that would allow him plenty of time to plow up a few acres of land for corn and a vegetable garden.

When they had finished eating, Fred Bradbury stood up and rubbed his belly. "That was a mighty fine breakfast," he said, "now I had better head for home. Come over to the wagon," he said to Wilson, "I want to show you something before I go."

They both walked over to the wagon that Wilson had just bought. Fred pulled back a tarp and pointed to four big sacks of feed.

"What's in the sacks?" Wilson asked.

"Oats for the horses," he said.

"Oats?"

"Yes, I want you to give the horses two double hands full oats every evening in a nose bag. They love it, so they'll eat it all with no problem. It supplements the hay and grass they eat and gives them a good coat and more energy. It's a secret I've used for years in raising horses. That's why my horses have always sold so well."

Wilson stood looking at the bags of oats. He said, "I'd like to try it, but I don't have any nose bags, and I probably couldn't afford it anyway."

Fred looked up and tapped Wilson on the shoulder. "I like you, Nichols," he said, "and I want those horses you bought to do well, that's why I brought the oats. Normally I get fifty cents a bag for them, but I'm giving you those four bags to get you started out on the right foot."

"Bu-but, I...

"Don't have any nose bags?" Fred interjected before Wilson could get it out. "Under all of that harness you'll find four nose bags big enough to feed the Percherons. You can use them to feed your other three horses too if you want, but you'll have to take the straps up so they'll fit. That's easy to do, and you can let them back out for the big horses."

"I appreciate your kindness," Wilson said, "but why are you doing this for me?"

"Because, like I said, I like you," Fred said, patting Wilson on the back. "I want you to do well where you're going. I wish I could be going with you, but I've got too big of an investment here to make the move right now. You're a square shooter, Nichols, you'll do fine in Missouri."

With that, he untied the one horses he was keeping from the wagon team, jumped astride it's bareback, and with a tip of his hat to Sarah rode off in the direction of his home singing the only words he could remember from an old folk song, "With a yoke of white oxen, an old yeller dog, a big

Shanghai rooster and one spotted hog….de de di de di dum dum..Sweet Bessie from Pike…”

CHAPTER 4

Monday, December 6, 1841

The day dawned cloudy and cold in Mercer County, Kentucky, with strong winds from the northeast. Wilson Nichols woke up at his usual time, about 5:30 A. M. He had laid out his clothes beside the down mattress where he and Sarah slept, the night before. This was the big day, the day they were to start their journey to Missouri. He slipped out from under the woolen blanket and sat up, being careful so as not to wake Sarah and Johnny. He sat there on the floor of the big wagon for a moment to get completely awake before he reached for the homespun woolen shirt that Sarah had made for him. He smiled when he heard the sucking noise coming from under the blanket. Sarah was already awake and giving Johnny his breakfast. Martha was sound asleep in her crib.

He dressed and climbed out of the wagon to check the weather. He looked up at the tree tops and smiled again. The wind was chilly and strong, but it was out of the east. It would be a big help to the horses pulling the wagons because it would be at their backs. He decided not to build a fire because of the wind. They would have to eat a cold breakfast, but they could get on the road sooner, and that would help.

He went to the rear of the wagon and pulled out the big tin container they kept their bread in. The container had to be tin to keep the mice from gnawing their way in and eating any leftover bread. Sarah had purposely baked three extra loaves last Saturday when she baked, to eat along the way. He pulled out another tin box where they kept their meat. He had stored three slabs of smoked bacon and some beef jerky in it for their trip. If they passed through any towns along the way, which he was sure they would, he planned to buy more supplies to supplement what they were bringing.

Sarah still had several quart mason jars full of peaches, green beans, beets, and peas left over from her canning last summer when they were still in their house. There were also several pint jars of strawberry and blackberry preserves to smear on their bread, plus some sorghum molasses.

Wilson had made a long wooden box with a hinged lid to store the glass jars in. He had packed them in straw so they wouldn't freeze or break from the constant jolting of the wagon. He fixed a tin plate of bread that he had sliced with his hunting knife and got a pint jar of strawberry preserves from the box. He took it to Sarah along with a quart jar of water from the big barrel strapped to shelf on the side of the wagon. There were four quart jars of milk from last night's milking that he had sat inside the back of the wagon to keep it from freezing. The weather was cool enough, especially at night, for the milk to keep at least two days. Wilson got a quart of it to drink with their bread and preserves. He wasn't sure how much their cow would continue to give during the trip, but they could get by.

Wilson, Sarah, and little Martha huddled in the wagon and ate their meager breakfast, and by 7:00 a.m. Wilson had the horses hitched up to their two wagons. Sarah took the reins of the smaller wagon and Wilson drove the big Conestoga, with the children wrapped safely in their blankets in back. By 7:15, with the wind at their back, the strange caravan headed west for Missouri.

The trek to Missouri had gone about like Wilson had planned, and at 2:35 in the afternoon of January 8, 1842 a cold rainy Sunday, they pulled up in front of a crossroads store at the junction of two trails. One was the east-west trail from St. Louis to Independence, Missouri, and the other was an old Indian trail that ran north and south from the Missouri River to Springfield, Missouri.

The store was in a log building, and it catered to the few scattered farms in the area plus the local Indians, mostly of the Osage Tribe. The owner and his wife lived in a log cabin in back of the store, with their three children. They survived, mostly, by trading blankets, rifles, corn meal, sugar and salt, to the Indians for beaver, fox, otter, and muskrat furs. They also carried gun powder, lead shot and primers for their rifles. The farmers bought the same things the Indians did plus flour, yard goods, needles, and thread. Every two or three months the owner would take his accumulated furs in his wagon to Arrow Rock, a small community on the Missouri River in Saline County, and trade them for the goods he sold in the store. Arrow Rock was a landing on the river that catered to the boats that carried supplies to and from St. Louis in the east and Independence and West Port, Missouri in the west. There was always a market for furs in St. Louis, so they were much in demand by the river boats that stopped at Arrow Rock.

Wilson got down from the big wagon, pulled his coat collar up against the rain, and went back to talk to Sarah. "This can't be Georgetown, the county seat of Pettis County," he said, "that's where we need to go to pay for our land and get our deed. The store is closed. I'll look around in back to see if anybody is here."

Sarah nodded and he walked around the store to try to raise somebody. He saw another log building in back with smoke coming from the chimney. He knocked on the heavy oak door. It wasn't raining hard, just a light sprinkle, and Wilson was grateful for that as he waited for a response to his knock.

The door swung open and small dark haired woman smiled at him. She was a rather dour looking woman who appeared to be about 30 years old, but her whimsical smile betrayed her playful nature.

He heard giggling coming from behind the door and a young girl's voice said "Who is it, Momma?"

The woman brushed her hair back out of her eyes, straightened her apron, and said, "I don't know honey, he's a stranger, but he seems nice."

Wilson took his hat off in spite of the rain, and said, "The name's Nichols, ma-am, Wilson Nichols, and I need some information if you don't mind. Is your husband home?"

She smiled even broader when she saw Wilson's handsome face. "He's taking a nap," she said, "won't you come in?"

"I won't disturb him, will I?"

"Oh, no, he sleeps like a log."

Wilson stepped into the room, after making sure that there was no mud on his boots. "Thank you, ma-am," he said.

She stepped back a few steps and two beautiful little girls, one about 6 and the other about 8 peeked from behind her. They giggled again. "What information do you need," she said, "maybe I can help?"

"I'm looking for the county seat ma-am, is this Georgetown?"

"Oh, no," she said, "it's about six miles north of here, but you can buy anything you need here, and save the trip."

"I have some business to do at the county courthouse, ma-am, and I was told that it is located in Georgetown.

"It is," she said, "but it ain't open today, it's Sunday."

"I know it is, ma-am, I was just making sure that it was close by, and that I hadn't missed it by 50 or 60 miles."

She laughed, "No, you're almost there," she said, "but the trail from here to Georgetown is pretty rough and hard to stay on in the best of weather. Why don't you spend the night here and go up in the morning, the weather will probably better by then?"

"Can we camp here in front of your store?"

"What kind of wagon do you have?"

"It would be hard to describe," he said, "if you don't mind, could you come look at it? Actually, we have two wagons, and some livestock."

She jumped at the chance to see what kind of rig this stranger was driving, "Let me get my coat," she said. She got her grey wool coat from a peg near the door and put it on. When the girls tried to follow her she said, "You girls stay in here with daddy, and if he wakes up, tell him I am out front with some people."

She followed Wilson around to the front of the store building, and when she saw the big Conestoga wagon and the equally large Percheron horses, she said, "My goodness gracious that is quite a rig."

She studied them for a minute, and then pointing to the smaller wagon asked, "Is that wagon yours, too?"

"Yes, it is," he said.

She studied again for a moment and then said, "I don't think your big wagon could make it to Georgetown on that winding, hilly trail. Why don't you spend the night here and you can work out some arrangements in the morning."

Wilson hesitated for a moment.

"You can pull around behind our house, we've got a shelter back there that we use to store hay under, but we ain't got much hay now, so it's about empty. You could unhitch your horses and put them under it, and they would be out of the weather. Your cow could go under there too. We kept a cow back there until two weeks ago when a farmer came by and wanted her real bad, so we sold her. You can let your stock eat what little hay that's left. There's enough to make them one good meal."

"Thank you, ma-am," he said, "I'll pay you for the hay."

"Naw," she said, "there ain't enough left to charge you for."

That did the trick. Wilson nodded and walked back to tell Sarah to follow him around the shelter.

CHAPTER 5

Sedalia, Missouri, Friday October 26, 2012

The bell ending the last hour of the day at Smith Cotton High School rang, and Mary Schroeder walked out into the hall from her classroom. She was heading for her locker when Jeanie Crabtree caught up with her. "Are you going to the game tonight?" she asked.

Mary shook her head, "No," she said.

"Why not?"

"Because Mizzou is playing Oklahoma at Columbia tomorrow, and Johnny really wants to see that game, so he's not coming home at all this weekend. I'll be staying at home."

"Darn," Jeanie said dejectedly, "I was hoping that you and Johnny could go with Brad and me and maybe we could do something after the game."

"Sorry," Mary said, "what are you guys going to do Halloween?"

"We haven't planned anything yet, why?"

Mary stopped walking and turned to face Jeanie to emphasize what she had to say. "Ever since we saw the ghost that night out on route AA Johnny has been doing a lot of research on Johnny Nichols. He has been spending some time at the State Historical Society in Columbia and he has found a lot of information on him. He wants to share it with me. He has even found an old photograph of him."

"So, is he coming home for Halloween?" Jeanie asked.

"Yes," she said, "he'll be here about five Wednesday afternoon, and he won't go back to school until early Friday morning. That will give us Wednesday evening and all day Thursday to go over his stuff. He wants my opinion on some things."

"So, what are you going to do Wednesday night?"

"Well, Johnny thought that, since it will be Halloween, that we would stand a good chance of seeing his ghost again."

"Did he say anything about Brad and me coming along?"

"Yes, he wanted me to see if you guys would like to join us, can you come?"

Jeanie hesitated for a moment. "It's up to Brad," she said, "but I feel sure that he'll want to come. How late do you plan on staying out?"

"Well," Mary said, "if the ghost shows up at midnight, like it did before, we can all be home and in bed by one."

"I think my folks will be okay with that, but it will all depend on Brad."

"Is he waiting for you in the parking lot as usual?"

"Yes, I'll talk to him at the game and call you after I get home this evening, probably between 9:00 and 10:00. We'll sure miss you guys at the game."

"I'm sorry to miss it too, but you know how Johnny is when he gets his mind set on doing something. He wants to find out what really happened to Johnny Nichols, and why he was hung without a trial by jury. Johnny, my Johnny, is taking pre-law at school, you know, and he worries about things like that."

At 5:05 P.M., Wednesday, October 31, Johnny Clayton pulled his Ford Mustang into the driveway of his parent's home on west Fifth Street in Sedalia and went into the house to call his girlfriend. "Hi, Honey," he said when Mary answered, "I'm home, do you want to hear my plans for this evening?"

"Yes," she said, "I've been waiting to hear from you."

"First, are Brad and Jeanie coming?"

"Yes, they're really looking forward to it."

"Good," he said, "I've asked my folks if I could borrow the van for this evening and they said I could. They use it to tailgate before the Mizzou football games and it's all rigged up for cooking hamburgers and hot dogs. I thought it would be fun for us to do a little tailgating this evening."

"Oh yes!" Mary exclaimed, "That would be fun. I'm sure that Brad and Jeanie would love it too. Where are we going, out to the park?"

"No," Johnny said, "I thought we'd go out to the cemetery, what do you think."

"The cemetery?" Mary asked, "What cemetery?"

"The one where Johnny Nichols is buried."

"Where is that?"

"Not far from where we saw his ghost that night. Do you remember seeing him turn down that lane from route AA and disappearing?"

"Yes."

"Well, I went to the County Extension Office in Columbia and got a plat map of Pettis

County. It shows all of the land in the county, the owners and the acreage in each piece. It even shows the location of all of the cemeteries."

"Do you think he's buried somewhere down that lane?"

"Yes, there is a little cemetery about a quarter of a mile down that lane called Hickory Point Cemetery. I feel sure that that's where he is buried.

Mary hesitated for a moment, "If we're going to have a tailgate party way out there, shouldn't we get started, it will be dark in an hour."

"Are you ready?" he asked.

"Yes, and Brad is over at Jeanie's house waiting for me to call."

"Will you call them and have them come to your house? I could pick the three of you up there in about 20 minutes. My mom packed the van packed for me and it's ready to go. Your house is only about 10 miles from the cemetery, so we can easily be there before dark."

"See you in 20 minutes," she said, and hung up.

"The Schroeder home is a typical two story farm house just three miles from the Sedalia city limits on the main road to Greenwood. Johnny wheeled into their lane and spotted Brad's 1973 Chevy Monte Carlo parked near the front porch. The 39 year old car had belonged to Brad's dad when he was dating his mother, and had been in their family all this time. They had decided to give it to Brad as an early graduation present, and since it was like new, and worth more than was paid for it originally, they had placed severe restrictions on his driving it. Mary, Brad and Jeanie were sitting on the steps waiting and they rose in unison when they saw the white Chrysler Town and Country van pull into the Schroeder lane.

It was 5:45 P.M. on that crisp clear October day when they reached the cemetery, and although the sun was near the horizon in the west, it was still light enough for them to take a brief tour of the small country cemetery.

Johnny found the lane off of county road AA without any trouble, and although the lane was narrow, it was graveled, and smooth enough that it was an easy drive to the spot where they turned off toward the cemetery. There actually wasn't a lane to the cemetery, but there was a small sign tacked to a fence post that read 'Hickory Point Cemetery' with an arrow pointing toward their left.

At the top of a low hill there was a small fenced in cemetery with a gate at the corner nearest the lane. Johnny stopped the van just short of the gate and they all got out. There was a short piece of a tree limb stuck in the hasp of the gate to keep it from coming open in the wind. Most country cemeteries are fenced in with hog wire to keep wild animals from digging in the graves. Coyotes, opossums, groundhogs, and raccoons are notorious for digging holes in the soft dirt that is used to fill the graves, and they can do a lot of damage in a short time.

Johnny removed the stick from the hasp and opened the gate. Jeanie was the first to spot the

Nichols' graves. There were two. Johnny was buried beside Wilson Nichols, his father. Their head stones were simple, upright, concrete slabs about 18 inches wide by 30 inches high and about 2 inches thick with their names, birth and death dates, and place of birth engraved on the side facing the grave.

They stood quietly for a few minutes contemplating the place and its quiet atmosphere. There is a certain reverence about a cemetery that usually makes people lower their voice while walking through it. Johnny broke the silence, "let's go fry some hamburgers," he said.

Chapter 6

Pettis County, Missouri, Monday, January 9th, 1842

It was a cold but sunny day in central Missouri when Wilson Nichols woke from a fitful sleep at the crack of dawn. The front carrying the rain had passed through during the night, and the temperature was near freezing. Wilson Nichols was not the first one awake in the big Conestoga wagon parked behind the storekeeper's cabin. Little Johnny was awake and fussing for his breakfast. Wilson and Sarah slept with him between them to keep him warm since they only had one crib and Martha slept in it.

Their plan was to build a fire to cook some oatmeal for their breakfast, and then put the children in the small wagon for the trip to Georgetown, the county seat. They would get the deed for their property at the courthouse there. Wilson pulled his clothes on and lowered himself down over the side of the big wagon. He scrounged around under some nearby trees and found some small limbs that were dry enough to build a fire. He took a handful of hay from under the shelter, arranged it under the sticks, and lit it with a match from his shirt pocket. It took three tries, but he finally got the fire blazing.

Sarah nursed Johnny, then put her clothes on and climbed out of the wagon to help Wilson with breakfast. It was 7:45 a.m. by Wilson's pocket watch when he climbed up into the smaller wagon beside Sarah. She was huddled on the seat, under a woolen blanket, with Johnny asleep on her lap. Wilson had transferred the crib into the smaller wagon and Martha was asleep in it.

Wilson shook the reins and the horses started pulling the wagon forward. As they pulled around to the front of the storekeeper's cabin, his wife opened the door and yelled "Have a safe trip, we'll look after your things while you're gone." Wilson waved and nodded in recognition. She closed the door.

It was only a six mile drive to Georgetown from the junction where they had spent the night, but the trail was every bit as rough as the storekeeper's wife had said. It took them nearly an hour of hard, bumpy riding in the wagon to get there. When they arrived, a blacksmith out in front of his shop shoeing a horse, paused long enough to point out which of the small cluster of buildings was the courthouse.

It took another hour of wrangling with the county clerk for Wilson and Sarah to get a clear title to the property. They had bought it in both his and Sarah's names so Sarah would have no problems if she was forced to sell the property in the event of Wilson's death. They paid the balance owed on land in gold to the lawyer representing the seller, and for another dollar, the clerk issued them a new deed to their land. With the deed there was a page with the legal description of the plot called the 'metes and bounds'. They would need this page to find their new property, so Wilson tucked the envelope containing the documents carefully under his coat. They gathered up the children, went out and got into their wagon, and by 11:15 A. M. they were back at the crossroads where they had left the big wagon and the rest of their horses.

The storekeeper and his wife insisted that Wilson and his family have dinner with them, which was a welcome invitation. After they had eaten, Sarah picked out some supplies that they would need at their new home including a sack of flour, some oatmeal and two pounds of sugar. Wilson picked out a five pound can of gunpowder and a double bitted axe. He knew he would be cutting logs for their new cabin, and a double bitted axe would make the cutting go much faster than with the old pole axe he had with him. He also bought a hand file to keep it sharp. The shopkeeper was happy when Wilson paid for the goods in gold. Gold was good anywhere, but some of the paper script issued by the local banks was hard to spend, especially over at Arrow Rock where he bought most of his wares.

It was after 1:00 p.m. when the two wagons started their trip southwest from the crossroads to find the acreage they had just bought. The trail to Green Ridge was not very heavily traveled, so it was rather obscure is places and hard to follow. It was, however, a much smoother ride than the one to Georgetown. The land was flatter, and they made much better time.

Wilson blazed the trail with the Conestoga wagon pulled by the big Percheron horses with his riding horse tied to the rear. It was followed closely by Sarah in the smaller wagon, pulling the cow behind it. He had the sheet of paper with the 'metes and bounds' to their land in one hand and the reins in the other.

Most of Missouri had been surveyed by U.S. government surveyors shortly after the Louisiana Purchase in 1803 when it was acquired from France, so Wilson would look out for the 'metes and bounds' as described by the surveyors in his contract. Mostly is was a tree here, a big rock there, or it followed a creek bed, but if he was lucky, he could find an iron pin at the corner of his property. These were left by the surveyors to mark the beginning of a tract, or to serve as a bench mark for an entire section. Iron pins are heavy and they could only carry a limited quantity on their pack mules, so the surveyors used them sparingly, mostly as bench marks for section corners.

Luckily, the property they had bought was in the very southeast corner of a section, and when Wilson saw a big boulder that was described in his contract he pulled hard on the reins and stopped the Conestoga wagon. He motioned for Sarah to wait while he wrapped the reins around the brake handle and jumped down to the ground. He got a spade from the back of the big wagon and walked over to the boulder.

"Walk ten paces due north from the center of the boulder and find an iron pin," the description on his contract read.

Wilson took the small compass, which he always carried when was travelling, from his pocket, and walked over to the big rock. From the center of the north side of the rock he carefully walked ten paces due north and dropped to his knees to look for an iron pin. When he was unsuccessful in finding a pin by feeling with his hands, he stood up and started scraping the grass back with the spade. It wasn't long before the tip of the spade struck something hard and made a pinging noise. It was an iron pin with the section number engraved on the top end. Wilson was elated. This was exactly what he was looking for.

He got back in the big wagon and waved for Sarah to follow him as he drove the four big draft horses pulling the Conestoga to the top of a knoll that overlooked the entire 42 acres they had just finished buying. Sarah pulled up behind the big wagon in the smaller rig, towing the cow behind her. They both got down from the wagons and Wilson took Sarah's hand as he led her to the very top of the knoll. They turned to survey their acreage and Sarah looked up at Wilson with a big smile on her face.

"Oh, Wilson!" she said, "It's beautiful, I'm so happy!"

He took her in his arms and hugged her tight. "I'm happy too," he said, as he tilted her chin up and kissed her tenderly.

Wilson took out his pocket watch and checked the time, it read 2:15. "We need to set up camp before it gets dark," he said, "I want to start cutting logs for a cabin in the morning."

"What's that over there?" Sarah asked, pointing to a level space just to their right.

They walked over to it to get a closer look. "It looks like there was a cabin here at one time," Wilson said.

There was a flat space about 10 feet by 15 feet that had been cleared for a cabin floor at one time. The tall prairie grass had overgrown it, but they could see the outline of a cabin. At one end of the space there were some flat rocks scattered about that had probably been part of a fireplace at one time. They even found a few logs scattered about in the grass.

Wilson rubbed his chin in thought, "It looks to me like the people who built a cabin here moved on west and the settlers around here just helped themselves to any usable logs and rocks," he said.

"Would this be a good spot for us to start our cabin?" she asked.

"It would be a very good place," he said. "Go look after the children, and I'll start a fire."

Sarah started back to the wagons and Wilson picked up the end of a broken log and drug it down after her. He got the axe out, split the log up into smaller pieces, and soon had a fire going. Sarah fried some potatoes and added several slices of bacon to the pan. She cooked a small pan of oatmeal with some raisins for Martha and they had milk from the cow. After they had eaten, he and Sarah snuggled before the fire, sitting on another log that Wilson had drug down from the old cabin site. He squeezed her tight, "This is our first meal in our new home," he said.

"Yes, such as it is," she said, smiling up at him, "Our new home."

CHAPTER 7

Johnny Clayton opened the back of the van and took out a folding table and four chairs. Brad helped him set up the grill and soon they had some charcoal briquettes starting to glow. One of the two coolers in the back contained hamburger patties already made up and ready to pop on the grill plus a package of hot dogs and a couple of bratwursts. In a paper sack were hamburger and hot dog buns, plus three bags of potato chips. There was something for everybody.

Apparently Johnny's mother really knew how to prepare for a tailgate party, because in the other cooler there were plastic zip-lock bags containing sliced pickles, onions, tomatoes and lettuce. There were squeeze bottles of ketchup, mayonnaise and mustard also, and sitting down in the ice were cans of soft drinks of every flavor. There was no beer.

Johnny's mother, Helen, didn't allow it. She barely allowed it when she and Johnny's father, John Clayton Sr., an attorney, would tailgate with their friends at football games. She maintained that tailgating was to have fun and celebrate the game by rooting for the Tigers, but not to get drunk and puke all over somebody's shoes.

By 8:30 P.M. the four of them had eaten and were listening to a CD on the player in the van. The CDs were out of Helen's collection from the 70s, and were mostly tunes like "Bridge Over Troubled Water", "The Sound of Silence", and "The 59th Street Bridge" sung by Simon and Garfunkel. The songs weren't familiar to the teenagers, but they liked the slower beat even tried to dance to them on the grass behind the van.

Time passed so fast that it was 10:30 before they realized it. Johnny turned the CD player off and raised his hands. "We need to start listening for Johnny Nichols and his horse," he said.

"Do you think they'll be back so early?' Brad asked.

"Yes, I do," Johnny said, "I don't think he's looking for Mary at all, I think he's out looking for the men who shot his father."

"Shot his father? When did that happen?"

"I don't have time to go into that now, but I'll tell you all about it tomorrow," Johnny said.

"What time tomorrow?" Jeanie asked, "I'll be in class until 3:20.

"Me too," Mary added.

"Can you skip one day?" Johnny asked. "This is very important to me, and I want your opinion on the material I have gathered up so far. It is so interesting to me that I'm using the story of Johnny Nichols as the subject of my term paper and my grade will depend on how well I research it."

Can't we get together around 3:30 after school lets out?" Mary asked.

"I'd like to," Johnny said, but I really need to start back to Columbia before then."

They sat in silence for a little while and then Mary said "Will we be through by noon?"

Johnny nodded, "Yes, we'll be through by noon," he said.

"Than count me in," Mary said, "my tough classes are all in the afternoon, so I can still make them."

"The same applies to me," Jeanie said, "so you can count me in."

"I'll be there too," Brad said, "where are we going to meet, and what time?"

"Let's meet in the main reading room of the Sedalia Library, and I was going to say at 10:00 A. M.., but to be sure that we're out by noon, we had better start at 9:00. What do you guys think?"

"Nine tomorrow morning would work better for all of us," Mary said.

They agreed on the meeting time, and when the chatter died down, they began to hear the clumpity clump of a horse's hoofs on sod, no doubt about it.

They sat up straight and strained to hear the sound of the horse's hoof beats as they got louder and louder, then they froze in their seats when the horse came right by the van and stopped at the fence in front of them. The rider dismounted, walked through the fence to his grave site and stood in the middle. The ground began to glow under his boots while he slowly disappeared into the grave.

When the glow of the grave had gone out and the horse had disappeared, they all sat in their seats in stunned disbelief of what they had seen. Mary could barely stifled a scream.

"Wow," Johnny said, "That was some sight." The other three sat in a dazed silence. After about five minutes of no sound, Johnny turned the key in the ignition and started the van's motor. "Let's go home and get some sleep," he said.

"Ye-yes," Mary stammered, "it's midnight, let's go home." She nestled close to Johnny, her body trembling, either from the cold night air, or fear, he couldn't tell which.

"Are you okay?" he asked, pulling her closer with his right arm while he drove with his left.

He felt her head nod. "Seeing his ghost scared the daylights out of me," she mumbled.

Sedalia, Missouri, November 1, 2012

Johnny Clayton slept until 8:00 A.M. that beautiful fall day in Sedalia, and he would have slept longer if his mother hadn't awakened him by knocking on his bedroom door.

"Johnny," she called through the door, "don't you have a nine o'clock appointment at the library?" She had been awake when he came in just after midnight and he had told her of his plans to meet with the others.

"Oh, my gosh, yes," he said, as he threw the covers back and wiped the sleep from his eyes with the sleeve of his pajamas. He was in and out of the shower in 10 minutes, and by ten to nine, was on his way to the library eating the egg sandwich his mother had made for him with his left hand and driving with his right.

There was plenty of parking around the library at that time of day, and Brad's Monte Carlo was parked right in front. Johnny pulled in behind it, grabbed his brief case off of the seat beside him, jumped out of his Mustang, and dashed up the front steps. It was 9:05 when he opened the big front door and glanced to his left. Mary, Jeanie and Brad had taken a table in front of one of the big windows that looked out on 3rd Street. He pulled up a chair and joined them.

Johnny opened his brief case, took out three yellow pads and a handful of pencils. He put one of each in front of them, "These are in case you want to take notes," he said. "As you know, my dad's a lawyer, so we always have lots of yellow pads lying around."

He also took some papers from the brief case and stacked them in front of him. On top of the stack were four Xerox copies of a photograph of a man sitting in a chair. He handed one to each of them. "Here's what Johnny Nichols looked like just before they hanged him," he said.

The four of them studied the pictures for a couple of minutes before anyone spoke. Johnny broke the silence. "This picture was taken by a sheriff at the County Jail in Jefferson City, right after he was recaptured. It was taken to use as proof to the people in the Missouri counties where he had been active in the past that he had been recaptured and was safely incarcerated.

"Recaptured?" Brad asked.

"Yes, he escaped from his captors at the county jail in Jefferson City, Missouri on May 18, 1863, shortly after he arrived there. After they recaptured him, he was sent to the Gratiot Street Federal Prison in St. Louis for safe keeping on May the 20$^{t.h}$. He was to be held there until the date he was scheduled to be hung, which was October 30, 1863. If you'll look at his right leg in the picture, you'll see that it is bandaged where they shot him while they were taking him into custody."

Mary looked up from the picture, "Is that a gun pointed at him? I can see what looks like a big gun sticking into the picture from the left side."

"Yes," Johnny said, "they must have been afraid of him because they were guarding him pretty close, even with his legs all bound up in shackles and chained to that big iron ball beside him on the table."

Mary squinted at the picture again "There must have been someone guarding, because I can see his leg in the bottom left hand corner, probably the man with the gun."

"Yes, and there were probably several more men in the room with guns that aren't in the picture. The information I have says that they were guarding him with a posse, probably eight or ten men. They couldn't afford to have him escape again, their reputations were at stake."

"He doesn't look very mean to me, in fact he was quite handsome," Mary added.

"He was probably six inches taller than most men, and when he stood up, he made a pretty imposing figure. They were afraid of him, that's for sure."

"What was this prison like?" Jeanie asked, "You said it was in St. Louis, do you have any pictures of it?"

"Yes." Johnny searched through his pile of papers and fished out a picture of an imposing building and brief history of the prison. He handed it to Jeanie.

*Gratiot Street Prison

Pronounced *Grass-Shut Located at the corner of South Eighth and Gratiot Streets on the south side of what is now the downtown area of St. Louis, the prison had originally been a medical college, built and operated by Dr. Joseph Nash McDowell. McDowell, although very eccentric, was actually a good physician and a fine surgeon.

McDowell came to St. Louis in 1840 to found the medical department of Kemper College, later known as McDowell Medical College. In 1847 he struck out on his own and erected the Greek revival building that was later to be used as a Confederate prison. He designed the building with two wings flanked by an octagonal tower. The tower was fitted with an unusual deck around which he placed six cannons to defend the school against possible attack by the Union Army. One of the cannons was said to have been the bow gun on the deck of Jean Lafitte's pirate ship. He also distributed muskets to his students for use in case they were attacked, and he kept a large supply of muskets, lead and powder in a basement of the college.

In spite of his imposing college building and reputation as one of the finest doctors of his day in a city where medical standards were high, it was his personality traits that made him the talk of the town.

He had an erratic temperament that some said approached insanity. He was said to be horribly jealous and suspicious of other doctors and schools. He was an ardent secessionist and was for the rights of southern states and the institution of slavery. He was a compassionate man, however, and he was known to be generous in the treatment of the poor and sick. He was also known for his hatred of immigrants (especially the Germans), colored people, and Catholics. He would often lecture on those subjects at street corners to anyone who would listen. He was also in the habit of wearing a breastplate of armor, thinking that his enemies might try to kill him at any time.

Because of Missouri's law against the dissection of bodies, it was almost impossible for medical colleges to get bodies for research. To get sufficient bodies for his classes, McDowell introduced the practice of 'body snatching' to St. Louis, although he preferred to call his student's night time forays into the city's cemeteries as 'resurrectionist activities.'

His euphemistic label for the reaping of corpses didn't deter the local residents and they were horrified when they found out what was going on behind the walls of the college, and where the cadavers were coming from. For the most part, the locals in the area avoided the college because they thought it was haunted, but occasionally one of them would stir up a mob action. That's when the canon and muskets were used to discourage them from entering the building. McDowell also kept a pet bear in the basement which he loosed on one mob. The mob scattered quickly, and the bear returned to its lair. The bear actually lived there until its death from natural causes some years later.

At the beginning of the Civil war, McDowell's son, Drake, joined the Confederate army under the command of General Meriwether Jeff Thompson. He took two of the school's canons with him. McDowell had already shipped the 1400 muskets that he had collected to the south in boxes that were labeled 'polished marble'. He also went south to serve the Confederacy as medical director for the trans-Mississippi Department. McDowell survived the war and after traveling and lecturing in Europe, returned to St. Louis.

In November of 1861, General Henry Halleck took over as a commander of the Union Army's Department of the West, headquartered in St. Louis. He suspected that the, now empty, McDowell Medical School building was being used to store Confederate munitions so he searched it. On finding it empty he took it over and converted it into a prison for captured Confederate soldiers.

The job of converting the medical college into a prison was given to a Major Butterworth. In December of 1861, 50 men, including 15 former slaves, were put to work renovating the college and cleaning out what the medical students had left behind. The former slaves were given the distasteful task of removing the three wagon loads of human bones and assorted medical specimens that were found in the basement. The crew installed cooking stoves and sleeping bunks and converted the dissecting room into a dining hall. General Halleck put Colonel James M. Tuttle in charge of the prison's operation.

When the first prisoners arrived on December 22, 1861, it was obvious that the prison had been poorly planned and constructed. Its capacity was about one third of the number that arrived on the first day. It was badly ventilated and not suited for large numbers of people. The latrine procedures were poorly planned, and quickly became useless. The waste buckets that had been placed in the rooms were insufficient for the number of men to use them, as was also the trench latrine in the fenced-in yard area. Renovation of other floors in the big building made more room for prisoners, but it didn't solve the sanitation problem.

Discipline in the prison was difficult and harsh. This was the beginning of the war and St. Louis was still embroiled in incidents of murder and shootings as the populace decided which side of the war they were on. Guards at the prison were ordered to shoot anyone who not only tried to escape, but even those who simply stuck a head or body part out of a window! The guards were often accused of showing no hesitancy to shoot, and it was said that they often took potshots at the prisoners just for target practice.

And if the fortress-like appearance of the outside and security of the prison were not enough, the interior had the look and smell of a medieval torture chamber. The two largest areas where prisoners were housed were called the 'round room' and the 'square room'. The 'round room' was described as a very dark, gloomy, and filthy place. It was the middle level of the octagonal tower section, the same tower atop which Dr. McDowell had mounted his cannons, and where he had constructed vaults to hold dead members of his family. The room was about 60 feet in diameter and usually had about 250 men crammed inside it.

Although crowed, it was actually better ventilated than the 'square room'. This room was about 70 feet by 15 feet and was home to another 250 or so prisoners. Normal rules of hygiene were disregarded so sickness and disease ran rampant in both rooms, but most especially in the square room. Captain Griffin Frost, a Confederate prisoner who spent some time in the 'square room' wrote in his journal that "all through the night can be heard coughing, swearing, singing and praying, sometimes drowned out by almost unearthly noises, issuing from uproarious gangs, laughing, shouting, stamping and howling, making night hideous with their unnatural clang. It is surely a hell on earth."

Federal officers and attendants occupied the first floor of the south wing which had been the McDowell home, and Confederate officers occupied the top floor. The north wing contained a divided basement where McDowell's pet bear had once lived. It now had a large room to hold prisoners. The middle floor was also divided, with one room for prisoners. An upper amphitheater, which had once been the pride of the medical school with its large area to view the dissection of cadavers and its six gothic windows, was later converted into two stories. One story was a convalescent hospital and the other, a dungeon. Above the dining room and extending the entire length of the north wing was the prison hospital. When the medical college had been in operation, this had been Dr. McDowell's wonderful museum of curiosities. There is no mention of what became of the exhibits once the Federal soldiers moved in to renovate the building. Perhaps they were tossed out with the three wagon loads of bones.

The hospital part contained 76 bunks arranged into four wards. Most of the sick were cared for by Confederate surgeons who had been taken prisoner and who had volunteered for sick duty under the direction of a Federal medical officer. Hospital attendants were detailed from among the prisoners. During the prison's operation, smallpox occurred here in almost epidemic proportions, along with outbreaks of measles, pneumonia, vermin infestations and the war's most accomplished killer, chronic diarrhea.

The prison itself continued to be a horrifying place. The population soared and the sanitary conditions and food rations further declined. Prisoners were dying at an alarming rate, sometimes as many as four a day. The conditions inside the rooms had collapsed beyond imagination.

CHAPTER 8

Jeanie looked the picture over and read the history out loud for the Brad and Mary. When she finished reading she looked up shaking her head. "What a terrible place to have to stay," she said. "How long was he locked up in that horrid place?"

Johnny checked his notes, "Let's see," he said, "he was recaptured the end of May, and was hung on October 30. That would be a little over five months."

"My goodness," Mary chimed in, "just staying in that place for five months would be punishment enough for most crimes, let alone hanging the poor guy. Do you have any more history on him?" she asked, "I've never cared much for history, but this story has whetted my appetite for more."

"I was hoping you would say that Mary, because I'm hooked on his history. I'm gathering information on his parents and his brothers and sisters now. I'm working on a story for my history class at the university, and his family will be the central theme for it. I'm doing it for credit, and hope to make an "A" for the semester. I need to have it done to turn in by the last of this month."

"The library has a lot of old newspapers on microfiche stored down in the basement," Jeanie said. "I can come down here after school and look through them for any items about the Nichols family. Would that help?"

"It sure would," Johnny said. "I plan to come home on the 9th of this month and stay until Tuesday the 13th. The schools will be closed on Monday the 12th for Veteran's Day, and we could get together then and go over our notes. How does that sound?"

"Sounds good to me," Mary said, and the others agreed.

"The 12th it is then," Johnny said, "do you want to start about 10:00 in the morning?"

The other three nodded, and Johnny marked his calendar. He pulled some more notes from his stack and passed them around. "Here's some information about the Civil War, and how it got started here in Missouri," he said. "Most people think it started at Fort Sumter near Charleston South Carolina on April of 12th, 1861, but it actually started right here in Missouri about four years earlier. You might start your newspaper searches in April of 1858 and see what you can come up with.

I'll help Jeanie and Mary with the newspaper search," Brad said. "The three of us can cover a lot of ground between now and the 12th."

Monday, January 10th, 1842.

As luck would have it, the sun was shining and the weather was mild for this part of Missouri. After a breakfast of pancakes, bacon, and hot coffee, Wilson Nichols started looking around their camp site for trees that he could cut down to start their log home. He picked a lodge-pole pine that was tall and straight, and started chopping. The pine was wood was soft, and Wilson's new double bitted axe was sharp, so he soon had it cut down and was trimming it when he heard a horse's hoofs down on the trail. Wilson stopped chopping and looked down at the trail. A man on a big sorrel horse was riding toward Green Ridge. When he saw Wilson and the two wagons parked nearby, he veered off of the trail and headed up the hill toward them.

When he got within shouting distance, the man pulled up and waved. "Hello," he said at the top of his voice, "I'm your neighbor, can I come up for a visit?"

Wilson propped his axe handle against the log he was trimming and turned to greet the visitor, "come ahead," he said. He took out his pocket watch and checked the time. It was 8:45 A.M.

The man rode to within ten feet of Wilson and dismounted. With his reins in his left hand, he took a couple of steps toward Wilson and offered his right hand, "My name's Ed McNeal," he said, "my farm's about a half mile north of here. I'm on my way to Green Ridge to buy some nails at the general store there."

Wilson looked Ed over as he took off his leather gloves and stepped close enough to him to grasp his hand. He liked what he saw. Ed was a tall man, about Wilson's height, with a pleasant face and a strong build. He had a firm grip when he took Wilson's hand, and he smiled a warm smile.

Wilson was taken with him at first sight, "My name's Wilson Nichols," he said, "do you have a family?"

"Yes sir, there's my wife Lucy, and we have three children. I say children, but they're pretty much grown up. Our oldest is

Mary Sue, she's 21, next is Harold, he's 19, and our youngest is Gabe, he's 17. How about you?

Wilson pointed to the big Conestoga wagon parked just down the hill from where they stood.

"My wife, Sarah, is in the wagon feeding our two children. Martha is the oldest, she's 19 months, and John is 5 months.

"Where are you from?"

"Mercer County Kentucky."

"How long did it take you to get here?"

Wilson scratched his head, "Well," he said, "We left early on December 6th and got here yesterday the 9th that would be 34 days in all."

"That's a long trip to be making in the dead of winter. Why didn't you wait until spring?"

Wilson studied for a minute, "Mainly because I had sold my farm and I didn't have anything to do except take care of my horses so I figured if we could get here in January, I could get a cabin built by planting time and we could move out of that wagon and into a decent house. It's hard on Sarah and the kids living like this.

"I know how you can save a lot of time building your cabin if you don't mind spending a little money," Ed told him.

"How's that?" Wilson asked.

Ed tied his horse to a scrub oak and propped one foot up on the tree Wilson was trimming. "I have a friend that farms just three miles down this trail, about half a mile from Green Ridge," he said. "He farms mostly, but last year he was in St. Louis visiting some relatives and he saw a steam driven saw mill being demonstrated by some outfit from Boston. There ain't a sawmill within 50 miles of here, so he figured he could make some money doing custom sawing for the farmers around this neck of the woods."

"Does he have any logs for sale?" Wilson asked.

Ed straightened up and said, "As a matter of fact, he has a lot of them, and if you're interested, you could save quite a bit of money. His name is Harley Clink, and after he had installed his new sawmill, he found out that the farmers around here just don't have any spare money. They wanted to pay their sawing bill with logs. The fee they usually agreed on was that if Harley trimmed and sawed 8 logs to various lengths, he was entitled to 4 logs for himself. He figured that he could eventually sell some of the logs and make a little money."

"How's he doing?" Wilson asked.

Ed shrugged his shoulders, "Not too well," he said. "I'll bet you could buy all the logs you need to build a nice cabin just for the price of cutting them."

"Are you going by his place on your way to Green Ridge?"

"I am, do you want to ride along with me?"

"Yes, I'd like to," Wilson said, "let me tell my wife, and saddle up my horse. I'll be ready in about 10 minutes."

Ed nodded and Wilson walked down to the big wagon. He leaned in to talk to Sarah.

"Honey, our neighbor, Ed McNeal, is going to take me to see a man who has some logs to sell that are already to cut. It'll save me a lot of work, and we can be in our new cabin in less than a month. What do you think?"

"How much money will it take?" she asked.

Wilson scratched his head while he thought. Finally, he said, "It'll probably take 30 logs to build what I want to build. I'll ask him to give us the logs for free, and I'll offer him a dollar a log to trim the sides and cut them to length. If he takes my offer, I may have to buy some boards to trim the windows and frame the doors. That might run another $10.00. I won't go over $40.00 for the whole cabin, can we spare it?"

Chapter 9

Sarah was holding little Johnnie over her shoulder to burp him, having just nursed him. She laid him, gently, on a pallet on the floor of the wagon and reached into the pocket of her apron. She took out the soft leather pouch that she always kept on her, it contained what money they had left over from selling their farm in Kentucky. After they had paid for their land in Missouri, there was still a small handful of gold coins in the pouch. She counted out a $20.00 piece, a $10.00 piece, and two $5.00 pieces and handed them to Wilson. She shook the pouch and peered in it. "I think there's a little over a thousand left," she said, "go ahead and buy the logs, it'll save you a lot of hard work, not to mention your time."

Wilson leaned in a little further and took the coins from her hand. He kissed her tenderly on the lips, "I should be back by noon," he said. He walked out to the temporary coral he had made by tying what rope he had around some trees and whistled to the big red stallion he always rode. He lifted the rope and let the stallion walk under it. He followed Wilson to the smaller wagon where his saddle and bridle were kept. In less than five minutes Wilson had him saddled and was sitting astride him ready to go. He motion for Ed to follow and they trotted their horses down to the main trail and headed south toward Green Ridge.

20 minutes of easy jogging brought them to the farm of Harley Clink about a quarter of a mile north of Green Ridge. Ed turned into the lane that led to the house and Wilson followed. They found Harley and his wife Esther at their kitchen table, sipping coffee and playing cards. Harley invited them in and offered them coffee.

Ed shook his head, "Thanks Harley," he said, "but we don't have time right now. This is my neighbor Wilson Nichols and he just moved here from Kentucky. He wants to get started building a cabin for his family right away, and he's looking for some good logs. Do you have any to spare right now?"

Harley shook Wilson's hand, "Pleased to meet you, Mr. Nichols," he said. "I do have some very good logs out by my saw mill, let me get my hat and coat and we'll go take a look at 'em."

Harley retrieved his hat and winter coat from a peg by the back door and walked with them out past his barn to a long open pole barn with a corrugated tin roof.

Harley was in his late 50s and he was about out of breath when they got to his sawmill which was housed in the big open barn. Pointing to a large, complex, machine in the barn, he said,

"That's my saw. I've got it under a roof to keep the weather off of it."

Wilson walked along the big saw rig, carefully looking it over. He had never seen a steam driven saw before, in fact, he didn't even know they existed. He had read about steam engines a lot, but this was the first one he had ever seen. "Where was this made?" he asked.

"It was made in England and shipped to Boston last year," Harley said. "I heard about it when the buyer in Boston turned it down for some reason. A shipping company in Boston bought it and shipped it to St. Louis through New Orleans, thinking that if they could get it out to where there was lots of timber, they could sell it for a profit. It turned out that they were wrong, and it sat on a dock in St. Louis for 6 months before I spotted it. I bought it for half the price they were asking, but it cost me a small fortune to have it hauled up here from St. Louis. If you're interested in it, I'll make you a very good price

Wilson continued walking along the side of the machine admiring it. The steam engine itself was in the far end of the building, and was connected to the saw by a wide leather belt. He turned to face Harley, "This does more than just saw logs doesn't it?" he asked.

"Yep," Harley said, "It's got a 6" plane and a band saw that's powered by the same engine. You need some planing done?"

Wilson continued walking. He admired the big machine, but he didn't want Harley to think that he was the least bit interested in buying it, that would come later. He walked all the way back to the steam engine and checked the water gauge on the boiler. It was full. He put his hand on the fire box to see if it had been fired up in the last few hours. It was cold. "Where are your logs?" he asked.

Harley pointed over to the other side of the mill, "They're piled over there," he said. They walked around the steam engine and Harley pointed to a big stack of logs about 8' high, and 25' wide. Without counting, Wilson estimated there to be at least 200 logs of every kind in the pile.

"How many do you need?" Harley asked.

Wilson took a sheet of paper from his shirt pocket and unfolded it. He had torn a blank sheet from the back of Sarah's journal last night and by lantern light had sketched a log cabin on it. It was to be 12' by 30' with a door and a window on each side of the middle part. It had a gabled roof and room for a loft under the rafters on the south end. He handed the page to Harley to look at.

Harley took a carpenter's pencil from the bib pocket of his overalls and started counting the logs in the sketch Wilson gave him. After about five minutes he looked up. "I figure it'll take between 40 and 45 logs to build a cabin this big," he said, "what number did you come up with?"

Wilson took the drawing back and glance at it for a minute, "That's about 10 more than I figured," he said, "It'll take ten, ten foot logs, just for the floor joists."

"Floor joists?" Harley said, a surprised look on his face, "are you planning on putting a wood floor in it? Why don't you just use the dirt floor like most people do, it would save you a lot of money."

"Because," Wilson said, "we have two small children and I don't want them running around on a dirt floor."

"What's wrong with that?"

"Well, worms for one thing," Wilson said firmly. Little children can pick up round worms, hook worms, tape worms and lots of diseases from putting dirt in their mouth. I want to avoid that by putting a wood floor in the cabin."

"What kind of money are you talking about?" Harley asked.

Wilson took his hat off and scratched his head in thought. He put his hat back on, looked

Harley in the eye and said, "I figured you would just give me the logs since you have such a big pile of them, and I would pay you $25.00 to cut them to the right lengths and notch the ends, how does that sound?"

Harley's eyebrows went up. "Twenty five dollars!" he exclaimed "that's ridiculous, I can't do it for less than $35.00.

"Let's talk about this," Wilson said. "Are you doing anything right now?" he asked.

"If you mean, am I working on anything right now, the answer is 'no'. It's winter, and there just isn't anything to do on a farm this time of the year, you should know that, Mr. Nichols."

"So, if you were sawing wood for me, you wouldn't be neglecting your other work, right?"

"I suppose you're right, but what about my sawmill? I would be using it, and that's worth something."

"Are you using the sawmill now?"

"No, but I would have to use it if I was sawing logs for you."

"Let me see now," Wilson said, "you're not working right now, and probably won't be doing much until about the first of April. You're not using your sawmill right now, and from the looks of that pile of logs, haven't used it much for the past several months. I'm offering you $25.00 to cut logs for me for the next two to three weeks. That's $25.00 more that you would make at your current rate, don't you think, so how about it?"

Harley stood and stared at Wilson. Just this morning his wife had reminded him that they were out of sugar, and the flour sack was about empty. That meant that she wouldn't be able to bake bread on Tuesday which was her usual chore, and that meant that they would be completely out of bread by Wednesday. He unsnapped the bib pocket of his overalls and took out the brown leather pocketbook where he kept what cash he had on hand. Snapping it open, he poured its contents into the palm of his hand. He counted 37 cents. It was enough for the sugar, but not the flour. Dropping the coins back into the pocketbook, he snapped it shut and put it back into his pocket. .

"Do you think we could cut what logs you need in three weeks?" he asked.

Wilson felt sorry for Harley. He had obviously sunk a lot of money into the sawmill and was hard up for cash. He reached into his pocket and took out the four gold coins that Sarah had given to him. He held up the $20.00 gold piece so Harley could get a good look at it. "I'll tell you what I'll do," he said, "I'll give you $20.00 to get started on my logs, and when you're half through, I'll give you $10.00 to finish the job. That's a total of $30.00, which is $5.00 more that I offered to begin with. How about it, do we have a deal?"

Harley stared at the $20.00 gold piece. As tight he was for cash, it looked as big as a saucer.

He reached out and took it from Wilson, "You've got a deal," he said.

Chapter 10

Wilson took his watch out and pushed the stem to open it. He glanced at it and looked up at Harley. "It's almost 10:00 now, how long would it take you to get enough steam up to turn the saw?" he asked.

"Oh, it would take a couple of hours," Harley replied.

"I'll tell you what," Wilson said, "I need to get back home by noon. Would you get up early in the morning and fire up the boiler so that we could start sawing about eight? I'll bring my wagon and stay all day, and maybe we can get a wagon load of logs sawed so that I can take them home with me tomorrow afternoon. What do you think?"

"I think I can do that," Harley said.

"I'll come with you," Ed said, "that is, if you don't mind."

"Not at all, are you sure your family won't mind?"

"I'm in the farming business, same as Harley, and all I have to do this time of the year is to look after my horses and feed some hay to a few head of cattle. My wife and daughter can do that for a few days while I help you build your cabin. If you don't mind, I'd like to bring my two sons along too. They're getting bored just sitting around, and they're good workers."

"Wilson thought for a minute, "Ed," he said, "I couldn't afford to pay them, and I sure wouldn't expect them to work for nothing."

"Why not?" Ed said, "we're neighbors, and that's what neighbors do, they help each other out. They would expect their dinner though."

Wilson looked over at Harley, "How about it Harley, could you feed us all lunch tomorrow?"

Harley felt his pocket to make sure the $20 gold piece was there. "Yes," he said, "I can kill a couple chickens in the morning and Esther can fry them up for dinner. Would that and some cornbread with mashed potatoes and white gravy be alright?"

"That sounds good to me," Wilson said. He looked over at Ed, who was nodding his head in agreement.

The three of them walked up to the house where Wilson and Ed had tied their horses. "We'll see you tomorrow morning about eight," Wilson said as he and Ed climbed into their saddles and headed down the lane to the main trail.

Harley went into his house to show Esther the $20.00 gold piece and to tell her he was going to hitch up the buggy and run into Green Ridge for some flour, cornmeal, and sugar for tomorrow's dinner. "We're about out of coffee too," she said, a big grin on her face.

When they got to the trail Ed turned his horse to the right, back toward Wilson's farm.

Wilson pulled Big Red up to a stop, "I thought you were going to Green Ridge," he said.

"I changed my mind," Ed said over his shoulder, "I just needed some nails to repair my corn crib, but that can wait until we get your cabin built."

"We?" Wilson said, spurring Big Red so he could catch up with Ed, "are you planning on helping me build the cabin too?"

"Of course," Ed replied, "I told you that me and the boys didn't have much to do until plantin' time, and they're bored to death. If the weather stays nice, the four of us could easily have it built in a couple of weeks.

The thought of having a nice dry cabin to live in, in two weeks, thrilled Wilson. "Ed, I really appreciate what you're doing for me," he said.

"Not at all," Ed said, "I plan to build a new barn in the fall, and you and some other neighbors would be a big help to me then."

"Put me down on your list," Wilson said.

Tuesday morning dawned cold and clear in Pettis County, Missouri, and the trail to Green Ridge was in good shape. At 7:30 A.M., Ed McNeal pulled up to Wilson Nichol's big Conestoga wagon in his own, slightly smaller, dray wagon. His two sons, Gabe and Harold, were scrunched up beside him on the seat with their coat collars pulled up around their ears. They had just pulled up when they heard Wilson in his average sized farm wagon rattling down the hill. He rounded the Conestoga and pulled up behind them. Ed motioned for him to follow and they were soon down on the trail to Harley Clink's farm.

Thirty minutes later they pulled off of the trail and stopped just short of Harley's sawmill. They could hear the whine of the big circular blade and saw smoke coming from the stack of the steam engine. "It sounds like Harley has started already," Wilson yelled over at Ed.

"Sounds like it," Ed replied. They drove their teams on down to the mill. Harley saw them coming and shut the saw down so they could talk.

The four of them gathered around Harley to listen to his plan about who was to do what, and when they were all in place, he started the saw up again. The five men had a lot of sawmill experience between them, mostly with horse driven saws, but it didn't take them long to come together as a team. When they stopped at noon for dinner, Wilson made a quick count of the logs that they had already sawed to their proper lengths, trimmed them on both sides, and had notched the ends. They were neatly stacked in Ed's wagon, so they were easy to count. The wagon was just about full, and Wilson counted eleven logs. They were cut to size according to the list Harley had made the night before. The list called for 43 logs, total.

Wilson smiled as he reported their progress. "If we can get one more log on Ed's wagon that will make 12 in all. My wagon isn't quite as big as Ed's, but it should hold about 10.

That would make 22 logs the first day, which would be half of all we need to build the cabin."

Ed reminded Harley, "Looks like we'll be through in two days instead of the two weeks like you figured," he said.

There was a touch of sarcasm in Harley's reply, "that's because there's 5 of us instead of just me doin' it all myself. We made a deal and shook on it, so I ain't givin' none of the money back," he said.

"I don't expect to get any of it back," Wilson said, "a deal's a deal. These friends of mine volunteered to help out, so I let them. I need to get the cabin done as soon as possible and I'm very grateful for their help. Let's go eat, I'm hungry."

There was a big sigh of relief from Harley as they walked up to the house. They stomped their feet before entering the kitchen, to shake the sawdust off of their clothing, and then they wiped their shoes on a gunny sack that Esther had placed in front of the door for that purpose.

It took less than 30 minutes for the five grown men to gobble up the two chickens that Esther had fried for their meal. They also devoured a big bowl each of mashed potatoes, and gravy, and a pan of cornbread. At 12:35 P.M. they rose from the table, excused themselves and thanked Esther for fixing the delicious meal. She acknowledged their thanks as they struggled into their coats and headed out the door.

The successful morning production of logs encouraged them to try even harder to have at least the 22 logs needed to make half the amount to build the cabin by the agreed time. By 4 P.M. they had filled both wagons and had piled some extra ones on the ground beside Wilson's wagon. He raised his hand and yelled for Harley to stop the saw. He checked his watch, it was 4:05 P. M.

"We got our wagons full," he said, "and if Ed and I leave now, we should get to my place with enough daylight left to unload them and have our wagons ready for tomorrow morning."

"For the same money?" Harley asked.

"For the same money," Wilson assured him.

By the time the two wagons arrived at the Nichols site, and had been unloaded, it was starting to get dark. Ed and his two sons saddled the horses that Wilson had loaned them, and headed home. "We'll see you in the morning," Ed yelled as they headed down the hill to the trail.

"I'll be ready," Wilson yelled back. He unhitched the horses from his wagon and turned them into the pen with the others. He had loaned three horses to Ed and his boys to ride home on. They had already unhitched their wagon and put Ed's horses in Wilson's pen with the others.

CHAPTER 11

Wednesday, January 12th.

When he got up about 6 A. M. to stir the embers and build a fire, Wilson noticed that the weather had warmed a little during the night. He had mixed emotions about that. The working conditions would be better at the sawmill, but if the trail thawed very much it would be harder for the horses to pull the heavy loads home.

Ed and his boys arrived at the Nichols' place at 7:30 A.M. on the dot. Soon they had rounded up their dray horses and unsaddled the three riding horses that Wilson had loaned them. They turned the riding horses back into the pen, and were hitching their dray horses to their wagon when Wilson climbed out of the Conestoga and walked over to the pen.

Sarah had fixed a good breakfast, so he had dressed, eaten and was ready to go.

"Good morning fellows," he said as he picked up two bridles that were draped over a small bush and ducked under the rope that served as a pen.

Ed and the boys each waved and said "Howdy" back to Wilson, as they finished hitching up the horses.

Wilson threw the bridles on the mares that he had used to pull the smaller wagon, and led them over to it. The horses and tack were so familiar to him that he was finished hitching them up by the time Ed and his sons were ready to go, and by 7:45 they were on their way to Harley Clink's sawmill.

They could smell the wood burning and hear the hiss of steam from the engine when they were about a quarter of a mile from the mill and Harley was waiting patiently for them when they pulled up. They soon took their places and Harley pushed the big lever that started the saw blade spinning.

The five men had a good day sawing, and by 4:30 they had sawed enough logs to fulfill

Wilson's agreement with Harley. Wilson started to climb up on his wagon seat to head home when he paused and turned to Harley.

"I'm going to need some milled lumber to make a door, put a deck on my roof, and a few other things, do you have some you could sell me?"

Harley motioned for Wilson to follow him and he walked up to the barn by the sawmill. He opened the door on the north end of the barn, wide so they could see in, and pointed to a stack of 1" x 6" boards in various lengths piled up against a stanchion in the middle of the barn. "Here's some that I sawed for a feller a couple of months ago but he ain't picked 'em up yet.

Wilson was awed by the number of boards in the big pile. He walked over and picked one of them up off of the top. He looked it over carefully and his heart skipped a beat. This was good lumber, exactly what he needed to finish out his cabin. He stooped down and took a rough count of the boards. When he got to 100, he stopped counting. There were at least 200 boards in the stack.

"Why did he want so many?" he asked.

"He said he was building a house in Green Ridge, and that he would probably need some more later. He said he was going to build some cabinets too, and he that needed some smooth lumber for that job, so I planed 30 of 'em for him."

Once again Wilson's heart skipped a beat. He could build Sarah some cabinets for her kitchen. She would like that very much. Wilson stood and faced Harley, "How much are you asking for all of this?" he said.

Harley paused to think. Finally he said, "The feller said he'd give me $7.00, but it's been a mite over two months now, and I ain't got a dime from him yet."

Wilson tapped his foot while he salivated over the lumber. He wanted it real bad. He thought about the $1,000 in gold coins that Sarah had salvaged from the sale of their home in Kentucky. Would she mind if he bought this lumber to finish their cabin out real nice? He didn't think so.

He turned to Harley and said, "I think I can scrape up another $5.00, would you take that?"

"Fer all of it?"

"Yes."

"That feller that had me cut it fer him said he'd give me $7.00."

"Have you seen any money yet?"

"No, not yet."

"I'll give you $5.00 for it, and pay you in gold tomorrow when I pick it up."

"In gold, you say?"

"That's what I said."

"I'll take it," Harley said.

"Done," Wilson replied, extending his hand to shake on the deal.

Wilson's heart was singing in his chest as he climbed up onto the seat of his wagon for the trip back home with the logs.

Ed and the boys had been waiting for him so they could make the trip back to his place together. That was in case one of them broke down along the way.

"What was that all about?" Ed asked.

"I'll tell you when we get home," Wilson replied.

The two wagons made the trip back okay, but it took them over an hour to go the three miles. The trail had softened some, and the horses had to go slow and pull hard to keep the wagons moving. Wilson gave a sigh of relief when they made it up the hill to the place where they had piled the other logs. While the four of them were unloading the wagons, Wilson told Ed about the deal he had made on the finished boards.

Ed whistled through his teeth when Wilson told him what he had paid Harley for over 200 finished boards.

"Well, I like things nice," Wilson said, "and the finished boards will allow me to trim the cabin up the way I want it."

"It will be nice when we're done," Ed replied.

Sarah came walking up the hill from their wagon carrying John on her hip with Martha toddling along beside her clinging to her dress. "Wilson!" she called.

"We're up here unloading the wagons," he called back.

When she saw the big pile of logs near the wagons, she was awed by their number. She looked at the men helping Ed unload the wagons, "Are these the McNeal's you've been telling me about?" she asked.

"Yes, dear," Wilson said, and pointing to each in order said, this is Ed, the patriarch of the clan, and these young men are Gabe and Harold."

"Please call me Harry," the eldest boy said, tipping his hat.

"My, what fine young men," Sarah commented to Ed, "you must be very proud."

"I am ma-am," he said. "My wife Lucy is home with our eldest child, Mary Sue."

"Wilson tells me that she's 21, is that right?"

"Yes ma-am, she turned 21 last September."

"Is she married?"

"No," he said, "she just hasn't met any decent men her age yet, but she's looking."

"I know exactly what you mean," Sarah replied, "She's the same age as I am, and I'd probably still be single too if I hadn't met Wilson at a pie supper his church put on one evening.

"She bakes the best pies," Wilson said, "I just couldn't resist."

He reached over, took John from Sarah, and cradled him in his arms. "This is our son, John, I was telling you about" he said smiling down at the boy, "and he's only five months old."

"Good Lord," Ed exclaimed, "you brought him all the way from Kentucky in that wagon?" That must have been a rough trip."

"It wasn't as bad as you might think," Sarah said, "fortunately it has been a pretty mild winter so far, and we have plenty of blankets." She took John back from Wilson and gave him Martha's hand.

He held her up for Ed to see, "This is my sweet little Martha that I told you about," he said, and she's 22 months.

"You folks have a nice family," Ed said in a very sincere voice. "I'd like you to meet Lucy and Mary Sue sometime."

Sarah smiled and said, "When we move into our new cabin, I'd like to have you folks over for dinner so we can get acquainted."

"We'd like that very much," Ed replied with a big grin on his face.

Chapter 12

The four man crew started on the Wilson cabin on Thursday, January 13, 1842, and with the pre-cut logs, made good time. Wilson and Sarah had brought quite a few tools from Indiana with them, and Ed brought most of his tools with him on the day they started construction.

The first day, Sarah cooked a big pot of beans and a pan of cornbread for their lunch, and it was plenty, but on Friday, Lucy and Mary Sue, sensing that Sarah had her hands full with two small children, came over with Ed and the boys in their wagon, bringing three chickens all cleaned and cut-up ready to fry, along with a big pot of mashed potatoes and two pans of rolls right out of the oven.

The families quickly formed a close friendship. Mary Sue took care of John and Martha while Lucy and Sarah fried the chicken in the big iron skillet Lucy had brought with her. They heated the rolls and mashed potatoes just before lunch time, and Sarah made a bowl of gravy. She also made a big pot of coffee. All of this was done on the outside fire pit that Wilson had built for Sarah to fix their meals on. The men had built a bon fire up near the cabin site to warm their hands.

That's the way they passed their days for the next two weeks. Farms were scarce in that part of Missouri in those days and the two families enjoyed each other's company. By slowly feeling each other out, it became apparent that the Nichols' and the McNeal's' thought a lot alike. They both approved of President Tyler, who had been elected in 1841 as a Whig, mainly because he was a Virginian and was for state's rights. None of them thought much of the radical 'abolitionists' that were moving into the Kansas Territory, and Western Missouri by the hundreds to assure that when Congress voted for Kansas Statehood, it would be voted in as a Free State instead of a Slave State.

The Missouri Compromise of 1820 which specified that the Louisiana Purchase territory north of latitude 36 degrees 30 minutes, and described Missouri's southern boundary, would be organized as free states and territory south of that line would be reserved for organization as slave states. As part of the compromise, the admission of Maine to the Union in 1820 as a free state was secured to balance Missouri's admission as a slave state.

The abolitionist that moved into that area between 1820 and 1860 were mainly from the more liberal northeastern states such as Connecticut, Vermont, New Hampshire, Rhode Island and Pennsylvania. They were outspoken in their abolitionist views, and didn't mind sharing them with their more conservative neighbors. This started a conflict that built up into a mini Civil War centered along the Kansas and Missouri border, especially from 1854 until 1861 when the Civil War started nationwide.

Bands of raiders, abolitionists and southern sympathizers, were formed to force their opposition into leaving the territory, both in Kansas and Missouri. It flamed into open warfare when a young, handsome, slightly built, son of an Ohio school teacher arrived in Kansas to do some farming and try to start a school. He wanted to educate the mostly illiterate Jayhawkers, as the Kansas abolitionists were known by their Missouri neighbors.

His name was William Clarke Quantrill, and He soon tired of the mundane life of a farmer and school teacher, so he joined a small group of Quaker abolitionists at Lawrence Kansas in December of 1860. The Quaker Jayhawkers proposed a raid on a prosperous Missouri farm to free their 26 slaves.

Bill Quantrill was much better educated than his co-conspirators, and he soon decided that their plan couldn't succeed. He then turned traitor and informed the Missouri farmer of the impending raid, and even helped kill the Quakers when they came to free the slaves. For this action, Bill Quantrill became a hero of the slaveholding farmers of Western Missouri. His intelligence and education, plus his skill and coldblooded readiness to use his pistols, soon caused him to become the natural leader of a small group of Jackson County farmers who were being driven into armed resistance by the outrages committed by the Kansans.

On Tuesday, February 1st, 1842, the Nichol's spacious new cabin was ready for them to move their things into it from the Conestoga wagon. The weather was cold but clear. Wilson got up early and built fires in both of the fire places in the new cabin and it was soon warm throughout. Lucy and

Mary Sue helped Sarah move their bedding and clothing and what other household furnishings they had brought with them from Kentucky into the warm cabin. During the last three days of construction Wilson let the others finish, while he built a bed frame, using some of the finished lumber he had bought. It would hold the down mattress that they had brought with them, so he and Sarah would have something to sleep on. He also built a rough cabinet for the kitchen with just shelves, no drawers, to store dishes, pots and pans, and what groceries they had on hand. He would build some nicer cabinets for Sarah later. They had brought three chairs with them from Kentucky, and by using a shelf from the big wagon, Wilson also built a table that would do until he had more time.

On Wednesday the 2nd, the McNeal's came over at 9:00 A.M., bringing more chickens to fry and potatoes to mash, and it was a lot handier cooking on the new fireplace indoors than on the outdoor fire pit. While the women were cooking dinner, the four men chopped wood for the fireplaces and stacked it by the back door. By the time they were called in for dinner at 1:00 P.M., they had quite a large pile built up, enough to last several weeks.

The food was set up on the new table that Wilson had built just yesterday, but the table was so covered with food that the seven adults and two children wound up sitting down and eating from their laps. They managed quite well, however, and no one complained.

Before they ate, Sarah had them join hands around the table while she said a few things.

"This is our first meal in our new home, and I just wanted all of you to know how grateful Wilson and I are to be able to eat inside, having eaten outdoors, or in the wagon for the past two months, and how grateful we are for all of the help we've had from our neighbors. Now, Wilson, if you will ask the blessing on the food, we can eat."

Wilson cleared his throat and they all bowed their heads. With moist eyes, he thanked God for their safe trip to Missouri, for their new home and for such good friends as the McNeal's. He thanked Him for the help that they had received from Harley Clink with the logs and lumber, and lastly, he asked God's blessing on the food. There were seven "Amen's."

"The plates are on the fireplace," Sarah announced, "help yourselves."

The McNeal boys sat on the rock hearth on either side of the fireplace while Sarah, Lucy, and Mary Sue occupied the three chairs. Ed and Wilson had rolled two, two foot sections of a tree into the cabin and set them on end for use as seats. It was a little uncomfortable, but nobody seemed to notice as they made the fried chicken, mashed potatoes and gravy, and two pans of cornbread disappear. The McNeal's kept two cows at their farm for fresh milk, cream and butter. Mary Sue had churned on Monday, so there was a small bowl piled high with real butter to put on the cornbread.

The small children had been fed before the adults sat down to eat, and Wilson and Sarah took turns holding John while the other one ate. Two-year-old Martha played on the new oak floor with blocks of wood Wilson had saved from cutting the one by six inch boards to fit in their spaces. He had sanded them so that they would be free of splinters, and Martha stayed busy stacking and unstacking them.

For the next thirty minutes the conversation died to mumbles between bites as the seven adults gobbled up the delicious food. All that was left was a pile of chicken bones and a tablespoon of butter in the bottom of the bowl. Susan took the dab of butter home with her, and

Sarah burned the chicken bones in the fireplace. She didn't want to throw them outside on the ground because they would attract raccoons, foxes and other varmints, and the six laying hens that they had brought from Kentucky, would be a big temptation for the wild animals, even though they were snug in the wire coop.

Chapter 13

Sedalia, Missouri, Friday, November 9, 2012.

Johnny Clayton got home from Columbia at 4:45 P.M., and after saying "Hi" to his mother, called Mary Schroeder to let her know that he was home. Mary had been camping by the phone ever since she got home from school at 3:45 P.M. She was waiting to hear from Johnny. Her parents had refused to buy her a cell phone, so she had no choice. "Is that you Johnny?" she asked.

"It's me," he said, "I just got home."

"Can you come over?" she asked.

"No I can't," he said, "and that's what I called about."

"What's up?"

"Well, my dad is a veteran of the Korean War, and his old Company is having a reunion at the Crown Plaza Hotel in Kansas City this week-end. All of his old Army buddies are in their 70s and 80s now, and this will probably be their last reunion. They have met every five years since 1960, and several of them have died off since then."

"I suppose he wants his family with him this time, is that what you're telling me?" Mary interrupted.

"Yes," Johnny said, "this one will be special, and they were all asked to bring their wives and children with them if they were still living and could come. I have to shower and pack a few things, then, I want to go over my notes one more time before our meeting Monday, or I'd come over now."

"Is your sister going too?"

"Yes," he said, "Dorothy and her family live in Kansas City, so they want to come. In fact, Mom, Dad, and I will be staying at their house tomorrow night so we won't have to drive back from Sedalia on Sunday. They live out in the Plaza area, so it will be handy to the hotel. We won't be home until around ten Sunday evening"

"So, I guess I won't be seeing you until ten o'clock on Monday morning?" she said, her voice carrying a note of dejection in it.

"I guess so, Honey," he said, "I'm sorry."

Monday, November 12, 2012

Johnny's alarm went off at 8:00 A.M., and he was awakened from a dream about hundreds of Confederate Soldiers imprisoned in a musty, smelly building in St. Louis. He raised up on his right elbow and shook his head to clear his mind. The odor of frying bacon wafted up to his bedroom. It was almost mid-night when they got home from Kansas City last night, so he found it hard to get out of bed.

He remembered his father telling his mother that he wanted to sleep in until 10:A.M. this morning, but he had reminded his mother that he had a meeting with Mary and Jeanie at that same time. "That's Mom fixing breakfast for me," he said to himself as he shed his pajamas on the way to the shower.

It was five minutes to ten when Johnny entered the front door of the library on west Third Street. He turned left into the main reading room, and spotted Mary, Brad and Jeanie seated at a table in front of a large window that looked out on Third Street. It was so quiet in the library at that hour, that they had heard the big front door open, and were looking for him when he walked in.

He walked over to them and tossed his brief case on the table in front of the only empty chair.

"Am I late?" he asked.

"No," Mary assured him, "We all got up a little early, I guess, it's just now ten o'clock."

"Okay," Johnny said, "I guess we can get started." He opened his brief case and took out a stack of papers. "I have some new information on Johnny Nichols," he said, "but first I'd like to hear any information you guys might have dug up since our last meeting."

Mary and Jeanie both had a stack papers in front of them, but Brad just had a pad to write on, and a ball point pen.

Mary went first. She took the top two sheets from her stack, held them in front of her for a minute or two to get everyone's attention, and said, "I think I have a surprise for you, Johnny." She looked down at the two sheets she held in her hand and said, "Did you know that you're related to Johnny Nichols?"

Johnny Clayton's eyebrows went up in surprise, "No, I did not," he said, "my father had mentioned once that we might be related, but nothing definite. How did you find that out?"

"Oh, it was quite by accident," she said. "I was building a file on the Wilson Nichols' family so I could compare it to your file and I asked the Director of the library if they had a copy of the 1860 Pettis County census, and they did.

In going through it, I found a listing of the Wilson Nichols family with all of their children. You knew they had nine children didn't you?" Johnny shook his head. She continued, "I knew that John S. Nichols had been hung in 1863 by the Union Government, but I wondered about the other eight siblings, so I got copies of the 1870 and 1880 Censuses too." She laid the two sheets of paper down in front of her to show them where she had worked on the Nichols' family tree.

She pointed to a paragraph on the second page in front of her and continued. "Their youngest child was a daughter named Mary, who was born in 1859 when Sarah was 42 years old. Mary was married to Clyde Shannon in1879 and they had four children, three sons and one daughter."

She looked up to see if Johnny was following her. He was, very intently, so she continued.

"The daughter was named Martha, after her great aunt. Here's where you come in," she said, looking up at Johnny. "In 1898 Martha married a James W. Clayton, and in 1901 they had a son that they named James W. Clayton Jr. In 1924, James Clayton Jr. married Louise Shelton, and in 1936 they had a son whom they named John Howard Clayton."..... Johnny's mouth flew open,

"That's my dad's name!" he exclaimed.

"Exactly," Mary said, her voice raising in excitement, "In 1953 he enlisted in the Marine Corps and in 1955 he came home from the war and enrolled at Missouri University under the G. I. Bill. After graduating from Law School, he came back to Sedalia and set up his practice.

Then in 1980, he married a very pretty young lady named Helen."…….

"My mom!" Johnny interrupted. He nearly shouted it as he bounced up and down in his chair.

"You got it!" Mary exclaimed, "And in July of 1990, they had a daughter they named Dorothy, and in July of 1993 they had a son, John H. Clayton Jr."

"Let me see that," Johnny exclaimed, as he reached over and took the two sheets from Mary's hand.

While he was looking at the family tree that Mary had written up, she said, "Your dad married late in life, didn't he?"

"Yes," Johnny said, "and when I asked him why he waited until he was 44 to get married, he told me that he wanted to get his law business going good before he took on the obligation of marriage. Actually," he continued, "I think that his business was going so well that he never would have married if my mom hadn't come along."

Mary smiled, "How come he married then?" she asked.

"Well," Johnny said, "he met my mom, and fell madly in love with her, and she with him. You've met her, and you know how pretty she is, even at age 56. She was 24 when they got married, and as she put it to me, she was looking for a more mature man to settle down with.

"And your dad is still a nice looking guy at age 76," Mary added. "I can see where they would make a good match."

CHAPTER 14

From February to September of 1842, Wilson Nichols busied himself with building a fence around 20 acres of his land to keep his livestock, especially his horses, from straying too far. There was no free range left in Missouri, and there was always the possibility of someone stealing his fine horses if they were allowed to stray onto someone else's land.

Barbed wire hadn't been invented yet, so the only practical way to fence in that much land was with a split rail fence. After consulting with Sarah, they agreed that they needed to use some of the $1,000 in gold left over from the sale of their farm in Kentucky to build the fence. Wilson bought the rails already split from Harley Clink and with Ed McNeal's help, he rounded up enough men to build the fence. It was finished by mid-September, and it was a proud moment when Wilson was able to herd his horses and his cow into the pasture that they had created with the fence.

In the fall of 1842, after their crops were all in Wilson Nichols, with the help of several neighbors built a barn from lumber purchased from Harley Clink. They finished it in time for Wilson to fill the loft with hay that he bought from some of his neighbors who had a surplus.

Wilson and Sarah were happy, though not content. They were set for the winter of 1842/43, with a nice new, warm cabin to live in and a new barn to keep their horses out of the weather. With a warm stall and plenty of good hay, their cow furnished them with milk, cream and butter all winter.

The next ten years were prosperous for the family of Wilson Nichols. The year 1843 had produced a good corn crop. He built a tight corn crib to keep what corn they would need to feed their chickens and to fatten the pig that Wilson bought in the spring of 1844 to assure meat for the winter of 1844/45. He sold the remainder of the corn.

Ed McNeal had put his barn project off until Wilson's barn was finished, so Wilson spent the fall of 1843 helping Ed put up a barn and corn crib. Wilson was a good carpenter and he had his own tools, so with Ed's two boys and two other neighbors who lived close, the six of them had the job done before Thanksgiving. While Wilson was helping Ed build his barn, Sarah brought her children over to help Lucy pick corn while Mary Sue watched the children.

The day before Thanksgiving, with the barn and corn crib done, the six men turned their attention to bringing in the rest of Ed's corn crop. Wilson hadn't had time to plant a crop that year, but his neighbors had enough surplus so that there was plenty of corn to buy to fill his crib.

In 1845, Sarah gave birth to another son, whom they named Nathanial. This pleased them very much because, with a growing farm and prospects of a bright future, they would need as many hands to do the work as they could get. They wanted more children and were delighted when, in 1846, Sarah gave birth to twins. They were both boys, and they were named, James Franklin, and William. In 1848, a son, George, was born, followed by a daughter, Sarah, in 1850.

By this time their oldest daughter, Martha was eleven, and was helping to care for her younger siblings. This was a big help to Sarah, and she needed all the help she could get because she bore two more children after Sarah was born, Charles Wilson in 1854, and Mary in 1859.

Wilson, with help from his older sons had spent the last five years of the decade building a nice home with overlapped siding and brick fireplaces. They had sanded and varnished the hardwood floors, and there were plans to paint the exterior. It was a mansion compared to the farm houses of his neighbors, but there was no jealousy among them because they all knew how hard Wilson and his sons had worked to build it. Besides, he had always been generous with his time, helping his neighbors build their homes, barns, and smokehouses.

By 1860 the Wilson Nichols family consisted of two adults, Wilson – 40, Sarah – 43, and nine children, ranging in age from 1 to 21 years old, 6 boys and 3 girls. The three oldest boys were 14, 15, and 19 years old, and could work the land side-by-side with their father. The twin boys were 13 and George was 12. The three girls were Martha, 20, Sarah, 10, and Mary 1. The twin boys were assigned to take care of the horses, which by 1860 numbered 20 head, 8 big Percheron draft horses, and 12 head of riding horses that could also pull the small dray wagon and the spring buggy. The buggy was used to run to town for what groceries they needed, such as flour and sugar, and to take Sarah to church with the two youngest children, Charles six and Mary one. Wilson and the seven older children all had their own horses to ride to church. The Reverend John O'Donnell, pastor of the Hickory Ridge Presbyterian Church joked that when the Nichol's family turned down the lane to the church on Sunday, it looked like a Calvary charge.

CHAPTER 15

Sunday, July 1, 1860 was a beautiful day in Pettis County, Missouri, and after church, Wilson Nichols gathered his clan on the porch of his home on the hill that was part of what was known as Hickory Point. About three miles northeast from there, on the other end of the ridge was a cemetery known as Hickory Point Cemetery.

When his family had gathered around him Wilson said, "Your mother already has our dinner prepared, and since it's such a beautiful day, I thought it would be nice to eat out in the yard. "What do you think?"

The Children jumped up and down and shouted with delight. "Yes, yes," they shouted.

"Good," he said, "Johnny, you and Nathan bring some planks and two saw horses from the barn , and set up the table here," he motioned a spot under a big Elm tree. "The rest of us can help your mother bring the food from the kitchen. It was one-twenty in the afternoon when the table was set up, and they all bowed their heads while Wilson asked a blessing on the food.

While he was praying, he heard horses coming up their lane from the main trail, and a chill went up his spine. Given the unsettled conditions along the Missouri-Kansas border, that many horses in such a sparse area of Pettis County could only mean trouble.

There were 12 mounted men in the group, and when Wilson turned to greet them, he froze. They were heavily armed, and they all wore kerchiefs over their faces that extended from their eyes to their chests. Their apparent leader held up his right hand, and without a word spoken, they came to a stop about five feet from Wilson. The dust kicked up by their horses' hoofs drifted over the table and settled on the food.

Sarah was as frightened as Wilson, but she managed to make a shooing motion with her apron and most of the children started to run to the house.

"Come back here!" the leader of the band shouted. The children continued to run for the house, so he pulled a pistol and fired it in the air. "I said 'come back here'," he shouted again.

They looked toward their mother, and fearful that this stranger would shoot one of her children, Sarah motioned for them to come back. While the children drifted back to their seats,

Wilson walked around to the side of the leader's horse and looked up to him.

"What's the meaning of all this?" he asked, with just a tinge of anger in his voice, after all, the riders had disrupted his family's dinner.

The leader smacked Wilson across the face with his riding whip. "I'll ask the questions," he snapped, "you'll talk when you're called upon."

Wilson raised his hand, "May I remind you, Sheriff, that you're on my land?" he said.

Whap, the man hit Wilson again with his whip, this time drawing blood from his left cheek.

Where did you get the idea that I was the Sheriff?" he roared.

"By your voice, mainly," Wilson said politely, "but I also recognized your saddle, I rebuilt it for you a year ago, don't you remember?"

"No, I don't remember," he said, "and if you call me Sheriff again, I'll shoot you."

Wilson lowered his head and wiped the blood from his face with the back of his hand. "I've got to be careful with this man," he said to himself, "he might start shooting my family." He lowered his head again, "Please don't shoot," he said humbly.

"That's more like it," the sheriff said, "Just give us all of your blankets and guns, any meat in your smokehouse, and we'll ride on.

"Please don't take our blankets," Sarah cried, "my baby's only one, and we'll need our blankets to keep us warm this winter!"

The Sheriff smacked his right boot with his riding whip and said, "Shut up, or I'll give you a whipping too!" He pointed to two of the men and said, "You two search the house for blankets and guns," and pointing to two more ordered them search the smoke house for meat, and anything else they could eat. The four men dismounted, handed their reins to another rider, and ran to do what the sheriff had ordered them to do.

Wilson clinched his fists, but he didn't dare speak. He didn't want to endanger his family, so he stood silent. Johnny glanced over at Martha as if to say, "I'm going to make a run for the barn."

She shook her head ever so slightly to warn him what a foolish move that would be. Wilson had bought Johnny and Martha each a new lever action Henry rifle last Christmas, and they were both hidden in the barn, fully loaded. They had talked about some renegade bushwhackers riding up to their farm to steal guns, so they both had hidden their rifles in the hayloft above the barn. These men were not from around Green Ridge, or they would have known that the Nichols family (the ones 10 and older who were big enough to shoot a gun) were all crack shots, and that most of them had guns of their own, including the Sarah and the girls.

Ever since 1854, when the war on the border had started between the Kansas Jayhawkers, and the Red Legs who were abolitionists, and the Missouri farmers and plantation owners, who were mostly pro-slavery, had started, Wilson had been preparing. He had hoped that it wouldn't spread as far east as his farm, but each year it got closer. Now, it seemed that the abolitionists had spread their operations into Pettis County, because the County Sheriff was riding with them. Wilson noticed that three of the men in the group wore red leather leggings over their trousers.

Wilson and his family stood silently and waited, with Sarah holding Mary, the baby. In less than ten minutes, the men were back. One of the two from the house was carrying four wool blankets, which was about all he could carry, and the other one carried an old Kentucky, muzzle loaded, long rifle, a double barrel muzzle loaded shotgun, and an Army Colt 44 caliber revolver.

"Is that all you found?" the sheriff yelled.

"Yes sir," they both said, almost in sync.

"Where are the rest of your guns", the sheriff said.

"That's all we have, Sheriff, Wilson said.

Blam! The sheriff's pistol went off, and the bullet hit Wilson in the middle of his forehead. His head jerked back with the impact and then he slumped forward to his knees and rolled over on his right side.

There was an audible gasp from several of the men in the group. They obviously hadn't planned to actually shoot anyone. Clyde Guderman, the sheriff's head deputy, shook his head in disbelief.

“Dammit I told you not to call me that,” the sheriff said, as he turned to look at his men, to see if they were still behind him. The two searching the smokehouse were coming back empty handed when they heard the shot. They quickly mounted their hoses and prepared to ride out of the yard.

“Wilson!” Sarah screamed, handing the baby to Martha, she rushed to the side of her husband and took his head in her apron clad lap. Seeing the hole in the middle of his forehead without much blood coming out, she feared the worst, that her beloved husband was dead.

“Coward!” Johnny screamed as he dashed forward.

Several of the men drew pistols, thinking that he was going to attack the sheriff, but he veered off toward the barn. Two shots were fired at him, but he zig-zagged as he ran and reached the barn safely. The sheriff waved his pistol toward the lane, “Let’s get out of here,” he said.

The two men with the blankets and guns finished stuffing them in the cloth bags hanging from the sides of the pack horse they had with them, and they turned to go. As they galloped down the lane, Johnny appeared at the barn loft window with his new Henry repeating rifle. He took careful aim at the sheriff’s hat and pulled the trigger.

As the men paused while one of them opened the gate, the sheriff's hat went flying from his head, with a hole completely through the crown. A half second later they heard a rifle report. The men instinctively ducked, but paused while the sheriff got off his horse to retrieve his hat.

Chapter 16

"That was a hell-of-a-shot," Clyde Guderman, the head deputy, said as the sheriff ran his finger through the holes to assess the damage.

"It wasn't much," the sheriff said placing the hat back on his head, "he missed me didn't he?"

"He meant to miss you" the deputy said, "I know about that boy, he's the oldest son of the man you just killed, and he's probably the best shot in the county. He wins every turkey shoot and shooting match in a three county area. He's got one of those new Henry repeating rifles, and he really knows how to use it. He could have killed you if he had wanted to."

The men rode through the gate, and didn't bother to close it. "Why the hell didn't he kill me then, if he's such a good shot?" the sheriff said sarcastically, "I had just shot his pa."

The deputy rode up next to the sheriff so he could talk to him without yelling, "Because he's a really smart kid too," he said.

The sheriff shot him a look that would have burned a hole in a wool blanket. "Are you implying that he's smarter than I am," he said.

"Well, look at it this way," Clyde said, "if he had shot you, and maybe killed you, every county sheriff in a 100 mile radius would have been after him. What good would he be to his family if he was on the run all the time? No, he's going to bide his time, and some day a year or two from now, they're going to find you in a ditch far away from here, your body riddled with bullet holes."

The Sheriff stood up in his stirrups and stared at his deputy, "Who's side are you on!" he yelled.

The deputy didn't flinch, he had lost all respect for his boss when he saw him shoot an unarmed man in cold blood in front of his entire family. "I'm in this with you whether I like it or not," he said, "but do you know who the second best shot in the whole area is?"

"Who, me?"

"No, it's Johnny's older sister, Martha, and she has a new Henry too."

Wednesday, November 21, 2012 was Thanksgiving Eve, and Johnny Clayton would be out of school until next Monday. He had turned his term paper titled *The Ghost* of *Johnny Nichols* into his History Professor for his semester grade just before he left the campus at Columbia and drove home with his fingers crossed. He was hoping to get an A grade on it.

At 2:15 P.M., he pulled into his parent's driveway on West Fifth Street in Sedalia.

Tomorrow, there would be a big Thanksgiving dinner. Dorothy and her family would be down from Kansas City, and Johnny's mother would put a leaf in the dining room table to accommodate everyone. It would be a big family day, and Johnny was looking forward to it. He smelled the ham baking in the oven as he walked in the door. His mom always baked a ham as well as a turkey, so there would be plenty to eat. After dinner, the men would gather in the living room to watch football, and Dorothy and her mom would clear the table from dinner, and then sit at the kitchen table and chat over pumpkin pie and coffee.

Johnny went into the kitchen and hugged his mom, his dad was still at the office, but would be home soon. He went into the living room and called Mary on his cell phone. She would be spending Thanksgiving at home with her parents, as would Brad and Jeanie. They had agreed to meet Friday at the library at 10:00 A.M. to go over Johnny's paper, and to do some more research into the Civil war. Johnny was preparing to write a full length book titled *The Ghost of Johnny Nichols*, and get it published, if he could. It would be an expansion of his term paper, and that's why he needed to do more research.

Mary was writing a paper on the subject too, for a grade in her high school history class. Because of Johnny, she had gotten very interested in the Civil War, and already had 12 pages written. She had until January to hand it in for a grade. Brad and Jeanie came to the meetings simply because Johnny and Mary did, although Jeanie admitted that she was starting to look forward to their history discussions.

Friday, November 23, 2012 dawned cloudy and blustery in Sedalia, with prospects of a sunny afternoon and warmer temperatures. The Clayton family Thanksgiving dinner had been a big success, as usual, and Johnny had stuffed himself, as usual. He lay in bed listening for activity in the kitchen, which would indicate that his mother was up. At 8:15 he heard her stirring and propped himself up on one elbow.

"Johnny, I'm up," she called up the stairs. She knew he had a meeting at 10:00 A.M. at the library and, as usual, she knew he would want some breakfast before he left. She was right, Johnny drank a glass of orange juice, ate three eggs, two slices of toast with homemade grape jelly, and four slices of bacon.

She smiled as he grabbed his brief case and headed for the door, giving his mother a peck on the cheek along the way. "What time will you be home?" she asked as she followed him to the door.

"Between one and two," he said with a smile, as he shut the front door and climbed into his

Mustang. He tossed his leather briefcase on the seat beside him, started the motor and backed out into the street. The leather briefcase was as expensive one, but it had seen a lot of wear. His father had used it for the past 30 years. He had gotten a new one as a Christmas present from Helen, and since his old one still had quite a lot of use left in it, he asked Johnny if he wanted it. Johnny was very happy to get it, and had used it this past semester at collage.

The library was busy at 10:00 A.M., so Johnny had to park his Mustang in the next block. He was hoping that Mary had gotten down earlier and had managed to reserve a table for the four of them. He was sure that Brad and Jeanie would be there too, because Brad had offered to pick Mary up and bring her as well as Jeanie. Johnny took the front steps of the library two at a time, opened the big front door and went in. He turned left into the reading room and Mary waved at him from their usual table. "I can always count on Mary," he said to himself, as he tossed his brief case onto the table and plopped himself onto the only vacant chair.

"Sorry I'm late," he said

"It's just three minutes after," Mary said, "we haven't been here long."

"Where are you in your research?" he asked Mary, as he took a copy of the paper he had turned to his professor out on his briefcase and laid it on the table before him.

"Quantrill is getting ready to sack Lawrence, Kansas," she said.

"That was in August of 1863," Johnny said, "you've come quite a ways."

"Yes, and I love it," she said. "Every-now-and-then I run across a name that looks familiar to me. I might have some had ancestors mixed up in this story somehow, I'll have to do some more research.

"This genealogy stuff kind of gets under your skin, doesn't it?" Johnny asked.

"It sure does."

For the next three hours the four of them compared notes. Even Brad had started to get interested, and made some notes on the pad in front of him.

"We have to be careful what we write," Johnny said.

"What do you mean?" Mary asked.

"Well," Johnny said, "we don't want to copy each other too closely. "In other words, we need to be original in what we write, even if you're using my notes, and I'm using yours, or someday, someone might compare our works and one of us could be accused of plagiarism.

"You're right," Mary said, "I hadn't thought of that."

At 1:15 they decided to call it a day, and they went to their separate homes for lunch of mostly left-overs from Thanksgiving dinners. "How about tomorrow at nine?" Johnny Clayton asked as they left the library. They all agreed.

Chapter 17

As devastated as Sarah was, she tried to comfort her family. With Martha, Nathan, James, and William, all helping her, she managed to get Wilson's body into the house and up on the kitchen table, where she bathed it and dressed it in his only suit. By then, it was three in the afternoon.

Leaving Wilson's body on the kitchen table, Sarah call her family around her out in the yard. Martha and Sarah had managed to salvage most of their dinner and carried it to the spring house to keep it cool. No one felt like eating then, but the fried chicken, baked potatoes and fresh baked rolls would keep until lunch on Monday.

Johnny was the best carpenter of all of the boys, so she delegated him, with Nathan's help, to build a coffin. Luckily, there was plenty of planed and sanded oak lumber stored in the barn to do the job, and all the tools they needed were in the tool box that Wilson had built years ago.

"James," Sarah said, turning to one of the twins, "saddle up, and go get the Reverend. Tell him what happened, and that we'll be burying Wilson tomorrow afternoon, but tell him that I'd like to talk to him this afternoon, if possible."

James nodded and headed for the barn.

"Oh!" she called after him, "stop by the McNeal's on your way also, and tell Ed that we'd be proud if he and his family could come to the service tomorrow too."

Johnny wiped his eyes with the red bandana he carried in his hip pocket as he pulled the pieces of lumber he would need from the stack in the barn. Nathan got two saw-horses ready, selected the tools they would need from the tool box, and they got busy building a coffin.

By five P.M. they had finished the coffin, and with William and Charlie's help, they carried it and the saw horses into the kitchen. Sarah handed Johnny a white silk-satin sheet that had been given to her and Wilson as a wedding gift when they were married in 1839. She had kept it wrapped all these years, and it was like new. She also handed him a sack of cotton batting that she had left over from her quilt making days.

She spread the batting evenly on the inside of the coffin and Johnny helped her spread the sheet over the batting and tack it in place with small furniture tacks. When they were through, the coffin looked as nice as any they could have bought in St. Louis.

After Sara had taken Wilson's boots off to give to Johnny who wore the same size, the five of them, including Martha, picked Wilson's body up and arranged it in the coffin with his hands crossed over his chest. She put a pair of grey woolen stockings, that she had knitted, on his feet, and draped a white woolen shawl over them. She and Martha stepped back, held each other's hands, and with tears in their eyes, nodded their approval. Johnny and Nathan placed the lid on the coffin and screwed it down tight.

"Take him out on the porch," Sarah said, "it will be cooler out there. We can load the coffin onto the wagon tomorrow."

At five fifteen, just after they had carried Wilson's coffin out on the porch and placed it on the saw-horses, their Pastor, John O'Donnell rode up with James at his side. They were followed closely by Ed McNeal and his two sons. Sarah and Martha heard their horses coming up the lane from the main trail and ran out into the yard to greet them. John and Ed were the first ones to dismount and they both gave the two ladies a big hug, all the time shaking their heads in disbelief. James rode on out to the barn to unsaddle his horse, and Ed's sons followed him.

Sarah led the preacher and Ed onto the porch where Wilson's coffin stood while Johnny and Martha brought chairs out from the kitchen. When they were seated, Sarah apologized for having sealed the coffin so soon. "I'm sorry that you can't view his body," she said, pointing to the coffin, but…

"That's alright," the Reverend O'Donnell was quick to interrupt, "I'd rather remember him as he looked in church this morning. Tell us how this tragic event came about," he said.

Sarah nodded as she dried her eyes with her handkerchief, and struggling to hold back the tears, she gave them an account of what had happened just four hours earlier. When she got to the place where the Sherriff shot Wilson in the head she could no longer hold them back, and sobbed openly.

Ed and John both got up and went to Sarah's side to comfort her. When she had calmed down enough to talk again, Ed, who had trouble controlling his temper, spoke up. "Can you identify the men who did this?" he asked.

Sarah nodded.

"All 12 of them?"

Again, Sarah nodded.

Martha and Johnny, who were standing in the kitchen doorway listening, both said "Yes," in sync, and nodded their heads vigorously.

"Can you give me a list of them?" Ed asked.

Martha held up a sheet of paper in her hand, "I've already started a list," she said, "and I can have it ready in half an hour. I just want to double check it with Mom and the boys first, to verify their names.

"How can you be sure of their names, Martha," the Reverend asked, "your mother said they were masked."

"Oh, mostly little things," she said. "Pa and the older boys have done work of one kind or another for just about every man in the county during the past three or four years."

"Give me an example," he said.

"Well," she said, looking at her list, "Joe Rainey was their leader, and dad fixed his saddle just this past spring, plus, he's the County Sheriff, and everybody in the county knows him."

Johnny interrupted, "That's the reason he shot pa, because he kept calling him Sheriff."

"Did he have a mask on?" The preacher asked.

"All if the men had red bandanas over their faces from their eyes down to their chests," Martha said, "it's like they had planned it that way, but the Sherriff's voice gave him away, as well as the saddle.

Martha looked at her list again, "Clyde Guderman, the chief Deputy was with them," she said, "we sold him a riding horse last year. He was riding her this morning, and you know he has a slight German accent. Peter Klingon was another one. We've shod all of his horse for the last four years or more. I would recognize him anywhere with that whiney voice of his. Then there was…"

"That's enough for now," Ed interrupted. "I trust you that you and the boys got all of them right. Could you copy your list off on another piece of paper for me?" he asked.

"Yes, I'll be glad to," she said.

"What are you going to do with it?" the Preacher asked.

Ed patted the Colt 45 on his hip and said, "I'm going to track 'em down and shoot every damn one of them in the head."

"You can't do that," the Preacher protested.

"I know it, but we've got to get our bluff in on them soon," Ed retorted, "because if we don't, my family might be next, or yours, John. They're a bunch of cut throats, and if they sense that we're weak, and won't fight back, they'll get all of us sooner or later. I'm just going to sidle up to them one at a time and show them the list. I'll let them know that we can identify every one of them, and if they don't turn the Sheriff in for prosecution, well give the list to the Sedalia newspaper so they can publish it."

Chapter 18

Monday morning, July 2nd, 1860 was a warm, cloudless day, with a slight breeze blowing across Hickory Point from the southwest. Twenty three people gathered around the grave of Wilson Nichols at the cemetery, waiting for the brief service to start at ten a.m. This group didn't include the pastor's wife, and Ed McNeal's wife, Lucy, who were at the Nichol's home preparing the food for a noon meal after the service Sarah had asked the Reverend John O'Donnell, Pastor at the Hickory Ridge Presbyterian Church, where the Nichols family attended services, to preside over the brief service. He started by reading the 23rd Psalm, and then he turned the service over to Ed McNeal whom Sarah had chosen to give the eulogy.

Ed was tall, and looked younger than his 66 years. He took his broad brimmed hat off and stood holding it by the brim in his hands, his feet apart, and a stern look on his weathered face. He looked over at Sarah, and then down at the coffin.

"Wilson was my best friend," he began in a voice that was surprisingly calm and well-modulated to suit the occasion. "He brought his family here from Kentucky to start a farm. He was a horse breeder, a carpenter, a blacksmith, and had many other talents. He leaves his lovely and caring wife, Sarah, and nine of the best children you'll find anywhere. We'll all miss him very much…" at this point, his stoic demeanor failed him, and his big shoulders began to shake as he fought to keep from crying.

He wiped his face with his bandana, got a tighter grip on the brim of his hat and went on. "He was prayin' over their Sunday dinner when twelve of the biggest cowards in Pettis County, including the Sherriff, rode up the hill to their house and demanded that they turn over all of their blankets and guns. Twelve heavily armed men against Wilson, Sarah, and their children, who were unarmed at the time. Joe Rainy, our High Sherriff, took out his 36 caliber Navy Colt pistol, and shot Wilson in the head from close range, just because

Wilson recognized him and called him Sheriff. There were 22 witnesses to the shooting, and I'm going to ask the County Prosecuting Attorney to swear out a warrant for his arrest. That same gang may shoot me too if I testify against him, but he has to pay for his terribly crime. There wasn't a better man in the whole county, or a better friend, than Wilson Nichols, and that's all I'm gonna say." He stepped back, nodded to the preacher, and put his hat back on.

John O'Donnell, their Preacher, stopped forward and said, "Let's all sing that wonderful hymn *Amazing Grace,* I know that you know the words. He started it off in a wonderful, clear, tenor voice and by the time they finished it, they were all singing it together, and with gusto.

He stepped back and nodded to the five eldest Nichols boys plus Martha who were holding on to the three ropes that ran under the coffin. The six of them strained at the ends of the ropes, and when Ed could see the coffin raise up enough to clear the three two-by-fours holding it out of the grave, he slipped them out and tossed them aside. The coffin sank slowly into the grave, as the ropes slipped through the fingers of the six siblings, and hit the bottom with a thump. Ed McNeal and John Nichols took opposite ends of the ropes one at a time and by jerking them slightly, managed to straighten the coffin up so that it lined up with the sides of the grave. When they had it right, they pulled the ropes out, and started shoveling the dirt back into the grave. It was 10:21 A.M.

Ed put his arm around Sarah and helped her back into her buggy. Martha got up beside her to drive the team, and everyone but Johnny and Ed followed them back to the Nichols' home for lunch. Johnny and Ed stayed behind to fill the grave in and smooth it down. Johnny would come back in the fall and sow the bare dirt mound with rye and fescue grass so it would be green and pretty in the spring.

Everyone adjourned to the Nichols home. It was just over three miles from the cemetery, and by 11:00 A.M., most of them had showed up and were milling around the yard, waiting for the ladies to call them in for dinner. Almost all of the attendees had been up since before six to do their chores, so they were getting hungry. The aroma of fried chicken wafted across the yard from the kitchen, and they began to salivate. With Sarah and Martha in the kitchen helping with the food, it was about ready.

The Nichols' kitchen and dining room were bigger than most, but even at that, it was going to be very crowded, and hot. Ed suggested that they move the food out into the yard, which was agreeable to all. Ed and the Nichols' boys went to the barn and brought up enough planks and saw horses to set up three tables, enough to seat 24 people. There weren't enough chairs available to seat that many people, so the men brought enough cement blocks and planks from the barn to make benches on both sides of two of the tables. It worked out real well, and by five minutes to noon, they were all seated around the tables with the food piled on platters in the middle, family style.

Sarah asked Reverend O'Donnell to say the blessing over the food, and he readily agreed. He stood at the head of the table where Sarah sat, and was about to start the blessing, when he heard the sound horses hoofs coming up the lane. "Oh, no!" he said and looked to Ed for help. Ed jumped up, to see for himself, who might be coming to the Nichols' place at this time of day.

"John, Nathan, Martha," he barked, "get your rifles, quickly"!

All eyes turned toward the lane in time to see a number of men on horseback galloping up the lane. Sarah jumped up, "Good Lord, they're masked," she said, gasping for air.

There were eight buggies parked around the yard, so the riders had to slow down to wend their way to where the tables were set up. Ed had time to get to his buggy and retrieve his rifle and six shooter from under the seat. He grabbed a pocket full of rifle cartridges, tucked his pistol in his waist band, and headed back to the tables.

John, Nathan and James had reached the barn and retrieved their rifles from the hay loft where they were hidden. Martha raced upstairs to her bedroom, got her Henry rifle from the closet, and grabbed a box of cartridges from her dresser drawer. Two other men in the group had rifles in their buggies, and both had them ready by the time the riders had reached the tables. Because of the number of buggies parked in the yard, and six extra horses tethered to the hitching rail by the kitchen door, the riders were almost single file when they stopped at the head table, where Sarah was seated with Reverend O'Donnell and his wife.

The lead rider spurred his horse up close to the table where Sarah was seated, and said, "We went by the cemetery to watch them put your old man in the ground, but I guess we were too late, so we figured we'd come by and eat with you."

Sarah was frightened and taken aback by the man's crude words, but Ed O'Neal wasn't. He stood and cocked his rifle in one motion. His words emphasized his anger, "Don't anybody go for his gun, you sons-of-bitches!" he barked.

"Why," the man said, as he put his hand on the butt of the pistol on his hip, there's 12 of us, and only one of you."

"Well," Ed said, gritting his teeth, "because, there's four expert riflemen with their guns pointed at your head, and they don't miss. You'll be the first to go, Sherriff, and they can pick off the rest of you before you can get to the gate at the foot of the hill."

"We'll see about that," the Sherriff said as he slowly eased his pistol out of its holster and raised it to eye level. Everyone jumped as a rifle shot went off from an upstairs window and the Sherriff's gun went flying. The rest of the men went for their guns, and at that moment another rifle fired, this time from the barn loft window, and the Sherriff's hat went forward and covered his eyes. Ed stood up in his stirrups and pointed his rifle at the Sherriff's head.

"Those were just warning shots," he growled, "if they hadn't been, there would be two of you lying in the grass, because those people just don't miss. Now let me tell you something Sherriff, yes, Sherriff, everybody here knows who you are in spite of the bandanas over your faces. We recognize every one of you here, and we're going to get all of you eventually, but not now. First, we're going to get our statements together, and take them to the prosecuting attorney. Then we're going to have all of you arrested and tried for the murder of Wilson Nichols. After you're all hung, then we're coming back here to celebrate with a big meal."

The sheriff pushed his hat back on his head so he could see again, stood up in his stirrups, and turned so he could see the men behind him. The last two men in the group had already turned their horses and were headed for the lane. He turned back to face Ed, "Hand me my pistol," he said, pointing to his gun lying on the ground.

"Get it yourself," Ed said, and he sat watching the sheriff as he got down from his saddle and retrieved his gun. By the time he got back in his saddle, most of his men had turned their horses and were heading back toward the lane that ran down to the main trail. The sheriff turned his horse to follow them, and said over his shoulder, "This won't be the last of this, you can bank on that."

"I hope not," Ed shouted at him, "it would give me a lot of pleasure to shoot you in the head, just like you shot my friend Wilson Nichols.

The Sherriff spurred his horse to catch up with his men, but they were all in full gallop by then, and they were half-way to the main trail before he caught them. As they rode through the gate, another rifle shot went off and the Sherriff's hat flew off and landed in the middle of the trail. He spurred his horse and raced off toward Sedalia. His deputy retrieved the hat and raced after him, the rest of the men followed in a fast gallop.

CHAPTER 19

Saturday morning November 24th, 2012. By ten minutes after nine, the four students had gathered at their regular table in the Sedalia public library for more research into the life of Johnny Nichols. After they had settled in, Johnny was the first to talk.

"I found something at the Missouri State Historical Society last week that I forgot to tell you about."

"What?" Mary asked.

"Well," he said, "the women who work there know that I have been researching the family of Wilson Nichols, and one of them found a letter written by Sarah that really floored me.

"Oh!" Mary exclaimed, bouncing up and down in her seat, do you have it with you?"

"Not the original, they won't let any of their documents go out of their office, but she made me a copy."

"Oh!" Mary exclaimed again as she scooted forward in her chair to hear better, "read it to us, please!"

Monday, July 2nd, 1860. It was a few minutes before everyone at the Nichols home had settled down enough to start eating again. The boys had returned from the barn and Martha had come down from her bedroom, but they all still had their rifles with them, in case the Sherriff and his band of trouble-makers returned. Ed could speak normally again as he turned to Preacher John.

"Reverend," he said, "would you take another shot at asking the blessing?"

The Reverend John O'Donnell nodded and stood up at the head of the table. "Let us pray," he said. They all bowed their heads as he asked an appropriate blessing on the food.

That evening, after all the guests had left, taking with them what left-overs there were from the food they had brought, and everyone was in bed, Sarah came to Martha's bedroom to talk. A peaceful quiet had settled over the house, and Martha was sitting on the edge of her bed combing her long hair out. She and her mother were the only ones with their own bedrooms. The two other girls shared one room, as 10 year old Sarah was old enough to look after little Mary. The six boys shared a big bunk-room across the back of the second floor. They each had their own bunk, and a chest to keep their spare clothing and personal items in. It worked out real well for them, and all six were pleased.

Sarah sat down beside Martha, "I have something I want to tell you," she said, softly. Martha turned to her mother and laid the comb in her lap.

Her heart started thumping in her chest as she thought about all of the things that had gone on that day. "What is it?" she asked.

Sarah hesitated for just a moment while she thought about how she would start her story. Finally, she said, "When I was just a girl, about my Sarah's age, I think I was about eleven at the time, something happened that might be an answer to the problem that happened today."

Martha held her hand up to stop her mother, then she got up, laid her comb on her vanity, and pulled a chair up to the bed facing her mother. She didn't want to miss a word of what she had to say. "Please go on," she said.

"As I said, I was about eleven or maybe twelve, and we were living in Butler County, Kentucky, this was before my dad moved us back to Mercer County, where I met your father. I'm pretty sure the year was 1828. No, it was 1829, because Andrew Jackson had just been sworn in as president of our country. He was the one who wanted to take the Cherokee Indian's land from them and trade it for the land in Indian Territory. Do you know where that is?"

Martha nodded, "It's that land between Kansas Territory and Texas isn't it?"

"Yes, that's it."

"Why would the President want to do that?"

"Well, it wasn't just the president who wanted to get the Indians off of their land, a lot of people agreed with him. In fact, Congress passed a law in May of 1830, and President Jackson signed it. I think it was, called *The Indian Removal Act*, which forced the Indians to vacate their land. It was very good land, and the new Indian Territory land that we gave them in exchange, was land we got when President Jefferson bought all of the territory where we live now, and a lot more, from Napoleon in 1803. France needed money, so we got the land at a very cheap price."

"So we forced the Cherokees off of their land in exchange for some unexplored land a thousand miles away?" Martha asked.

"That's right, Martha, but it wasn't only the Cherokee who were forced off of their land, it was a group called the Five Civilized Tribes, which also included the Cherokee, Choctaw, Chickasaw, Muscogee, also known as the Creek Indians, plus the Seminole."

"How do you know all of this?" Martha asked.

"Well, I came from an educated family", Sarah said, "my father was a school teacher as well as a farmer, and my mother taught school too. You know, when I was growing up, girls weren't allowed by most families, to get an education. They usually went through the third grade, just far enough to learn to read and write, and to do simple arithmetic. Some didn't even learn to read and write. It just wasn't considered necessary, because girls were supposed to help their mother keep house until they married, and then they stayed home to nurse and nurture their own children, and keep their own home neat and clean."

"But you gave us older kids the equivalent of a high school education, and I'm grateful for that, mother."

"Well, we had the books to teach from, thanks to my parents, and I love to teach, so it was a pleasure to me to see you children learning so much. Now, with your help, Martha, we can continue the tradition with the younger children. There is another small box of books that we haven't gotten to yet and it contains twelve of the old classic stories handed down to me. I want you to start reading them so you can get an idea how the great writers of my youth wrote stories. As you finish them, you can pass them on down to George, and Sarah, and Charlie, and even little Mary when she gets old enough."

"Who wrote them, Mother?"

"Well, I have three by the Bronte sisters, including Emilie's Wuthering Heights, two by Nathanial Hawthorn, and several by English writers that you will love. I'll get them down tomorrow and give them to you to start reading."

"Oh, Mother, I can't wait to start reading them."

"Handle them carefully dear, so the other children can read them too. Now, back to my story.

As I said, we were living in Butler County, Kentucky in 1839. My parents had bought a tobacco farm from a family who moved back to Virginia. They didn't want to grow tobacco, but it was good soil and my dad wanted to grow corn. The year 1839 was just a fair year for crops, and my dad was disappointed, but he decided that we would stay another year or two, and if it didn't work out, we would move back to Mercer County. The winter of 1838/1839, was cold with quite a bit of snow. We were comfortable because we had plenty of wood for our stove, and the smoke-house was full of meat from the two hogs we had butchered, so we weren't worried, just bored. Fortunately, I had books to read.

Chapter 20

Saturday, November 24th, 2012. Johnny Clayton took four sheets of paper from the top of the pile in front of him and cleared his throat. Holding the sheets up so we all could see them, he said, "As near as I can find out, this is a letter from Johnny Nichols' mother Sarah to her sister in Indiana. It's dated July 4th, 1860, and it's addressed to Evangeline Todd. I don't know how the Missouri State Historical Society got hold of it, but they have ways of getting documents from other states. They belong to a National Historical Society, and they have conventions where they all get together and swap information. I imagine that's where they got it, at one of those meetings.

The letter began with Sarah telling her sister of Wilson's murder by the masked thugs who interrupted their picnic dinner. It covered the graveside funeral service and the gathering for dinner afterward. She told how Ed O'Neal had stood up to the same thugs when they interrupted that dinner, and how good shots from Martha and Johnny had hastened their departure. She told how she was afraid that they would come back, and then she related her plan to stop them by putting the *Curse of George Red Hawk* on all twelve of them. Finally, she promised that she would write more as soon as she knew how the curse worked out. It took Johnny 30 minutes to read the letter, and when he had finished it, he sat back to get their reaction, especially Mary's.

July 2nd, 1860, Martha's bedroom in the Wilson Nichols home.

Sarah started her story…"It was the 4th of January in 1839, and I was sitting on the couch by our big bay window reading a book, when I glanced out the window and saw a group of people coming toward our house. I called for my father to come quickly, and he came and stood by the window with me and watched them approach. "They're Indians," he said. We stood by the window and watched a group of about twenty Indians in their usual Indian attire approach the front of our house. They stopped about ten feet from our porch, and looked as if they didn't know what to do next. Father opened the front door and went out on the porch to try to talk to them. Their leader was on horseback, wrapped in a blanket, and looked like a Tribal Chief. Father raised his hand in a friendly gesture.

The old Chief raised his hand in answer, and said something in Cherokee that my father didn't understand. A young male who appeared to be in his mid-twenties, was holding the reins to the Chief's horse, apparently leading it. He handed the reins up to the old man, and stepped forward.

"I am John Red Fox, grandson of Chief George Red Hawk," he said pointing to the old man on the horse.

"I see that you speak English." My father said to the young man.

The young man nodded.

"What brings you to my home?" father asked.

"We have been on a long forced journey, and we are cold and hungry. Can you furnish us with some food?"

"You look cold and wet from the snow," my father said, looking at the small children in their mothers' arms, some with rags wrapped around their feet instead of shoes.

The young man nodded, "Yes, we are cold and wet also," he said.

My father pointed to a big empty barn behind and to the left of our house. The farm had originally been a tobacco farm, but my father had bought it to raise corn and wheat, and had never used the tobacco drying barn, except to store his farm machinery in one end of it. It was made of split logs, the same as the house, except it was bigger, and had large windows that could be opened in the summer so the wind could blow through and dry the tobacco. The main thing was that it had a good roof and was dry on the inside. "I'll go open that barn up," he said, "and you can go in there to get in out of the wind."

The young man nodded and they all headed for the barn.

"My father, my older brother, and me, put our coats on and went out to open up the barn. We opened the big door on the south end of it and after the Indians had all filed through it, we closed and secured it. There was a big cast iron stove in the middle of the barn with a tin flu going up through the roof. When the air outside was too damp, the tobacco farmer would build a fire in the stove so the tobacco would dry faster. While my brother took a wheelbarrow and went to the woodpile for wood, my father and I spread a couple of tarps on the floor so the Indians wouldn't have to sit in the dirt.

Two of the Indians, one of which was the Chief's grandson, helped us bring buckets of water from the well, and gourd dippers from the kitchen, so they would have drinking water. Mother got busy and mixed up a big pan of cornmeal mush and put it on the kitchen stove to heat. Corn meal was the only ingredient she had enough of in the kitchen that would feed that many people. She had baked bread that morning, so she had several loaves of fresh baked bread to go with the mush. My father went to the smokehouse and brought out the biggest ham he could find and carried it to the kitchen and started carving it into strips about an inch wide and three inches long. When he had finished carving the ham, the mush was warm enough to serve, so with help from the Indians, and my brother, we carried the food to the barn.

Although starved for food, the Indians remained orderly, until Red Fox fed the old Chief first. The rest squatted cross legged in circles on the tarps and began to dip the bread in the mush and eat. The ham didn't last long, but each one got at least one strip.

When night came, father showed Red Fox how to bank the fire in the stove so that it would burn slowly most of the night. My mother brought out three spare blankets from our closet to spread over them, especially the children.

"I woke up early the next morning, but my mother was already up and fixing another pan of mush. It took all of our cornmeal, and she had to make it thinner to make a full pan, but they could dip it with a gourd and sip it. At least it would be warm and still have some nourishment. Mother sliced up one whole slab of bacon and fried it in her big iron skillet. There was enough for each of the Indians to have two slices.

Our family ate the six eggs we had on hand, and some of the bacon. Mother sliced four slices off of a loaf of bread for our toast and sent the rest of the loaf out to the Indians.

We had just finished eating, when there was a loud rap on the front door. When my father opened it, two men dressed like soldiers, except there were no insignias on their uniforms, were at the door. There were two more on horseback out in the yard, holding two saddled horses and a pack horse.

"What can I do for you?" my father asked.

"Where are them Indians," the taller of the two demanded gruffly, "and don't try to tell us you ain't seen 'em!

"My father told them about the ones who slept in the barn last night, and asked them what interest they had in them."

"We're in charge of 'em," the taller man said, "and they ran off from us three days ago. We've got to take 'em back to the rest of the tribe so we can get on our way to the Indian Territory out west."

"Are you from the United States Army?" father asked.

"No," the man said, "but we've been contracted by the Army to make sure these heathens get to where they're supposed to be. We got over 300 more waitin' down on the trail south of here, and these renegades is holding us up. It took us three days to track 'em down, and if it weren't for the snow, we never would have found them."

"Don't you feed them?"

"Sure, we feed 'em, but the Army jest don't give us enough food to go around.

"Do you give them all of the food the Army provides, or do you eat most of it?

"You sure are nosy, aint you? Are you goin' to turn 'em over to us, or do we have to burn your house and barn down to get 'em to come out?"

"Father remained calm, but he was mad as hops. He opened the barn and allowed the four men to herd the Indians back toward the main trail where the rest of the tribe waited under the guard of 10 more armed men. Chief Red Hawk spoke to Red Fox and refused to mount his horse until he had talked to father and me. Since the Indians wouldn't move on until Chief Red Hawk bade them to, the four guards allowed them to talk in private.

Through Red Fox, Chief Red Hawk asked if there was some way he could repay us for the food and shelter from the cold.

Father told him no, that it was only the humane thing to do, and he was grateful for the opportunity.

Chief Red Hawk said through Red Fox that he had nothing left to repay him with at this time, except his horse, and some curses given to him many years ago by the Nunnehi, who are the Little People in our culture. I had freed a Red Tailed Hawk from some brambles where he had flown to catch a rabbit and gotten tangled up. I had just freed the hawk when a Nunnehi appeared to me and said for my kindness to the hawk, he was going to give me 15 curses to be used against my enemies. A curse will destroy one enemy, so I had the power to destroy 15 of my enemies. I am old now, he continued to relate through Red Fox, and I have only used two of the curses in the 60 years that I have had them. I destroyed two soldiers who had beaten a squaw who was with child, killing both the squaw and her child. I gave the curses a week to work their task on the soldiers. The next day, one accidently shot himself with his own rifle and the other one fell off of a path into a river below and drowned.

I have 13 curses left and I have the power to give them to you if you will take them from me. They could protect you from your enemies.

Father refused, and the guards were pressing Red Hawk to get the tribe moving, so, silly me, I held up my hand and asked father if Red Hawk could give them to me. I figured we might need them some day against the Yankee Soldiers since we were southern sympathizers. My father looked at Chief Red Hawk when Red Fox asked him if he could give them to me, the Chief nodded and took out a very sharp knife. Red Fox said I could have the curses, but first I would have to be a blood sister to him, and since he was the grandson of Red Hawk, that act would make me a member of the Cherokee nation.

Red Fox held out his right hand, palm up, and Chief George Red Hawk, Chief of the Manassas tribe of the

Cherokee Nation made a small cut in it, enough to make it bleed. Red Fox took my hand and held it out to his grandfather, and when I flinched, he assured me that it wouldn't hurt much, so I let Red Hawk make a small slit in my palm. When the slit in my hand started to bleed, Red Fox pressed his hand to mind so that our blood mingled. While our blood mixed, the old Chief raised his hands and said three syllables in the Cherokee language. Red Fox gave my hand back to me and said that, now, I was his blood sister, and a member of the Cherokee.

The old Chief then put his hands on my shoulders, looked up at the sky and said three more syllables. You now have 13 curses to use, Red Fox said. Red Fox helped his grandfather on to his horse, took the reins in his hand, and led it down the trail toward the south with the rest of the tribe following behind. The four guards glared at my father as they rode along beside and behind the Indians.

I was standing there bewildered, looking at my right hand, when my father took it in his and wrapped a handkerchief around it to stop the bleeding. 'That's a lot of power, use it wisely,' he told me as we walked back into the house."

Chapter 21

"Wow, that was some letter," Mary gasped when Johnny Clayton had finished reading it. "I remember reading about the removal of the five civilized to Oklahoma in history class. That was sure a cruel thing to do."

"Yes," Johnny said, "but supposedly, it was all done legally through treaties and other agreements, all ratified by congress, signed by our president and the various Indian Chiefs. The biggest tribe were the Cherokee, who settled in northeastern Oklahoma, but I found out from reading about them that there are two bands of Cherokee. A group of them living in what is now North Carolina, avoided removal because the land they were living on was ceded to them by some earlier treaties. The treaties held up in court, so they stayed. Today, they are known as the Eastern Band of Cherokee.

Brad Compton spoke up, "I never cared much for history until we got into this ghost thing, and now, I really like it."

Jeanie nodded her approval, "Me too," she said.

"What say we get together during Christmas break and work on this some more?" Johnny said. "I should know what kind of a grade I got on my history paper by then, and we can judge the scope of our work a little better by that. Is that okay with you guys? My first semester ends on December 21st, and my second semester doesn't start until mid-January, so I'll have nearly a month to work here at home. How about it?" he asked.

The other three agreed.

"Are you going to use the curses on those men who shot father?" Martha asked.

"Well, it came to me," she said, "that it would be a good way to end our problems with them, and nobody would know what really happened. What do you think, will it work?"

"I think it would, and they deserve to go that way," Martha said, "they're just a bunch of border ruffians who don't like southern sympathizers, and except for the sheriff, I doubt if they'd be missed by most people."

"I think I'll try it on one first, and if it works, I could curse the rest, what do you think?"

"Yes," Martha answered, "try it on the sheriff first since he's the ring leader, and if he dies, the gang might just disband."

The next morning, July 3rd, 1860, after the Nichols family had all had breakfast, Sarah motioned for Martha to follow her. She led her into the edge of the woods behind their house and stopped at a small clearing. Martha watched as her mother raised her hands up toward the brilliant blue sky and repeated the three syllables of Cherokee that Chief Red Hawk and taught her. Then she lowered her hands and said the name of the cursed person, "Joe Rainey, by 3:00 P.M. tomorrow, July 4th." She raised her hands again and repeated three more syllables of Cherokee the Chief had taught her. She lowered her hands and said, "That should do it, Martha, now we'll wait to see if it works."

They walked back into the house and continued their chores with anxious longings. It was hard to keep their minds on their work as they waited for the curse to work.

They didn't hear about the results of the curse until nearly 6:00 P.M. on Wednesday July 4th when Ed McNeal came home from a trip to the hardware store in Sedalia to buy a new handle for his axe. He could have made one, but as he said to Lucy, "They just don't fit like the store bought ones do."

"They had a parade in town today," he said, "in celebration of today being Independence Day, and there was quite a commotion during the parade."

"What happened," Martha asked anxiously.

"Well," Ed said, "the sheriff was leading the parade on his horse, when he had a heart attack right in the middle of the street."

"Did he die?" Sarah asked.

"He sure did, he slid out of his saddle, and was dead when he hit the ground."

"What time did it happen?" Martha asked.

"Oh, I reckon it was about three o'clock," Ed said.

Martha looked at Sarah and smiled, "I guess he won't be leading another posse into our yard," she said.

"I guess not," Ed said, as he wheeled his horse around and started back to the lane. "Thanks, Ed," Sarah yelled after him.

"You're welcome," he yelled back over his shoulder, "I just thought you'd like to know."

The next day, July 5th, 1860, right after breakfast, Sarah and Martha went out into the woods behind their house, and Sarah put her curse on the other11 men in the gang that had murdered her husband. She had listed them, by date, in the order that she wanted them to die, on a sheet of paper, and had spaced them out so as not to raise any suspicion with the public. She didn't want to start a rumor that a mysterious epidemic was spreading in the area. She saved Robert Brownley, and Henry Heimsoth for last. They both lived in Sedalia, and were close friends of the Sheriff. She scheduled them both to die on December 31st, 1863, at 3:00 P.M.

In December of 1860, 15 year old Nathan Nichols rode to Jefferson City, Missouri on his big red stallion and enlisted in General Price's Missouri State Guards, telling his mother that he couldn't wait any longer to fight back at the people who killed his father. By joining the State Guard, he thought he could do it legally, instead of joining one of the many bands of renegade confederates roaming up and down the Missouri-Kansas border raiding and killing at random. His mother cried to see him go, but she gave him her blessing. Their Christmas was less joyful without him.

Another shock came for Sarah in January of 1861, when 14 year old James followed his older brother to Jefferson City and enlisted also. Since both boys were so far advanced in their riding skills and in marksmanship, they were placed in a new unit called the Mounted Infantry which was a fast moving infantry unit. They didn't fight on horseback, but would dismount when they got to their destination and fight like the other infantry units.

Then again, after the spring crops were planted, in May of 1861, Sarah's oldest son, John 19, rode to Jefferson City and enlisted in the State Guard on the 18th of that month. It grieved Sarah to have her three oldest sons gone at the same time, but she completely agreed with their mission. She knew that if war broke out, they would give a good accounting of themselves.

When Ed McNeal's wife, Lucy, died of cancer in June of 1861, he turned his farm over to his two sons and retired at age 64. By that time, his grandchildren were old enough to help with the work, so he didn't worry about it. The McNeal and Nichols families had been good friends for 20 years, and Ed missed Wilson almost as much as Sarah did. He would ride over to see her two or three times a week, and their friendship meant a lot to both of them. Neither of them had any desire to re-marry, but they enjoyed their friendship very much. It helped fill the big void each of them had when their spouses died. Ed treated the Nichols children like they were his own, and Sarah felt the same way about his children and grandchildren.

The U.S. Postal service was originated by the Continental Congress in July of 1775, with Benjamin Franklin as postmaster, and the power to place posts as needed from Massachusetts to Georgia. Postal service was scarce and slow in those days, but by 1861, with the use of faster river boats instead of the old packet boats, and railroads instead of horse drawn vehicles, the speed and reliability had vastly improved. When the southern states seceded from the Union, they were forced to create their own Postal Service, and it was erratic at best. After the war, however, the Southern Postal Service was rejoined to the U.S. Service, and normal service to the southern states was restored.

Once a week, Sarah would send one of her children to the Post Office in Sedalia to see if there was any mail, but letters from her sons were scarce, and she worried about them. Martha was a big help and a comfort to her mother, but she found herself nearly in tears on occasions when her mind wandered back to the days when she and Johnny would play together as children.

Their worries increased when the entire year of 1862 went by with no word from Nathan or James. John, on the other hand, was sent home for a rest period in March of 1861. His unit was in a battle at Cole Camp, Missouri, and John contracted pneumonia during the fighting. Since there was no medical service available for him in his unit, his commanding officer sent him home for three months to recover. Sarah was happy to have him home, albeit with a serious illness, but she and Martha nursed him back to good health.

He rejoined General Price's Army in June of 1861 just in time to engage in the battle of Dry Wood, Missouri. After that battle, he was assigned to General Price's body guard. From Dry Wood, they engaged in the Battle of Lexington, Missouri where they captured General Mulligan's Union

Army. From there, General Price fell back and established winter quarters at Springfield Missouri. Sarah got a letter from him in March of 1862 dated in February, saying that he was alright, but they might be retreating further south.

CHAPTER 22

Sedalia, Missouri, Saturday, December 22, 2012. Johnny Clayton was home on semester break, and had called his group together to compare notes concerning their history project about John S. Nichols. They met at the library at nine A.M. to go over additional material they had gleaned since their last meeting in November.

Johnny had received an A+ on his semester paper for his history class, and was very happy about that. Mary had found a lot of new information about the Nichols family in the library, and on-line, and was anxious to share it with the rest.

The year 1863 was a very eventful year for the Nichols family and Mary started off by telling of John's capture and trial.

"First, I need to see if you three have ever heard of General Order Number 10?" she asked. Johnny had, but Jeanie and Brad had not. Mary held up a copy of it, and since it had played such a big part in Johnny's future, she chose to read it to the rest.

General Order Number 10.

This order was issued by Brigadier General Ewing, Commanding Officer of the Headquarters District of the Border, Kansas City, Missouri, August the18th, 1863.

I. Officers commanding companies and detachments, will give escort and subsistence, as far as practicable, through that part of Missouri included in the District, to all loyal free persons desiring to remove to the state of Kansas or to a permanent military stations in Missouri-including all persons who have been ascertained, in the manor provided in General Order No. 9 of this District, to have been the slaves of persons engaged in aiding the rebellion since July 23, 1862, will be taken to help such removal , and after being used for that purpose, will be turned over to the officer commanding the nearest military station, who will at once report them to an Assistant Provost Marshall, or to the District Provost Marshall and hold them subject to this order.

II. Such officers will arrest and send to the District Provost Marshall for punishment, all men (and all women, not heads of families) who willfully aid and encourage guerillas; with a written statement of the names and residences of such persons and of the proof against them. They will discriminate as carefully as possible between those who are compelled by threats or fears to aid the rebels and those and those who aid them from disloyal motives.

The wives and the children of known guerillas, and also women who are heads of families and are willfully engaged in aiding guerillas, will be notified by such officers to move out of this district and out of the State of Missouri forthwith. They will be permitted unmolested, their stock, provisions and household goods. If they fail to remove promptly they will be sent by such officers under escort to Kansas City for shipment south, with their cloths and such necessary household furniture as may be worth removing.

III. Persons who have borne arms against the government and voluntarily lay them down and surrender themselves at a military station, will be sent under escort to the District Provost Marshall at these Head Quarters. Such persons will be banished with their families to such State or district out of this department as the General Commanding the

Department may direct, and will there remain exempt from civil trial for treason.

IV. No officer or enlisted man, without special instructions from these Head Quarters will burn or destroy any buildings, fences, crops or other property. But all furnaces and fixtures of blacksmith shops in that part of Missouri included in the District, not at military stations, will be destroyed and the tools either removed to such stations or destroyed.

V. Commanders of companies and detachments serving in Missouri will not allow persons not in the military service of the United States to accompany them on duty except when employed as guides, and will be held responsible for the good conduct of such men employed as guides and for their obedience to orders.

VI. Officers and enlisted men belonging to regiment or companies, organized or unorganized, are prohibited going from Kansas to the District of Northern Missouri without written permission or order from these Head Quarters or from the Assistant Provost Marshall at Leavenworth City or the Commanding officer at Fort Leavenworth or some officer commanding a military station in the District of Northern Missouri.

By Order of Brigadier General Ewing

P.B. Plumb, Major and Chief of Staff

"Wow!" Johnny exclaimed when Mary put her copy of General Order Number 10 down and looked to Johnny, and the others for comment. "General Ewing must not have heard of our Constitution."

"That's what I thought when I read it the first time," Mary said, "it puts a lot of power into the hands of people who have no experience in using it."

"I'll bet it was grossly abused" Johnny commented more to himself than to the other three.

"Oh, it was," Mary said. "From what I can glean from the history books in the library, the order wasn't obeyed as written, and the Deputy Provost Marshalls used it to get even with people they just didn't like."

Brad shook his head in disgust, "Can you imagine having someone sent to prison, or even hung, just because you didn't like the way they combed their hair, or had a different opinion from yours?"

Mary picked the document up and handed it to Brad. "Just look at it," she said, "it's full of grammatical errors. If the General was a West Point grad, which I imagine he was, it seems to me that he didn't even have it proof read, much less given a whole lot of thought as to its effect on people's lives."

Johnny searched through the pile of papers in front of him. "Here are some things I dug up that have been written about General Order Number 10" he said. "These are some comments from a forum called "Civil War Talk" on the Internet. Shall I read them?" He asked.

They all nodded.

He read from a copy taken from the forum;

"Despite the seemingly well-meaning tone of this order and the warnings against depredations contained in it, the order when carried out was not strictly obeyed and as he would when he implemented General Order Number 11, Ewing would allow units of the Kansas Red Legs and Jayhawkers to take part in putting this order into effect. While General Ewing bears most of the blame, as he should, one must remember that prior to the war Ewing was a politician, and he continued to harbor political aspirations."

"There's your answer as to whether General Ewing attended the Military Academy at West Point, Mary," Johnny pointed out.

He continued – "The most powerful politician in the region at this time was Senator Jim Lane of Kansas, also the commander of the Kansas Brigade AKA The Red Legs. There is ample evidence that Lane used his political power to badger Ewing into both issuing this order, and General Order #11 as well, as using "selected" Kansas Units to take part. In any event, this is the order that kicked off an ungodly period of bloodshed and heartbreak in Missouri and Kansas."

"Who were the Kansas Red Legs?" Brad asked.

CHAPTER 23

"I put this paper together from several sources on the internet," Johnny said, "It pretty much tells us who the Red Legs were." He started to read.

Kansas Red Legs – During the early part of the Civil War, Missouri was infested with bands of guerillas, and it was no uncommon occurrence for some of these lawless gangs to cross the border and commit depredations in Kansas. To guard against these incursions, and otherwise to aid the Union cause, a company of borders scouts was formed sometime in the year 1862. As it was an independent organization, and never regularly mustered into the United States service, no official record of it has been preserved. The men composing the company became known as "Red Legs," from the fact that they wore leggings of red or tan-colored leather.

Johnny looked up, "The date the company was actually formed is confusing," he said. "I have read it was formed in June of 1862, and there is one claim made by a member of the company who claimed that it was organized in October of 1862. There is still another account that says it was organized in either Dec of 1862 or January of 1863. All of the accounts agree that Senator Lane from Kansas was their commander, but the field commander, under Lane, was Capt. George H. Hoyt and the size of the company is listed as from 50 to 163 men, take your pick.

The Red Legs were organized, under the Provost Marshal in Leavenworth, Kansas, but when Ewing took over from Gen. James G. Blunt in the spring of 1863, he hired Hoyt as his chief detective, and a lot of Red Legs got detective papers and really unheard of legal powers – they could search anything, demand anything, and kill anyone who refused to comply. Doubtless, they took great pleasure in illegally punishing many Missourians. There is no wonder that the people of Western Missouri hated the Red Legs.

The qualifications for membership in the company were, unquestioned loyalty to the Union cause, undaunted courage, and the skillful use of the rifle or revolver. Their headquarters in Kansas was the "*Six-Mile House*, so called because it was six miles from Wyandotte, Kansas on the Leavenworth road. This house was erected in the winter of 1860-61 by Joseph A. Bartels, whose son, Theodore, one of the best pistol shots on the border, was a member of the Red Legs. The commander of the Red Legs, Capt. George H. Hoyt, was the Lawyer who defended John Brown at Charleston, Va.

There were redlegs before there were Red Legs, so to speak. In September of 1861, before the Seventh Kansas was officially mustered into the Union Service, Charles R. Jennison and a couple of hundred future "Jayhawkers" raided independence, Mo., ostensibly to protect Unionists who were being harassed by local secessionists, but actually, in typical Jennison style, it was to make a profit. They gathered all the nearby men into the Independence town square, then went about looting the local shops. In one of them, a shoe store owned by a man named William P. Duke, they came across about 100 red sheepskins, designated for boot tops. Covering their own boots with these, they assumed a distinct look and founded a feared name: thenceforth, marauders from Kansas were known as redlegs. And there were plenty of Kansas marauders and multiple gangs of redlegs, leading to further generalization of the name.

In September of 1862, Senator Lane led the "Red Legs" on a pillaging march through western Missouri, burning and looting as they went. The climax of Lane's march occurred at the little town of Osceola, Missouri, about 60 miles south of Sedalia in Saint Clair County, on September 23. After exchanging a few shots with some Confederates on the outskirts, his men entered the town and proceeded to ransack it. They robbed the bank, pillaged stores and private houses, and looted the courthouse. Captain Thomas Moonlight bombarded this last building with a cannon, and others set fire to the town, almost totally destroying it. Many of the Kansans got so drunk that when it came time to leave they were unable to march and had to ride in wagons and carriages. They carried off with them a tremendous load of plunder, including as Lane's personal share, a piano, and a quantity of silk dresses. The "Sack of Osceola" henceforth became the prime cause of the bitter hatred of Lane and Kansans in general by the people of West Missouri.

"Does that answer your question, Brad," Johnny asked.

"Yes," Brad said, "but what kind of power did General Order Number 11 give to the military?"

"A lot," Johnny said as he looked over another handful of papers that he had taken from his stack. "I have a copy of General Order Number 11 here if you want me to read it," he said. They all nodded, so Johnny read from his copy of General Order Number 11.

General Order Number 11 Headquarters, District of the Border, Kansas City, August 25, 1863.

1. All persons living in Jackson, Cass, and Bates counties, Missouri, and in that part of Vernon included in the district, except those living within one mile of the limits of Independence, Hickman Mills, Pleasant Hill, and Harrison, and except those in that part of Kaw Township, Jackson County, north of Brush Creek and west of Big Blue, are hereby ordered to remove from their present places of residence within fifteen days from the date hereof. Those who within that time establish their loyalty to the satisfaction of the commanding officer of the military station near their present place of residence will receive from him a certificate stating the fact of their loyalty, and the names of the witnesses by whom it can be shown. All who receive such certificates will be permitted to remove to any military station in this district, or to any part of the state of Kansas, except the counties of the eastern border of the state. All

others shall remove out of the district. Officers commanding companies and detachments serving in the counties named will see that this paragraph is promptly obeyed.

All grain and hay in the field or under shelter, in the district from which inhabitants are required to remove, within reach of military stations after the 9th day of September next, will be taken to such stations and turned over to the proper officers there and report of the amount so turned over made to district headquarters, specifying the names of all loyal owners and amount of such product taken from them. All grain and hay found in such district after the 9th day of September next, not convenient to such stations, will be destroyed.

The provisions of General Order No. 10 from these headquarters will be at once vigorously executed by the officers commanding in the parts of the district and at the station not subject to the operations of paragraph 1 of this order, especially the towns of Independence, Westport and Kansas City.

Paragraph 3, General Order No. 10 is revoked as to all who have borne arms against the Government in the district since the 20th day of August, 1863.

By order of Brigadier General Ewing

H. Hannahs, Adjt – Gen'l

Mary held up her hand, "There was so much hate between the Kansans and Missourians back then, that this order only agitated an already bad situation, don't you think so?" she said.

Johnny nodded his head vigorously, "Yes, I do," he said. "You know that just two days before this order came out, William Quantrill and his band of renegades sacked and burned Lawrence Kansas in retaliation for some of the things the Union troops did under General Order Number 10. They ran the farmers out of the district, and sent most of their wives to Kansas City and locked them up. They were being held in an old building in Kansas City that collapsed and killed several of the women, one of whom was the wife of Bloody Bill Anderson. Anderson rode with Quantrill at the time, and I think that the death of the women in Kansas City triggered the sacking of Lawrence."

"I read about that," Mary said. "I think that between the Red Legs and Union Soldiers gone rogue, they caused most of the problems in Western Missouri. Senator Lane and his Red Legs from Kansas sacked and burned three towns in Southwestern Missouri, Including Osceola, which was burned to the ground.

Brad entered the conversation, "There's an old Clint Eastwood movie out about the Red Legs and some of the terrible things they did," he said. I think it's called *The Outlaw Josie Wales*, or something like that."

"I've seen that movie," Jeanie said, it was on the late show the other night. I liked it."

"I've seen that movie several times," Johnny said, "I think it's a great movie, and it's sure true to history."

"Here's my opinion of the effect of General Order Number 11, he said as he consulted the notes he had put together for his book.

He read from his notes;

"Order No. 11 was not only intended to retard the pro-Southern depredations, but the renegade pro-Union activity, as well. Gen Ewing not only had his hands full with Confederate raiders; he equally had troubles with Unionist Jayhawkers, led by the radical Kansas Senator

James Lane. There was a lot of anger sweeping over Kansas following Quantrill's raid.

Convinced that Ewing was not retaliating enough against the Missourians, Lane threatened to lead a Kansas force into Missouri, laying waste to the four counties named in Ewing's decree, and more. On September 9th, 1863, Lane gathered nearly a thousand Kansans at Paola, Kansas, and marched towards Westport, Missouri, with an eye towards destruction of the pro-slavery town. Ewing sent several companies of his old Eleventh Kansas Infantry (now mounted as cavalry) to stop Lane's advance, by force, if necessary. Faced with superior Federal force, Lane ultimately backed down.

Order No. 11 was partially intended to demonstrate that the Union forces intended to act forcefully against Quantrill and other bushwhackers, thus rendering vigilante actions (such as the one contemplated by Lane) unnecessary, and thereby preventing their occurrence, which Ewing was determined to do at all cost."

Johnny paused and looked up at the clock, "It's five minutes after twelve," he said, "do you want to take a break and run up to Eddies and get a hamburger?"

Jeanie looked up from her note taking, "I'd rather wait until one," she said, "I ate such a late breakfast that I'm just not hungry right now."

"I'm with her," Mary said, "let's wait until one."

Johnny looked over at Brad, who nodded his approval. "Okay," he said, we'll go at one."

He look back down at his notes, "Shall I continue reading?" he asked. The other three nodded, so he cleared his throat and continued.

"General Ewing ordered his troops not to engage in looting or other depredations, but he was not able to control them. Most of them were Kansas volunteers, who regarded all Missourians as "rebels" to be punished, even though many residents of the four counties named in Ewing's orders were pro-Union or at least neutral on the subject of slavery. Animals and farm property were stolen or destroyed; houses, barns and other outbuildings were burned to the ground.

Some civilians were summarily executed – a few as old as seventy. Ewing's four counties became a devastated "no man's land," with only charred chimneys and burnt stubble showing where homes and thriving communities had once stood, earning them the sobriquet "The Burnt District." There are few remaining antebellum homes in this area due to the order."

CHAPTER 24

"Ironically," Johnny continued, "Ewing's order had the opposite military effect from what he intended: instead of eliminating the guerrillas, it gave them immediate and practically unlimited access to supplies.

For instance, the Bushwhackers were able to help themselves to abandoned chickens, hogs, and cattle, left behind when the owners were forced to flee. Smokehouses were sometimes found to contain hams and bacon, while barns often held feed for horses. Although Federal troops ultimately burned most of the outlying farms and houses, they were unable to prevent Confederates from initially acquiring vast amounts of food and other useful material from abandoned dwellings."

Johnny looked up, "Things were really a mess on the Missouri, Kansas border, with so much power in the hands of so many inexperienced people, there's no wonder that there was so much killing and looting going on."

"Do you blame General Ewing for the problems?" Jeanie asked.

"Not entirely," Johnny said, "I think that some Kansans like Senator Lane and Col. Charles Jennison had a lot to do with the trouble too. There was enough blame to go around, don't you think so?"

"I do," Mary said emphatically.

"Me too," Jeanie added.

"I made some notes for my book about what some of the historians have said about those two General Orders," Johnny said. "Shall I read them?"

"Please do," Mary said, her anxiety building.

Johnny sifted through the notes he had taken for his book, and read from several sheets he had marked for the occasion.

"Gen. Ewing eased his order in November of 1863, issuing General Order Number 20, which permitted the return of those who could prove their loyalty to the Union. In January of 1864, command over the border counties passed to General Egbert Brown, who disapproved of Order No. 11. He almost immediately replaced it with a new directive, one that allowed anyone who would take the oath of allegiance to the Union to return and rebuild their homes.

Ewing's controversial order had disrupted the lives of civilians, most of whom were entirely innocent of any guerilla collaboration. Furthermore, there is no evidence that Order No. 11 ever seriously hindered Confederate military operations. No raids into Kansas took place after its issuance, but historian Albert Castel credits this not to Order No. 11, but rather to strengthened border defenses, and better organized Home Guard, plus guerrilla focus on operations in northern and central Missouri in preparation for General Sterling Price's 1864 invasion.

The infamous destruction and hatred inspired by Ewing's Order No. 11 would persist throughout western Missouri for many decades as the affected counties slowly tried to recover."

"That's all I have on the effects on General Order Number 11," Johnny said, "does anyone else have anything?"

Mary held up her hand, "I found an article take from an old Kansas City newspaper dated August 26, 1863 written by George Caleb Bingham," she said, "do you all want me to read it?" she asked.

The other three nodded their agreement.

Mary laid the article on the table in front of her and began to read...

American artist George Caleb Bingham, who was staunchly pro-Union, called Order No. 11

"an act if imbecility" and wrote letters protesting it. Bingham wrote to Gen. Ewing, "If you execute this order, I shall make you infamous with pen and brush," and in 1968 he created his famous painting reflecting the consequences of Ewing's harsh edict. Former guerilla Frank James, a participant in the Lawrence, Kansas raid, is said to have commented: "This a picture that talks."

Bingham, who was in Kansas City at the time, described the events as follows:

It is well-known that men were shot down in the very act of obeying the order, and their wagons and effects seized by their murderers. Large trains of wagons, extending over the prairies for miles in length, moving toward Kansas, were freighted with every description of household furniture and wearing apparel belonging to the exiled inhabitants. Dense columns of smoke arising in every direction marked the conflagrations of dwellings, many of the evidences of which are yet to be seen in the remains of seared and blackened chimneys, standing as melancholy monuments of a ruthless military despotism which spared neither age, sex, character, nor condition. There was neither aid nor protection afforded to the banished inhabitants by the heartless authority which expelled them from their rightful possessions. They crowded by the hundreds upon the banks of the Missouri, and were indebted to the charity of benevolent steamboat conductors for transportation to places of safety where friendly aid could be extended to them without danger to those who ventured to contribute it.

Mary glanced up with a look of disgust on her face, "I shudder to think what those poor people went through," she said.

"I do too," Johnny remarked. He glanced up at the clock ticking away on the east wall of the library, and said, "It's one o'clock, folks, shall we go up to Eddies and get a bite to eat?"

"Yes," Brad said, "I'm starved."

There was a scraping of chairs of the hard wood floor of the reading room as the four of them stood and filed out front door to their cars.

Springfield, Missouri, March 1st, 1862. John Nichols was awakened by the sun peeking through the flap of the tent that he shared with three other Confederate soldiers. They were part of General Sterling Price's Missouri Militia, now part of the Confederate Army. They had come back to Springfield after a successful battle at Lexington, Mo., with stops along the way at Neosho, Cassville, and Osceola on the Osage River. John Nichols and the other three men in the tent were General Price's body guards, and had been selected because they were all four excellent horsemen, good marksmen, and fierce fighters. The four of them usually stuck pretty close together, and by seven A.M. they were all up, dressed, and heading for the mess tent for breakfast.

While they were waiting in line for their bowl of oatmeal and two slices of hard bread, Col. Burns, (Gen. Price's executive officer) came through the tent to tell the men to pack their gear and be ready to march by ten A.M. "General Samuel Curtis' Union army is within a half day's march from Springfield," he told them, "and we're going to pull back further south to Arkansas, maybe as far as Fayetteville."

Johnny gulped down his oatmeal and stuffed the bread into his shirt pocket to eat later. He and his friends would be mounted, so they would move out when General Price left the camp. Promptly at ten A.M., the cannon boomed the signal for the soldiers start marching. Two drummer boys and two flag bearers led the first company on their long march south.

It was a three day march, and late in the afternoon of March 3rd, General Prices' army joined a big Confederate force at Cove Creek, Arkansas, near Fayetteville. The addition of General

Prices' army and 800 Indians, mostly Cherokee, brought the Confederate force's numbers to

16,500. The overall commander of this big force, part of the Trans-Mississippi District, was Major General Earl Van Dorn. He had been appointed overall Commander of this joint force to quell a simmering conflict between General Sterling Price of Missouri and General Benjamin McCulloch of Texas.

Johnny Nichols had never seen so many men in one place before, and he was very grateful for the fact that he was assigned to guard General Price, and that he was allowed to ride his big red stallion that he had raised from a colt. He was also grateful for the fact that he had his Henry semi-automatic rifle with him.

Van Dorn was aware of the Union Army's movements into Arkansas, and his intentions were to destroy Curtis'

Army of the Southwest and to reopen a route to St. Louis, the gateway into

Missouri. He intended to flank Curtis and attack his rear guard, forcing Curtis to move north or else be encircled and destroyed. He ordered his army to travel light, with each soldier carrying three days rations, forty rounds of ammunition, and a blanket. Each division was allowed an ammunition train and an additional day of rations. All other supplies, including tents and cooking utensils, were left behind.

On March 4th, 1862, instead of attacking Curtis' position head on, Van Dorn split his army into two divisions under Price and McCulloch, ordering a march north along the Bentonville Detour to get behind Curtis and cut his communication lines. For Speed, Van Dorn left his supply trains behind, which proved to be a bad decision. Amid a freezing storm, the Confederates made a three-day forced march from Fayetteville through Elm Springs and Osage Spring to Bentonville, arriving stretched out along the road, hungry and tired.

Warned by scouts and Arkansas Unionists, Curtis rapidly concentrated his outlying units behind Little Sugar Creek. On March 6th, William Vandever's 700-man brigade marched a remarkable 42 miles in 16 hours from Huntsville to Little Sugar Creek. Curtis' right flank suffered from the mistake if his second-in-command, Sigel, who sent a 360-man task force west, where they would miss the next three days fighting. Sigel also withdrew a cavalry patrol from the road on which the Confederate army was advancing; however, Colonel Frederick Schaefer of the 2nd Missouri Infantry, on his own initiative, extended his patrols to cover the gap. When Van

Dorn's advance guard blundered into one of these patrols near Elm Springs, the Federals were alerted. Still, Sigel was so slow in evacuating Bentonville that his rear guard was nearly trapped by Van Dorn on March 6th.

Waiting until the Confederates advance was nearly upon him, Sigel ordered his 600 men and six guns to fall back on a road leading northeast toward Curtis' position. The 1st Missouri

Cavalry led by Elijah Gates attacked from the south to cut off Sigel's retreat. Gates' men surprised and captured a company of the 36th Illinois, but many were freed when Sigel's withdrawing men unexpectedly bumped into the group. Sigel managed to fight his way through

Gates' men, helped by a blunder by Brig. Gen. James M. McIntosh.

McIntosh planned to envelop Sigel's force from the northwest while Gates closed the trap on the south. However, McIntosh mistakenly took his 3,000-man cavalry brigade too far up the northerly road. After marching three miles out of his way, he turned his troopers onto the road leading east into Little Creek valley. By the time they reached the place where Sigel's northeast road met McIntosh's east-bound road, the Union general's men had just passed the intersection.

A Southern attempt to press the pursuit was repelled when the 3rd Texas Cavalry charged, only to run smack into Sigel's main line. The Confederates lost 10 killed and about 20 wounded to Union artillery and rifle fire.

Curtis placed his four small divisions astride the Telegraph, or Wire Road, in a fortified position atop the bluffs north of Little Sugar Creek. From the creek, the Telegraph Road went northeast to Elkhorn Tavern where it intersected the Huntsville Road leading east, and Ford Road leading west. From Elkhorn, the Wire Road continued north and down into Cross Timber Hollow before crossing the border into Missouri. From there the Union supply line followed the Telegraph Road northeast to St. Louis. The hamlet of Leetown lay northwest of the Telegraph Road, about halfway between Curtis' position on the bluffs and Ford Road. Curtis made his headquarters at Pratt's Store, located on the Wire Road between Elkhorn and Little Sugar Creek.

CHAPTER 25

Sedalia Mo. Public Library, Saturday, December 22nd, 2012. By 2:00 P.M., the four friends had eaten their lunch and reconvened at the library to continue their research into the life of John S. Nichols. They traced John's travels with General Price's Confederate army from the time he joined it in May of 1861 to Springfield, Missouri in December of 1862. They had fought many battles all over Missouri in the interim, but their biggest battle was yet to come, *The Battle of Pea Ridge.*

Johnny Clayton dug into his brief case and pulled out a folder. "Here's my version of *The Battle of Pea Ridge*", he said. And since John Nichols was a body guard for General Price, and Price's army had such a big part on that battle, we need to add an account of it to our story."

"Yes," Mary said, "but isn't that a pretty big folder?"

"Yes it is," Johnny said, "so I thought I would just give a brief account of the battle and the results, and any part that John Nichols had in it. What do you think?"

"I think that would be okay," Mary replied, "otherwise, it would take up half of your book.

Looking through his folder on the *Battle of Pea Ridge*, Johnny Clayton gave this account. "It is generally conceded that the Union army under General Curtis got the better of the battle, and he was considered the best general officer of the battle by the way he managed his troops. Even though he was greatly outnumbered, he maneuvered his troops well and managed to rout the Confederates on the third day of the battle."

Johnny paused to look through his notes, then continued.

"The main body of the Confederate army under General Van Dorn retreated through sparsely settled country for a week, taking what food they could from the inhabitants, since he had become separated from his supply train. He was finally united with his supply train south of the Boston Mountains.

Thousands of General Price's troops deserted and returned to Missouri. Van Dorn refused to admit that he was defeated, 'but only failed in my intentions'.

"The casualty count was, 203 killed, 980 wounded and 201 missing for the Federal forces, and 800 killed and wounded and between 200 and 300 prisoners for the Confederates. A later estimate for the Confederates put their losses at 2,000 killed and wounded. Those losses included a large proportion of senior officers. General's McCulloch, McIntosh, and William Y Slack were killed or mortally wounded, and General Price was wounded. Also four colonels, were killed, and Colonel Hebert was captured.

After General Price was wounded, he managed to continue to direct his division in battle with the aid of his four man body guard, with John Nichols directing them. It was at this point that John got the reputation for mutilating corpses. When they were ambushed by a platoon of Union Infantry, John quickly dismounted while grabbing his Henry rifle. He hit the ground firing and killed three of them so fast that the other side thought he had fired three shots into one man, when actually he had killed three men, and each with a single shot through the head. Two of the Union soldiers testified later at his trial that they saw him fire two more shots into an already dead soldier. After the battle was over and Price had retreated back into Arkansas, John Nichols fell sick again and was left with a family in Crawford County to heal. They were southern sympathizers and they took good care of him. After he was well again, he re-enlisted in a Confederate unit led by General Rains.

Because the Confederates were short of men after their losses at Pea Ridge, and because of John's recruiting skills, he was asked to go back to Missouri to raise another company of men, which he did. He went back to Pettis County and recruited 29 men, turning them over to Colonel Corcoral. He then joined Colonel Corcoral's unit as Captain of the new company on their raid at Lone Jack, Missouri. After Lone Jack, they retreated back to Bentonville, Arkansas to join General Price."

On September the 5th, 1862, John once again left his army unit to raise another company of men. He recruited 40 men in Johnson, Henry, and Saline Counties and turned them over to Colonel Corcoral who was camped on the Osage River in Missouri. From there, he rode with Corcaral back to Arkansas where they reported to General Hindman at Bentonville. There he rejoined Company E in Thompson's regiment which was a company he had recruited before, and had commanded it with the rank of Captain, before turning it over to someone else to go raise another company.

He served with this company during the winter of 1862-63, making a raid on Springfield, Missouri, on the 8th of January, 1863. After the Springfield raid, they fell back to Batesville, Arkansas, and waited until spring. In their down time, John continued to train the men in his company to be better riders and marksmen, so they would be more affective in battle. In the spring, they moved to Cape Girardeau, Missouri on the Mississippi River with General Marmaduke's division. Then they fell back to Arkansas again.

He left the army for the last time on May 4th, 1863 to raise yet another company, and went back to Missouri. On the 14th of May, he was captured in Morgan County, and put in jail at Tuscumbia, Missouri in Miller County. On May 16, he was taken to Jefferson City, Missouri and, imprisoned while he waited for his trial. He was no sooner locked up than attempted to escape from his cell. He was shot in his left calf by a guard, and thrown back into the prison under a heavy guard. His wound was bandaged, and no further medical attention was given. The local sheriff, who was in charge of the prison, however, decided to put him in shackles with a ball and chain attached to satisfy the many complaints from local citizens that he might escape and do them harm. This fear was mostly brought on by stories put forth by the sheriff's office that John was a very cruel and dangerous man, when actually, he was just the opposite.

Johnny Clayton paused to pose a question to Mary, Brad, and Jeanie. "I don't have a transcript of John Nichol's trial, but I do have a copy of his confession, which tells about the trial, but none of the details, do you want me to read it?"

"He confessed to the charges brought against him?" Mary asked in an astonished voice.

"Not exactly," Johnny said, "but when he found out that there would be no one appointed by the court to defend him, and that he wouldn't be able to testify in his own behalf, or have witnesses testify for him, he wanted to get his story out somehow; so when a reporter from the Missouri State Times came to see him on the morning of his execution, John gave a lengthy statement which was published the next day under the headline of *Confession of John S. Nichols.* Actually, it was more of a brief auto-biography than it was a confession."

Mary held up her hand, "Aren't we guaranteed a fair trial before a jury of our peers by the constitution?" she asked.

"Yes," Johnny said, "and we're also supposed to have a lawyer to defend us even if the state has to furnish one, but remember that this was in 1863 in Missouri, and General Order Number 10 was in effect. There was no trial, per se, just a hearing before a Deputy Provost Marshall, who had all power. He had the power to arrest on any charge he dreamed up, he could try the defendant by himself, sentence the defendant, and carry out the sentence without consulting anyone. In this case, the Deputy Provost Marshall hated all southerners, so, naturally, he found Johnny guilty of being a "Bushwhacker," and sentenced him to be hung."

"Did he actually confess to any of the accusations?"

"Yes," he was accused of killing a Negro named George, owned by a Mr. Gray in Johnson County. He admitted to shooting the unarmed man twice in the head without even getting off of his horse. He justified it because George was leading a group of men to him who were looking to kill him. The men were unfamiliar with the territory, and did not know where John was, so John claimed he killed George in self-defense to keep the men from finding and killing him."

"Anything else?" Mary asked.

"Yes, he admitted to taking horses from Union soldiers to mount the men he had recruited, but said that he did it as a Confederate soldier, and not as a band of guerillas or bushwhackers. In the matter of mutilating Union soldiers, he was not charged with that, but it was brought up by two witnesses in the trial, and he wanted to set the matter straight. Also, he admitted to going into homes of Union sympathizers and taking blankets and guns. But he claimed that he was following orders from his superiors to take any such loot to help his own troops survive. This was a common practice on both sides of the war.

He also shed some doubt on the veracity of the State's witnesses. It turns out that two of them were with the band of renegades who shot his father and stole their blankets and guns."

"Oh my Lord," Mary exclaimed, "no wonder they got rid of General Order Number 10, it opened the door for a lot of abuse."

Johnny shook his head in disgust, "It was also cause for a lot of burning and looting of Union sympathizer's homes in retaliation, especially the burning of Lawrence, Kansas," he said. "Let me read from some notes I made for my book about how John Nichols was treated, okay?"

The other three nodded, so Johnny Clayton picked up a paper from the stack in front of him, and started to read.

On May 19th, 1863 John Nichols was brought before a military commission presided over by a deputy Provost

Marshall. The only ones present were the Deputy Provost Marshall, the Federal Prosecutor, and several witnesses for the prosecution. John was not allowed to have a lawyer to defend him, nor witnesses to testify in his behalf. Neither was he allowed to testify for himself on the witness stand. All of this, of course, would be allowed in a regular trial in a Federal court or a county circuit court. It was all so unfair that it caused a lot of animosity toward the Provost Marshall, and General Order Number 10.

CHAPTER 26

"Oh!" Johnny interrupted himself, "I almost forgot, I found a picture of John Nichols that the sheriff had a photographer take of him after he put a ball-and-chain on him. He had it taken so he could send copies to the sheriffs of the surrounding counties to assure them that John Nichols could not escape a second time." Johnny passed the copy around so the rest could see what John looked like.

"He seems very calm," Mary said, "and I would say that he was quite handsome."

Jeanie squinted at the picture when it was her turn. "Is that a gun pointed at him?" she asked.

"Yes," Johnny said, "I'm sure that several guards were nearby with guns drawn. If you will look closely at the left side of the picture, you will also see the leg and foot of one of the guards, probably the one holding the gun. They were so afraid he would try to escape again. They made him seem to the public as being mean and dangerous, but actually, he was very resourceful, and I think that they were more afraid that he would out-fox them and escape than anything else."

When the picture got back to Mary, she studied it again, "He looks so shabby," she remarked.

Johnny took the picture from her and held it for all to see. "Actually, I think that what he is wearing is what's left of a Confederate officer's uniform. Remember, that after the battle of Pea Ridge, he made several recruiting trips to Missouri from his base in Arkansas. He was on the road constantly, riding through trees and brush, and sleeping on the ground. Of course, his clothing is ripped and torn with buttons missing. He had no needles or thread to fix them, and this was 1863 in sparsely settled country, so there were no dry cleaners or laundries on the nearest corner. He bathed in creeks and ate on the run. You'd look a bit shabby too, after months of living like that."

"He looks very calm to me, for a man about ready to die," Brad said.

"Yes," Johnny said, "and he remained that way right up to the moment that they released the trap door from under him. For a man of only 22 years, he showed remarkable self-control."

"Did they send him to prison right after the Provost Marshall sentenced him?" Mary asked.

"Yes, they couldn't hang him right away because the sentence had to be approved by both the Governor of Missouri, Hamilton Gamble, and President Abraham Lincoln before he could be executed, so they sent him to the Gratiot Street Prison in St. Louis to be held until his sentence had been approved. Both the Governor, and President Lincoln approved the sentence, saying that the trial was fair, and the sentence was appropriate, so he was hung on October 30th, 1863."

"Back to his story," Johnny said as he continued reading from his notes. "On Wednesday, May 20th, John Nichols was escorted by six guards working for the Deputy Provost Marshall, to St. Louis on the train, still wearing the ball-and-chain on his leg. He was booked into the notorious Gratiot Street prison, and locked up in one of their most secure cells on the third floor of the tower which was reserved for their most feared prisoners.

His mother knew nothing of his capture and trial until Ed McNeal happened to be in Sedalia on May 20th to buy some things, and he read about the trial in the Sedalia newspaper. He rode as fast as he could to the Nichols home. He got there at 11:30 A.M., found Sarah in the kitchen, and told her what he had read."

"Oh Lord!" she exclaimed, and shaking all over, she collapsed into a chair. "Can we visit him?"

"No," Ed told her, "he's already in St. Louis by now."

"Can we visit him in St. Louis?" she asked, bursting into tears. Her hands were trembling so bad that she couldn't take her glasses off to wipe her eyes. Ed walked around to her side of the table, gently removed her glasses and laid them on the table in front of her. Ed pulled out a chair and sat down beside her. He took both of her hands in his, "Possibly," he said, "but it's a long way from here. I'll go get Martha so we can all sit down and make some plans."

She nodded, too tearful to answer him. Ed found Martha in the barn and told her the news about John. She was as upset as her mother, but able to control her emotions a bit better. She walked back to the house with Ed, dabbing at her eyes with the corner of her apron. The three of them sat around the kitchen table, and when they were able to talk again, Ed made a suggestion.

"Why don't Martha and I go down now to see if John is alright, and if he is allowed to have visitors? There is no use for all of us to go 200 miles to St. Louis and not be able to see him. We can take him some clothing, and a couple of towels to make him feel better. I doubt that they will allow him to have a razor, or scissors, to shave and trim his hair. We can find out what he is allowed to have, and then in August, on his birthday, we can all go down and take some more things to him. He'll be there for five months, what do you think?"

"Oh my poor Johnny," Sarah sniffed, I'm sure that he didn't do anything to warrant being hung like a horse thief. I want to go with you and Martha, I want to see my Johnny."

Ed looked at Martha. She nodded, "William and George are old enough to run the place for a few days while we're gone, I think mom should go with us."

Ed shoved his chair back and stood up, "Good," he said, "I'll ride back to town and buy three round trip train tickets to St. Louis. Would you like to leave on Friday the 22nd, and come back on Monday, the 25th?" he asked.

"If you can get tickets for those days, that would be fine," Martha said.

Ed nodded and pulling his broad brimmed straw hat down over his eyes, walked out into the bright May sunlight. He mounted the big red horse that he had bought from Wilson four years ago and started down the lane to the road that led to Sedalia.

When he got back to the Wilson farm at 3:30 that afternoon, the six remaining family members were all seated around the dining room table, including little Mary who was only four. Sarah had calmed down some, but it didn't take much to start the tears flowing again. They were having a family meeting, with Martha leading the discussion. Mary was the most upset. She and Johnny had bonded from the day she was born. When he came home for three months with pneumonia, she had camped by his side the entire time.

Martha had explained to her siblings about the situation with John, and as calmly as she could manage, told them that they would never see John again, because in October, he was going to be with their father in a good place, where there was no war.

With trembling lips she continued, "Uncle Ed, your mother, and I are going to travel to St. Louis this week-end to see him while he is still alive, and can visit with is. We will leave Friday morning on the train, and we'll be back by Monday afternoon.

William, James' twin brother, a handsome lad of 17, stood up to assure his mother and sister that he would take good care of the farm while they were gone. George, 15, and Sarah, 13 both pledged to William that they would help too. Even Charlie, who was just 9, and very good at tending the horses, told his mother that they would be well taken care of in her and Martha's absence. This made Sarah feel better because the horses were a big part of their income.

Ed Showed Sarah and the rest of the family the three tickets to St. Louis that he had bought.

"We leave at 8:30 Friday morning, and we'll get back Monday afternoon at 3:15," he said.

Sarah turned to Martha, "Get my purse will you please, it's upstairs on my bed."

"Oh, no!" Ed said, holding up both hands in a motion for Martha stop, "I'm paying for this trip. John is like my own son, and I want to see him as much as you do."

Sarah insisted, but Ed would have no part of it. He was going to foot the bill for the three of them, and that was that. Sarah finally consented and gave into Ed.

Friday Morning, May 22nd, 1863, at 8:00 A.M, Ed McNeal's surrey drove up to the Sedalia train station and Sarah Nichols, Martha Nichols and Ed McNeal got out. Ed had offered the use of his surrey because the Nichols' buggy wasn't big enough to carry four adults plus their luggage. He had driven it to the Nichols' farm to pick up Sarah and Martha, and then William Nichols had driven them to Sedalia. After Sarah, Martha and Ed got out, William drove it back to the Nichols' farm with instructions to meet the 3:15 train from St. Louis on Monday, the 25th, to take them all home. Sarah had packed a change of clothes for her and Martha plus a clean shirt and trousers for John in one small bag, and Ed had brought a change of clothes in a small bag also, so their luggage was minimal.

They waved at William as they got on the train, and settled into their seats for the five hour train ride. It was a three day trip by horse and buggy, before the railroad had been extended to Sedalia in 1862. Between the click, click, click, of the wheels on the rails, and the swaying of the coaches, the three of them had soon dozed off. They were awakened only once during the trip, when the conductor came through the car and punched their tickets.

At 11:20 that morning, the train pulled into the railway station on Market Street in St. Louis. Ed hailed a cab and asked the driver to take them to the Gratiot Street Prison. He nodded, and without a word, drove them out Eighth Street to Gratiot Street, and there on the Northwest corner of the intersection was big two story brick and stucco building. The driver stopped his cab at the very corner of the building at a single door marked Provost Marshall. He wrapped is reins around the brake handle and climbed down to the street. Opening the cab door, he looked at Ed,

"Is this where you wanted to go?" he asked.

Ed got out and looked the building over, "I think so," he said, "will you wait for us?"

"Yes sir," the cab driver said, "but it will cost you."

"How much?" Ed asked.

"One dollar an hour," the driver said without blinking an eye, "and that's on top of the seventy five cents you already owe me."

Ed thought his price was out of line, but what could he do considering that he was a complete stranger in the city. He took out his wallet and handed the driver a one dollar bill, "This is just a retainer," he said, "you'll get the rest when we get to our hotel."

“Shall I leave your bags in cab?” he asked, tucking the dollar into his vest pocket.

“No,” Ed replied, “we’ll take them in with us, but wait just a minute or two while I go check to see if this is the right door.” Ed walked up to the door on the Gratiot Street side and tried the knob. It was locked, so he rapped on the door. A man in a Union Soldier’s uniform with sergeant’s stripes opened the door, and looked surprised at seeing a big man in civilian clothing standing there.

“What do you want?” he asked in a rather rude voice.

Ed raised himself up to his full 6’- 3” height and said, very firmly, “We’re here to visit one of your prisoners,” he said.

“Who?” the soldier asked.

“John Nichols.”

“That’s impossible,” the soldier answered.

Chapter 27

"Why would that be impossible?" Ed asked, "He's here isn't he?"

"Yes, but Mr. Broadhead says he can't have any visitors."

Ed was starting to lose his temper, but wisely decided not to show it. "Who is this Mr. Broadhead?" he asked.

"His name is James O. Broadhead," the sergeant said indignantly, "and he's the Provost

Marshall General."

Ed had heard the term 'Provost Marshall' used before in reference to John's so-called trial, so he deduced that a Provost Marshall General must be pretty important. "Is he here," he asked.

"No he ain't here," the sergeant said with an air of finality.

Ed was not easily discouraged, "Well, who's in charge when he's not here?" he asked.

Without a word the sergeant turned and yelled "Major, will you come here please?"

The door opened up wider and a Union Officer stepped in front of the sergeant. "What can I do for you?" he asked.

His face clouded when Ed told him that he, along with John's mother and sister had come all the way from Sedalia in Pettis, County to see him, and that they would be very grateful if he could arrange it."

He studied Ed for a moment, "I hate to give you bad news," he said, "but he's such a dangerous man that we have him locked up on the third floor of the tower with our other murderers, with orders not to let him out under any circumstances."

"Dangerous? Murderer?" Ed exclaimed, "I watched him grow up, and a nicer young man never lived."

The major stepped out onto the stoop beside Ed and closed the door behind him, as if to keep their conversation private. "Not according to the transcript we have of his trial." He said.

Ed motioned toward the waiting cab and said, "Would you mind telling what you told me to his mother and sister, they're waiting in the cab?" He stepped down off the stoop and took a couple of steps toward the cab, expecting the major to follow him.

The major was trying to make up his mind as to whether to follow Ed, or remain on the stoop when a well-dressed man walked up from across Eighth Street and approached Ed. "Hello," he said, tipping his hat, "My name is William Bull, is there something I can do to help?"

A surprised Ed held out his hand, "My name is Ed McNeal," he said, "and yes, I do need help."

"Tell me what I can do," Mr. Bull said, "I live just up the street, and I could see that you were having trouble."

The officer on the stoop stood with his mouth open while Ed told his new friend what their problem was, ending with "We came all this way, and they won't even let us see him."

Mr. Bull stepped up to Ed, and taking him by the arm, turned him around so that he was looking up Eighth Street. Pointing to a big three story colonial style home on the east side of Eighth Street, he said, "That's where I live with my family, and we're about to have lunch, would you and your friends like to come eat with us?"

A flabbergasted Ed stammered, "B-But there's t-three of us."

"I know," William Bull said, "I saw the two ladies in the cab, and I suspected that you had something to do with the new prisoner who came in last Wednesday, so when I saw them turn you away at the door, I thought that I might be of some help. Why don't I ride in the cab with you to my house, and you can dismiss the cab and come in for lunch with us?"

Completely stunned, Ed nodded and the two of them walked over to the cab. William Bull introduced himself to Sarah and Martha and got into the cab with Ed. When the cab got to the Bull home, they all got out. Ed paid the driver and unloaded their two bags. He was wondering where they would spend the night.

William Bull took a few minutes to explain why he had been so brash as to butt in on Ed's dealings with the major. He told them that this neighborhood had developed when the prison was a medical college. The Bulls had built their home in this area so they could be among southern sympathizers. He said that most of the big comfortable homes surrounding the prison were occupied by former cotton plantation owners and slave holders who had sold out and moved to St. Louis for the convenience of the big city. When the medical college was converted to a Federal Prison, they saw an opportunity to help the prisoners by furnishing them with some decent food from time to time, and if a Confederate prisoner was able to escape, it was no trick at all to see that he simply melted quickly into the surroundings and was then furnished with a way to get out of town.

William Bull laughed and said, "I don't think the Federal soldiers have realized to this day that they're among the enemy."

He picked up the ladies' bag and Ed picked up his and they all walked into the sumptuous home. William's mother and father were very sincere in welcoming Sarah, Martha and ED to their home, and while the maid set three more places at the dinner table, William explained their predicament to his parents.

"Did your son actually kill someone?" his mother asked.

Sarah nodded, and explained about George and why John was obliged to shoot him. It was actually an act of self-defense, she explained.

The Bulls understood perfectly, and seemed to sympathize with her. Mrs. Bull explained that they watched the prison carefully for opportunities to help those who had been imprisoned for fighting for the southern cause. "I don't know what we can do for your son, because of his sentence, but we are more than willing to try."

"What about Judge Harrison?" William suggested, "He and the Provost Marshall General are good friends, even though the Judge is a Confederate sympathizer. Maybe he can help."

"It's worth a try," Mrs. Bull said, "Why don't you and Mr. McNeal walk up to his house to see if he's home, and if he is, invite him to come down and have lunch with us?"

William stood, "Ed, would you like to walk up to the Harrison home with me? It's just half a block away up on the corner of eighth and Chouteau Avenue, and he might be able to help."

Sarah and Martha were astonished at the hospitality the Bulls had shown them, and they stood also, not knowing what to do next.

"No, no," Mr. Bull said, "they'll be right back, please just sit down, and we'll have some lunch when they return."

Ed and William Bull walked out the front door of the palatial home and down the broad steps to the sidewalk. William guided Ed to the right toward Chouteau Avenue, the next street north of Gratiot. On the corner was another big imposing home that had an armed soldier stationed by the front door.

"Who lives there?" Ed asked.

William chuckled, "That's the headquarters of General John Fremont," he said.

"I've heard of him," Ed remarked.

William chuckled again, "You probably have," he said, "he has had quite a career in the Union Army. Two years ago, he led an army into battle at Wilson's Creek down near Springfield, and the got whipped by General Price's army."

"Oh, yes," Ed remarked, that's where I heard about him, in the newspaper account of that battle. Sarah had two sons in that battle, they were with General Price's army."

"Well, President Lincoln fired him from the army soon after that for insubordination," William said, "but he got back in somehow. I think he started his own army by some means, and this is his headquarters."

"Is he there now?" Ed asked.

"I don't think so," William replied, "The last I heard, he was over in Tennessee somewhere, fighting with General Grant, but I'm not sure." He pointed across Chouteau Avenue at another big southern colonial style home on the northeast corner of the intersection, "There's the Judge's home," he said.

They walked across Chouteau Avenue and up the steps of the mansion to the front door. William rapped the big brass door knocker, and soon the door was opened by a colored maid in a black uniform with a white lace-trimmed apron and matching cap. "Massa Williams," she said in a surprised voice. She opening the door wide, beckoned them in. "Ifen you'all will jus wait here fo a minute, I'll tell the Judge yo here. He's in the library." She disappeared down the vast foyer and through a door on the left.

Ed couldn't believe the huge foyer and the big winding staircase that followed the right wall up to the second floor rooms.

Soon, they heard the plodding footsteps of the Judge and the door to the foyer opened. Ed got a good look at him as he carefully negotiated the length of the foyer to where they stood. He was a rather large man, and he appeared to Ed to be his late 60s. He had a mane of snow white hair that reached to his shirt collar, and he was dressed in a black smoking jacket with gold trim around the cuffs. He wore black trousers and shoes to match the jacket, and he grimaced as he walked, as if in pain, but the twinkle in his eyes belied the stern look on his face. He was leaning on a shiny black cane with a brass handle, and he plopped his feet down in front of him as if he had trouble controlling them. "Hello, William," he said as soon as he recognized him, "who is your friend?"

"Hello Judge," William said, and pointing to Ed, replied, "this is Ed McNeal from Pettis County, and he has a problem that perhaps you can help us with."

The judge extended his right hand while his left hand held the cane steady. "Hello Mr. McNeal," he said, "I'm Judge Harrison, it's nice to meet you." He shook hands with Ed and William, and then motioning to a door on his right said, "Let's go in the sitting room here, where we can have some privacy." They stepped into a cozy room with a fireplace in the rear wall and book shelves on either side. The room was dominated by a round mahogany table with four upholstered chairs around it

"My, what a lovely sitting room," Ed remarked as they each took a chair around the table.

"Thank you," the judge said, "would you like some tea?"

"No thanks, Judge," William said, "mother is waiting lunch for us, and we would like for you to join us if you would, please."

The Judge stroked his chin for a moment while he thought about the invitation. Finally, he said, "Well, Lillian, that's my wife," he said to Ed, "is visiting her sister in Chicago, and I wasn't looking forward to dining alone, so I think I will join you. Let me tell the cook so she won't fix my lunch here, and we can go."

He pulled a tasseled cord dangling beside the fireplace, and when the maid appeared, he said,

"Constance, will you please tell Nettie that I'll be having lunch with the Bull family down the street, so there will be no need for her to prepare my lunch here."

The maid nodded and left. The three of them walked out onto the porch, and with William and Ed on either side to steady him, the judge managed to negotiate the steps down to the sidewalk. When they reached the street level, however, he surprised them with his ability to keep up with their pace.

Chapter 28

It was nearly one P.M. when the five of them were seated around the Bull dining room table for lunch. Mr. Bull signaled the need for a blessing by bowing his head and clasping his hands in front of him. After the others followed suit, he recited a brief prayer that he had obviously memorized, and then nodded to the butler to start serving their lunch.

The butler started off by ladling each of them a cup of thick, cold, potato soup from a tureen on the buffet. Ed had never eaten cold soup before, so he tasted it rather tentatively. It was surprisingly delicious. What is this soup?" he asked, "I like it."

Mrs. Bull smiled and said, "It's vichyssoise, Mr. McNeal, from an old family recipe, I'm glad you like it."

When they were about finished with lunch, Judge Harrison turned to Ed and said, "What was it you wanted me to help you with?"

Ed explained to the judge that they had come all the way from Pettis County to visit with Mrs.

Nichols' son, John, and weren't permitted to see him.

"Who told you couldn't see him?" the judge asked.

"I don't know his name, but it was the major that's in charge of the military guards. He told us that since John Nichols was a murderer, he was too dangerous to be let out of his cell."

"On whose orders?" the judge asked.

"By orders of the Provost Marshall General" Ed replied.

"That would be Jim Broadhead,"

"Yes, that's his name."

"He's an acquaintance of mine," the judge said, "I may be able to persuade him into letting you visit with your son Mrs. Nichols," he said, turning to Sarah.

She looked at the little watch that was pinned to her blouse. "It's nearly two," she said, "can we go now?"

The judge wiped his mouth with his napkin, and laid it by his plate, "I don't see why not," he said, as he rose from his chair.

The five of them, Ed McNeal, Sarah and Martha Nichols, William Bull, and Judge Harrison all walked the half block, south, down Eighth Street to the corner and then crossed over to the office entrance of the prison.

"Let me do the talking," Judge Harrison said as he rapped on the door with the head of his cane.

The door swung open and the same sergeant as before stood before them. "Judge Harrison," he exclaimed, when he recognized the big man with the cane, "what can I do for you?"

The judge didn't hesitate, "We're here to visit with John Nichols," he said in a stern voice.

The sergeant hesitated when he saw he saw Ed McNeal standing with the judge. *"So that's what this is all about,"* he said to himself, *"he went and got himself some help, well, the answer is the same."* "I'm sorry, Judge, but he is not allowed to have visitors," he said, in the same stern voice.

Unwilling to go through the chain of command, the judge said in an equally stern voice, "Let me talk to Jim Broadhead."

"D-do you know him p-personally?" the sergeant stammered.

"We see each other quite regularly," the Judge answered.

"J-just a m-minute," the sergeant murmured, he closed the door.

Judge Harrison was just about to rap on the door again, when it swung open, and there stood the major. Before he could say anything, the judge put his hands on his hips and said, "I don't want to go through the whole garrison, take us to Mr. Broadhead!"

The major was just about to tell the judge off when a voice came from behind him. "Is that you Judge Harrison?"

"Yes," the Judge replied, "James, is that you?"

Someone pushed the major aside and a rather handsome man in a navy blue suit appeared. He looked to be in his 50s and had a demeanor of authority about him. "What's on your mind, Judge?" he asked.

Judge Harrison introduced the man to Ed, Sarah and Martha, and said, "Of course, you know William Bull."

"Yes, I do," he said, "how are you William?"

"I'm quite well thank you," William said. He started to make small talk when Judge Harrison interjected.

"May we see you in your office privately," he said.

"Of course," Mr. Broadhead said as he opened the door wide, and with a sweeping arm motioned for them to follow him.

The major stood, open mouthed, with one hand on the door knob, as the five of them filed past him on their way to the Provost Marshall General's office.

The major, still gaping, ordered the once sarcastic sergeant to take three more chairs into the

Provost Marshall General's office. When they were all seated and the sergeant had left and closed the door behind him, Judge Harrison explained the reason for his visit.

"I did give the order for John Nichols to be held in solitary," Mr. Broadhead said," because he came to us from the Deputy Provost Marshall in Jefferson City with his orders marked *dangerous murderer, guard carefully.*"

"Have you seen the prisoner, or talked to him?" Ed asked.

"No sir, I haven't," the Provost Marshall admitted.

"Were you aware that he is a captain in General Price's Confederate army?" Ed asked.

"No sir, his orders didn't mention that."

"Were you aware that he was not allowed to testify in his own behalf, or call any witnesses to support his position?"

"No sir," Mr. Broadhead said, "and if that's true, it doesn't appear that he got a very fair hearing,"

"It wasn't a hearing, Mr. Broadhead," Ed said, "it was a railroading."

"But he was accused of murder, and that's a very serious charge," James Broadhead countered.

Sarah held up her hand, "May I speak, your honor," she said.

"You certainly may," he said, "and I'm not a judge, and this isn't a hearing, so I would appreciate it if you would just call me Jim"

"Yes sir," she said nodding, "but I just wanted to point out that the Negro he shot was working for the Union Army, and he was on his way turn John in, so it was actually an act of self-defense as a Confederate soldier."

"Didn't he tell the Deputy Provost Marshall that?"

Martha spoke up, "Sir," she said, "he wasn't permitted to speak at all, but there were two witnesses against him who were part of a gang the raided our home, shot our father in the head, and killed him. They were allowed to speak, but he wasn't."

"I'd like to talk to this young man," Broadhead said. He arose from his chair, went to the door, opened it, and, in a loud voice said, "Major, come here please."

"Yes sir," the major answered as he appeared at the door.

"Take the sergeant and a couple of guards, and go bring John Nichols down here, I want to talk to him."

"Now! Sir," the major said in amazement.

"Yes, right now, we'll be waiting,"

The major saluted, turned, and grabbed the sergeant on his way through the office. He grabbed two more guards from their recreation room as he passed through the south wing of the prison, and the four of them went to the second floor of the tower. To get to the floor where John was being held, they had to exit the second floor through a door that led to an outside stairway. The outside stairway had been built to reach the third floor when it was added to the tower. There was no other way to do it without major reconstruction of the tower.

The major pounded on the door until one of the three guards on duty opened it. "I have orders from the Provost Marshall General to take John Nichols to his office right now!" he demanded.

The totally surprised guard led them down the aisle between the iron cages that served as cells on that floor. The floor was divided down the middle with one big cell on the right and two smaller cells on the left. The main door on each cell was secured with a large padlock, and there was a guard posted at each of the three doors.

The guard leading the major and his three helpers down to John Nicholls' cell suddenly stopped. "Wait," he said, "you said you wanted to take him from his cell?"

"Yes," the major snapped, "why?"

"Because," the guard said meekly, "we don't have keys to these cells."

"You don't have keys to these cells?" the exasperated major yelled, "why the hell not?"

"Because the major thought it would be too dangerous for us to carry keys to the cells in case we were overcome by the prisoners some way. They could take a key from one of us and all of them could escape."

"Oh damn!" the red faced Major said, "those were my orders. Sergeant, run down to our office, and you will find three big keys on a ring in the middle drawer of my desk. Bring them to me, we'll just have to wait here 'til you get back."

While they were waiting, the major and his three helpers sauntered on down the aisle to the cage that held John Nichols, just to get a look at him through the bars. They found him in the last cage on the left, with four other prisoners. He was writing on a sheet of paper, using the small wooden table by his cot for a writing surface.

"John Nichols?" the major said in as gruff a voice as he could muster, "come over here so I can get a look at you."

John stood up and laid the paper and pencil on his cot. He bent over and picked up the iron ball that was attached to the shackles on his legs, and painstakingly hobbled over to the bars where the major was standing. "I'm John Nichols, Sir," he said, in a quiet, calm voice.

The Major was quite taken aback by John's appearance. Here was a young man in his early 20s with a calm demeanor and a mild voice, not the raging maniac he had expected to find. One of the other prisoners, who did fit the major's expectations for appearance, picked up his ball and chain and started toward the cage door where the Major stood. "You stay right where you're at," the major growled, pointing his finger at the man, "don't come any closer." The man growled something back, dropped the heavy ball on the floor with a loud thud, and sat back down on his cot.

CHAPTER 29

The major turned to John, "You have some visitors," he said, "and as soon as the sergeant gets up here with the key, we'll take you down to see them."

John had been told that he would not be allowed to have any visitors, so the actions of the major surprised him. He had managed to talk the guard into getting him a sheet of paper and a short stub of a pencil, and was writing to his mother when he was interrupted by the major.

"Who are they?" he asked.

The major couldn't remember all of their names, so he said, "I don't know them, you'll just have to wait until you get down there." Also, the major couldn't believe that a confederate prisoner would be able to write, so he asked John, "What are you writing?"

"I was writing a letter to my mother," John said.

"Let me see what you have written," the major demanded.

John walked over to his bunk and picked up the sheet of paper he had been writing on. He stuck it through the bars and the major took it. His curiosity quickly turned to amazement when he saw what

John had written. "Dear Mother," had written, "I was able to procure a sheet of paper and a pencil so I could write you to let you know…."

Not only had John written something that made sense, but his handwriting was clear and legible. Most prisoners that the major had been in contact with could neither read nor write, and the ones that could write were barely legible. John's writing put the major's own handwriting to shame. "Are you an educated man?" he asked.

"Yes," John replied.

"How far did you go?"

"Through high school, and some college."

"Where?"

"At home, my mother was a school teacher before she married my father, and we have all of the books needed to teach the courses in our library."

The major was impressed, and as he handed the paper back to John said, "I'd like to talk to you sometime, just to visit."

"It will have to be before the end of October," John reminded him.

"I know," the major said, shaking his head sadly.

The sergeant rushed up to the major, out of breath, and handed him three keys on a heavy ring. By trial and error, the major found the key to John's cell and unlocked the door. With a guard on either side of him to keep him from falling, John managed to walk slowly, with the shackles on his ankles, and carrying the heavy iron ball in both hands.

Some ten minutes late, when they finally managed to get to the outside stairway, the major called a halt. There just wasn't any way that the four of them could get John down the steep stairs with the shackles on his legs, and carrying the heavy ball. He turned to one of the third floor guards, "Who has a key to these shackles?" he asked.

"All three of us do," the guard said, "these men all have shackles and iron balls on them, and sometimes we have to take them off so they can bathe."

"Well, take these off of this man," the major ordered.

"But Sir," the guard said, "the orders were..."

"I don't care what the orders were concerning the shackles, I'm in charge here, and I want them off!"

The guard produced a key from his pocket, and shaking his head in utter confusion, unlocked the shackles and took them off along with the attached iron ball. "I never know who's in charge around here," he muttered to himself.

"Sergeant, pick up those shackles and the ball, and bring them with you, just in case," the major said in a commanding voice.

The sergeant turned to one of the guards that they had gathered up on their way to the top of the tower, "Guard," he ordered, "pick up those shackles and the ball and bring them along with us."

The guard knew that he was at the bottom of the chain of command, so he reluctantly picked up the shackles, and since they were all he could carry by himself, motioned for the other guard to bring along the heavy ball. John and the two officers made it down the step okay, but the two guards struggled as they could get no further than three feet apart because of the chain.

They somehow managed to get to the Provost Marshall's office, and the major rapped on the door. "Come in," the Provost Marshall said in a loud voice.

The major opened the door, but hesitated to enter. "I have prisoner Nichols with me, sir," he said, "but there is not room for all of us in your office, what shall we do?"

"Just send Nichols in, and close the door," Provost Marshall Broadhead said.

"But sir, shouldn't we be guarding him?" was the answer.

"Just stay outside by the door, we'll be alright," Broadhead said.

Provost Marshall Broadhead was just as surprised as the major had been when he got a good look at John Nichols. This was not a wild unkempt ruffian killer standing before him, but a tall, slender, mild mannered young man in his early twenties. He didn't fit the role of a killer at all. Ed McNeal stood up so that John could have his chair next to his mother Sarah.

Sarah threw her arms around him and wept. John hugged and patted his mother, "I'll be alright," he assured her, "I'll be alright."

Martha went around her mother and stood by John's chair, patting and kissing him, tears running down her cheeks.

The Provost Marshall General stood up and said, "I think I'll step out into the other room for a few minutes," and nodding at Ed, Judge Harrison, and William, said, "Why don't you gentlemen join me for a cup of coffee? Let's give these ladies a few minutes in private with John, shall we?"

Ed was quickly changing his opinion of Provost Marshalls in general, and this one in particular, as the four of them filed out into the other room to have a cup of coffee. The major and sergeant with the two guards were sitting in chairs just outside of the door when they filed out.

"Sir," demanded the major, "Who's guarding the prisoner?"

"His mother and his sister, Major," Mr. Broadhead replied, "and that's all he needs right now."

The major got the message, and since the Provost Marshall was in charge at this point, he sat down quietly to wait.

After about thirty minutes, Mr. Broadhead stood, placed his coffee mug on one of the desks in the room and walked to the door of his office. He rapped gently on the door, and opened it about half way. Peering around the door, he said, "We need to get John back to his cell, so I'll give you ten minutes to say your good-byes, then we'll have to take him back upstairs." He closed the door and picked his coffee mug back up. He didn't want any more coffee, he was just killing time.

After ten minutes, he motioned to the major, and tapped on the door again. This time, he opened it wide, and the major, sergeant and two guards brought John out of the office with Sarah and Martha close behind. They both gave John a big hug, "We'll see you on your birthday," Martha said, as she gave him one last hug.

"We might see you again tomorrow if they will let us," Sarah said, "we're not going back until Monday morning."

All eyes turned to James Broadhead, "Check with me in the morning," he said to Judge Harrison, "and we'll see."

The two guards picked up the shackles and iron ball laying by the door, and followed the sergeant, the major, and John out of the door leading to the tower. When they got to John's cell, they put the shackles and ball back on him and watched him as he hobbled back to his bunk. He picked up his paper and pencil and laid them on the small table by his bunk. No need to finish it now, because he had just seen his mother and sister. He would wait a couple of weeks and finish it then.

Ed, the judge, William Bull, Sarah and Martha all went back to the Bull home. By the time they got there, it was 3:30 p.m. They were met at the front door by William's mother, who said, "I assume you got to see John?"

"Yes," William replied, "and we have Judge Harrison to thank for setting it up."

The judge said, "I know Jim Broadhead well enough to know that when he heard about Sarah's plight he would show some compassion. He's not an evil man."

"He certainly isn't, and we're very grateful," Sarah added.

"William," Ed said as he took hold of William Bull's sleeve, "could I prevail on you to help us find a suitable hotel close by, we won't be going back to Sedalia until Monday morning?"

"Oh," William said, "no need for a hotel, please stay with us, we have plenty of room, and it would be an honor to have you."

"Yes, please do," his mother said.

"Oh, thank you," Sarah said, "you have been so gracious to us."

"It's been a pleasure being with you folks, and I was happy to have had a chance to meet your son," William said.

"Did I hear one of you say that you will be back here on his birthday," he continued, "when will that be?"

Martha spoke up, "It's August the 23rd," she said, "It's on a Sunday this year."

"Good", William said, plan on staying with us in August also."

"That would be very nice," Sarah said, "your home is so handy to the prison. It makes me feel good to know that there are people near John who care."

"It makes us feel good too," William said.

"Indeed it does," said his mother.

CHAPTER 30

Martha and Sarah slept together in a large bedroom upstairs in the Bull home. They slept in a big canopy bed with a goose down mattress, and since Friday had been such a long tiring day, they both slept like logs. Ed slept in a smaller bedroom just down the hall, also on a goose down mattress.

William's bedroom was next to Ed's, and his parents slept downstairs in the master suite. There were two more bedrooms, not in use, on the second floor, so there was, indeed, plenty of room.

They were having breakfast, buffet style, in dining room at 8:30 Saturday morning, when Judge

Harrison's butler knocked on the front door. William answered the door, and took the note the butler handed him. He walked back into the dining room and opened it. "Well," he said, "it looks like Judge Harrison has been busy." He handed the note to Sarah.

A smile crossed her face as she read it and then handed it to Martha. "The judge has arranged for us to see John again this afternoon at two, and also Sunday afternoon" she said, her voice evidencing her joy.

Martha read the note and handed it to Ed, who read it and handed it back to Sarah, who put it in her purse. There was a happy mood around the table as they finished eating.

After breakfast, William had their footman bring the Bull family carriage around to the front door, and from ten A.M. until noon, he took their three guests on a tour of that part of St. Louis. Sarah, Martha, and, Ed were surprised to see so many Union soldiers on the streets.

"It looks as though the entire town has been taken over by the Union Army," Martha said.

"It looks that way around the prison," William said, "that's mainly because Jefferson Barracks, an old army post, is just about ten miles south of here, and for the time being it is being occupied by the Union Army. They staff the prison with guards from the post, so you see them coming and going all of the time. Actually, St. Louis is about half Union and half Confederate right now."

Ed spoke up, "If the city is half and half, why isn't there any fighting going on in town right now?" he asked.

"The main reason, is because the General in charge of all the Federal troops in St. Louis, and including

Jefferson Barracks, has declared martial law in this area. That means that he thinks the Federals are in charge, and he doesn't want any shooting going on around so many civilians. If you'll notice, none of the Federal troops are armed, and the Confederate troops in the area are cooperating by not carrying arms in public either. It's sort of an unofficial cease fire."

"I see," Ed replied, "good idea."

"Yes it is," William said, "It's too bad that we can't do this all over the country until we can reach some kind of agreement about the slavery issue. It would sure save a lot of lives."

At noon, the carriage pulled up in front of the Bull home, and the four of them got out. The footman took the carriage to the stable in back of the house while William took the guests into the sitting room. "Why don't we all take about 15 minutes to wash our hands and freshen up a bit, and then meet in the dining room at fifteen after? I'm sure the cook is waiting lunch for us, and we can continue our conversation while we eat."

The cook had made a beef stew that smelled delicious as they all sat down. There was fresh baked cornbread, and since strawberries were in season, there was strawberry short cake for desert. William's father sat at one end of the long walnut dining table, and his mother at the other end. William and Ed sat on one side, with Sarah and Martha facing them on the other. William's father asked Sarah what she thought about St. Louis as the butler served the stew.

"It's nice enough," she said, "but I was raised on a farm, and St. Louis is just too big for me, I prefer smaller towns. I don't mean to run your city down, especially since you folks have shown us such wonderful hospitality, but I am more comfortable in smaller towns like Sedalia."

"If you promise not to tell anyone, I'll let you in on a little secret that Mrs. Bull and I share," he said with a friendly twinkle in his eyes.

"I promise," Sarah said, suspecting that he was going to make some kind of a joke.

"Mrs. Bull and I don't like it here either, especially since the war broke out. We'd be back on a cotton plantation in the southeastern part of Missouri if we hadn't made such a big investment in this house."

"Can't you sell it?" Ed asked.

"I suppose so," he said, "but we would take a big loss on it now."

"Why is that?" Ed asked.

Mr. Bull took a big bite of the stew and topped off with a bite of cornbread. "Mmm, excellent," he said. There was a minute's pause while he cleared his mouth. Then he said, "When we moved here after we sold our cotton plantation twenty years ago, the prison was a medical school, and the neighborhood was a nice, peaceful place to live. Most of the families living here at that time were southerners, just like us. The homes were all nice, and the neighbors were friendly, so we took some of the money we got for our plantation and built this house."

"It's such a wonderful house too," Sarah interjected.

Another pause while Mr. Bull savored another mouthful of stew. Finally he said, "Our family was larger back then. We had two other sons and a daughter living at home besides William, and that's why we have so many bedrooms."

Where are your children now?" Sarah asked.

"Well," he said, "our daughter married a cotton broker from Memphis, and she lives down there. Our oldest son is married and living in Columbia, Missouri. He's a professor at the university there, and our middle son bought some land in southern Missouri with the thought of farming it, but they discovered a big vein of galena on it. Galina is basically lead ore, and he's selling it as fast as he can mine it."

"Why is that?" Ed asked.

"Well," Mr. Bull said, there's a big war going on right now, and both sides are shooting lead balls at each other as fast as they can, plus they use it in making paint, and a lot of other products.

"I should have thought of that," Ed said.

Mr. Bull jerked his thumb in William's direction, "and William manages some property for the family here in St. Louis, he said. "We own a couple of office buildings downtown, and William keeps them rented. He also maintains them and that's a job in itself, just keeping the roofs from leaking is a big job.

Also, we still own some land near Sikeston Missouri that we rent out to a cotton farmer, and William looks after that too. What do you do Ed?"

"Basically, I'm retired," Ed replied. "I used to farm, but I'm more or less retired from that now, and my two sons are running the farm. They're excellent farmers, and they make a good living from it with a little left over for me. My wife is dead, and Sarah's husband is deceased also, so that's why I came to St. Louis with her and Martha, just to escort them down on the train. Plus, I wanted to see John also. He's been almost like a son to me."

At one-forty-five, the four of them, walked down Eighth Street and crossed over to the door of the prison. William rapped hard on the door and they waited. "Since this is Saturday," he said, "I don't know who we will find on duty here today." They hadn't waited long when a young Lieutenant opened the door.

"Is there something you want?" he asked, rather brusquely.

"Yes," William said, "James Broadhead said we could visit with a prisoner by the name of John Nichols today at two, is Mr. Broadhead in?"

"No," the lieutenant said, "Mr. Broadhead isn't here, and we're not to take John Nichols out of his cell for any reason."

William pushed his way through the door and beckoned the others to follow him. "Well then, may we visit him in his cell?" he asked.

"Who are you people?" the curious lieutenant asked in a gruff voice.

William spoke up. "I'm William Bull," he said, "and I live across the street in the big colonial house in the middle of the block, you may have noticed it." Then pointing to Ed and the two women, he said, "This is Sarah Nichols, John's mother, and the lovely young lady beside her is John's sister, Martha. The gentleman here is Mr. Ed McNeal, and he escorted these ladies clear across the state of Missouri, so they could visit John before he is executed for a crime he did not commit."

Sarah fished through her purse and came up with the note from Judge Harrison stating that Mr. Broadhead told him that they could visit John at two. She handed it to William, who in turn handed it to the lieutenant. "Here is a note from Judge Harrison," he said, "who also lives in this neighborhood. It states that Provost Marshall General, James Broadhead, who is a good friend of the judge, told him that we could see John Nichols this afternoon at two."

The Lieutenant read the note and handed it back to William. "Corporal", he shouted over his shoulder. A young corporal, barely old enough to shave, appeared.

"Yes sir," he said as he saluted the lieutenant, "Corporal Short reporting, sir."

"Was there any kind of an order in our box this morning when you reported for duty concerning some people coming here at two this afternoon to visit prisoner John Nichols?"

The young corporal's face reddened, "Yu-yes Sir," he stammered, "as a matter of fact there was."

"Where is that order now?" the lieutenant demanded.

"On your desk sir," was the reply.

This time it was the lieutenant's turn to turn red-faced. "I uh missed it I guess," he stammered, then recovering quickly, said, "go get it for me."

The Corporal disappeared and swiftly returned with the order in his hand. He gave it to the Lieutenant and disappeared again. The lieutenant scanned the order and addressing William, said, "It seems that the Provost Marshall did leave an order to allow the four of you to visit prisoner Nichols today. However, there is a catch, he doesn't say anything in this order about taking him out of his cell, and the last order I have is that he is not to be removed from his cell under any circumstances. What are we going to do about that?"

Ed spoke up, "It looks like we only have two choices here, Lieutenant, either we get in touch with the Provost Marshall and have him issue new orders allowing you to take the prisoner out of his cell, or we can go up to his cell block and visit him there."

Not wanting to disturb his boss at home on a day off, the lieutenant opted for the second choice. Looking at Sarah, he said, "If you think you can climb those steps up to the third floor of the tower, I would prefer that you visit your son in his cell. Is that alright with you Mrs. Nichols," he asked.

"I'm sure that I can make up to his cell," she said, "shall we go now?"

"Yes," the lieutenant said, then turning around, he shouted, "Corporal!"

The Corporal had obviously decided to make himself scarce. When he didn't come after the second call, the lieutenant turned to Sarah. "Hell," he said, "oh excuse me for cursing ladies, but that corporal makes me so angry sometimes. I guess I'll have to take you up there myself." He started for the door to the barracks when Ed interrupted him.

"Lieutenant, I think there is a set of keys in the major's desk that opens the three cells on that floor, and since they are the only keys that fit those locks, don't you think we'll need to take them with us?"

"No," the lieutenant said without hesitating, "because I'm not going to open his cell. You'll have to visit him through the bars. I'm not going to take the chance of having the Provost Marshall get all over me for opening his cell when I have orders not to."

Chapter 31

When the five of them got to the steps up to the third floor of the tower, Ed turned to Sarah, "What do you think," he said, "can you make it up these steps?"

Her answer was to hand her purse to Ed, pull the bottom hem of her dress up over her shoe tops with her left hand, and grasp the hand rail with her right. She led the way, and wasn't panting nearly as hard as the rest of them when they reached the landing at the top. The lieutenant pounded on the heavy door with his fist, and soon it was opened by one of the guards on duty. This was obviously the lieutenant's first visit to the third floor, because he had to ask the guard for the location of John's cell.

It was at the far end of the aisle that divided the big circular room down the middle. This floor was occupied by, supposedly, the most dangerous men in the prison, and therefore, was not as crowded, or as noisy.

John heard them coming, and was standing at the door of the cell when they walked up.

"John Nichols?" the lieutenant asked.

"Yes sir," was John's soft reply.

"Your family is her to see you again," the lieutenant said, "but you will have to visit through the bars, because I can't let you out of your cell." He looked up and down the wide aisle, and could only see four chairs. "Guard," he called at the nearest man on duty.

The guard hurried to his side, "Yes sir?" he asked.

The lieutenant pointed up and down the aisle. "I count four chairs, and there are five of us," he said. "Gather those chairs up and place them in front of John Nichols' cell so our guests can sit while they visit. I'm going back down to the office, and when they are through visiting, send one of the guards down to get me so I can escort them back downstairs. You men will have to stand for a couple of hours while these people visit. Do you understand what I want you to do?"

"Yes sir," the guard said.

Turning to the four standing at John's cell door, the lieutenant said, "You have two hours to visit. The guard will come get me when the two hours are up, and I will take you back to the entrance. I'll see you then."

"Thank you Lieutenant," Sarah said, as he marched off toward the outside stairway.

They had a good visit with John, and Sarah promised that they would come back on Sunday.

"I'll look forward to it," he said as he blinked back his tears.

Sunday morning, Sarah, Martha and Ed were having breakfast with the Bull family when William spoke up, "Would you folks like to attend church with us?" he asked.

Sarah thought for a moment, then she said, "We would love to, but would we be back in time for us to see John again this afternoon?"

"Probably not," William volunteered, "the church we attend is about a 30 minute carriage ride from here, and it would be hard to get back in time to arrange for you to meet with John."

"We had better not chance it, William," she said, "but if there is a minister from your church who could come with us this afternoon and minister to John, I'm sure he would appreciate it, and so would we."

"Yes, William said, we have an outreach minister in our church who does that very thing. I'll talk to him first thing this morning, and I'm sure he will come with you when you go to see John. His name is Rev. Wilson Farrar, and I'll tell him to be here at the house by 1:30, is that alright?"

"That would be wonderful," Sarah said, "we'll be waiting for him.

At exactly 1:30 p.m. the door chimes at the Bull home rang out, and the butler answered it. He ushered the Rev. Wilson Farrar into the Bull sitting room where Sarah, Martha and Ed were waiting. He introduced himself, and they soon get acquainted. At 1:45 P.M., the four of them walked down to the entrance of the Prison and Ed knocked, rather loudly, on the big oak door. When no one answered after a few minutes, he knocked again, only louder.

The door opened slowly, and the corporal from Saturday peered around it as if he didn't quite know what to do.

"Hello Corporal," Ed said in a firm, but pleasant voice, "we're back again to see John Nichols."

"Did, uh, the order say Sunday too?" the surprised corporal stammered.

"It sure did," Ed said, in a voice a little firmer than before, "it's probably on the lieutenant's desk, why don't you go look for it?"

"Uh, yes sir," the uncertain corporal said, "but I'm here all by myself today, and I don't know if it would be permissible to allow visitors to come in here with just one person on duty.

"Well," Ed said, "We can call the Provost Marshall General's home and see if it would be alright, or you could just let us go up and see John and take the chance that no one would mind.

Rev. Wilson Farrar spoke up, "Corporal," he said, "My name is Wilson Farrar, and I'm an associate pastor at the Delmar Street Presbyterian Church. I come here often to minister to prisoners. I know the Provost Marshall General quite well, personally, and I'm sure that he wouldn't mind if we went up to the cell where John Nichols is being held so I can minister to him. Let us in, and I will take personal responsibility for our visit."

The corporal hesitated for a moment, then swung the door all the way open, "The worst they could do would be to bust me down to private," he said, "come on in."

The foursome had no trouble negotiating the steep stairs to the third floor of the tower, and when Ed pounded on the door, the lone guard on duty opened it. When he recognized Ed and the two ladies with him, he beckoned them to come in.

By 2:05 that Sunday afternoon, they were standing in front of John's cell. He had heard them coming down the wide aisle between the cell blocks, and was waiting for them when they got to the door of his cell. Ed introduced the Reverend Farrar to John who nodded in recognition. The reverend put his hands between the bars and took John's hands in his. "How are you doing, John," he asked.

"I'm doing okay," John answered, "It's my mother and sister who need ministering to."

"I'll do that too," Reverend Farrar said," but you need some ministering also, and that's mainly why I'm here. Don't you feel like you would want me to at least pray with you?"

John shook his head, "The Federal Government is going to inflict their punishment on me on October 30th for what they consider were my sins to the state," he said. "It's up to God to decide if I get his acceptance or not. I have never belonged to a regular church," he continued, "my mother and father and all of my siblings have been baptized into the Hickory Ridge Presbyterian Church, but for some reason, I never was. So I guess I'm just a heathen."

"No, John," the reverend said, "we're all sinners, and that's what we need to pray about, that our sins will be forgiven. Let me go first, okay?"

John nodded, and Reverend Farrar held his hands and prayed that his sins would be forgiven so that he could join his father in paradise. John was too emotional to speak when it came his turn to pray. He could only nod his head as tears trickled down his cheeks.

"That's alright, John," the reverend said, "pray it in your heart, God will hear you."

"Oh John," Sarah said, her emotion evidenced by her trembling voice, "we all love you so." She pushed the reverend aside so that she could reach through the bars and take John's hands. "God loves you too, don't be afraid."

"I'm not afraid, mother" he managed to say between sobs, "I just wish that things could have turned out better."

Martha came up behind her mother and put one hand through the bars. She patted her brother's arm affectionately, "We'll all join you in Heaven one day," she said.

ED stood back watching, and wiping his eyes on his sleeves.

Chapter 32

Saturday, December 22, 2012, 5:00 p.m., Sedalia Public Library

Johnny," Mary asked, "did you get all of that information from Sarah Nichols' letters?"

"Most of it," he said, "but William Bull kept a diary, and I got some good information from it. Also, John Nichols' so-called confession was a good source."

"Do you have more there to share with us?" she asked, pointing at the stack of papers in front of him.

Johnny glanced up at the wall clock, it read 5:05. "Yes, I do," he said, "but it's after five now, and I need to get home. We have dinner at six at our house, that's when my dad usually gets home from the office."

"How about the 26th, the day after Christmas?" Jeanie asked, "we'll still be out of school, and I'd like to learn more about Johnny Nichols, I'm really getting interested."

Johnny Clayton looked around the table to get a consensus, and Brad, Jeanie, and Mary were nodding their heads. "Okay," he said, "how about meeting here Wednesday morning, the 26th, at nine? We can have lunch at my house because we always have tons of food left over from Christmas dinner."

"You don't think your mom would mind?" Mary asked.

"Mind?" Johnny said, "she would be delighted. She's always looking around for someone to give food to after our Christmas dinner. She'll be glad for us to help eat it up so she won't have to throw any out."

"Great, than it's all set," Mary said, clapping your hands, "I can hardly wait."

Monday, May 25th, 1863, 7:30 a.m., home of the Bull family on South Eighth Street, St. Louis, Mo. Everyone had finished breakfast early so the Bull family could see their guests off to catch the train to Sedalia. The butler had the footman bring the carriage around to the front door, and it was waiting to take Sarah, Martha, and Ed to the station.

William's parents said their good-byes to them at the front door, and both insisted that their guests stay with them when they came back to St. Louis in August for John's birthday. William rode with them to the train station, and would say his good-byes there.

He watched them get on the train, and stood by the carriage and waved at them as the train pulled away from the station. The trip home would take three hours longer than the one from Sedalia to St. Louis, because it was a local instead of an express, and would be stopping at several towns along the way to unload and load freight and passengers.

It was 3:18 p.m. when they arrived at the Sedalia station, and William was there with Ed's surrey to pick them up. It took another hour and 15 minutes to traverse the 12 miles from the station to the Wilson farm in the surrey. William let them out at the kitchen door and took the surrey on out to the barn. The three of them were very tired, but pleased with the way their trip had gone. They had enjoyed their visit with John, even though it was very sad at times, considering the circumstances.

It was almost 5:00 p.m. so Sarah and Martha busied themselves with fixing supper for the clan. They all went to bed about 8:30 that evening to rest up from their trip. In her mind, Sarah was already planning their trip to St. Louis in August.

On August 1st, 1863, the Nichols clan got some good news, and some sad news. That morning at 10:30 a bedraggled figure came trudging up the lane to the Nichols' house. Martha saw him first, through the kitchen window.

She turned to Sarah, "Mother," she said, "there's a man coming up the lane, and he sure looks familiar."

Sarah looked out the window and almost dropped the pan she was holding, "Good Lord, it's James," she said. Setting the pan on the kitchen table, she rushed out the back door, and drying her hands on her apron as she went, ran across the yard toward the oncoming figure.

His clothing was ragged and torn, he had a week's growth of beard on his face, and needed a haircut, which combined to make him look worse that he actually felt. "Mother!" He shouted when he saw Sarah rushing toward him. He held out his arms and they collided with enough force to almost knock James down.

Martha came running up and the three of them held each other and jumped up and down with glee. Arm in arm, they walked back to the house. Sarah and James went into the kitchen, while Martha ran to the barn to spread the news to the rest of the clan. They all had chores to do so she found them scattered about the barn and garden, but in less than ten minutes they were all crowded into the kitchen listening to James' explanation why he was home from the Confederate Army so soon.

First, he gave them the bad news, that Nathan had been killed at the battle of Vicksburg, Mississippi on May 23rd.

Sarah sucked in her breath when she heard the news. "That's when we were in St. Louis, visiting John," she exclaimed.

While Sarah composed herself from the news about Nathan, Martha explained to James about what had happened to John, and why he had been taken to St. Louis. The news that John was to be hung in October upset James to the extent that he had to be consoled by Martha, and his twin brother William. They were all in tears when Ed rode up, tied his horse at the rail, and came into the kitchen. He was as surprised as the rest of them to see James home from the war.

When they had sorted it all out, this was James' story. After his enlistment in the Confederate

Army in Springfield, he fought with General Price's army at Wilson's Creek. Although all three of the Nichols' brothers were in General Price's Army of Missouri, they were in different regiments and companies. They were in an army of over 8,000 men, and would occasionally see one another, but had no close contact to speak of. Nathan was a private in Company E of the Second Regiment, Missouri Infantry, while James was a private in Company K Sixth Regiment, Missouri Infantry. John, of course, was one of an elite guard that guarded General Price.

After the battle of Wilson's Creek, John went up to central Missouri with General Price, while Nathan and James went as part of a detachment to the Army of the Mississippi. In 1862, James was taken prisoner at Corinth, Mississippi, and sent to a Union prisoner of war camp in Ohio. He escaped from there and was recaptured in Tennessee. He escaped again, and since all of the Union POW camps were full they had no place to send him. They decided to offer him a pardon if he would swear not to take up arms against the Union again.

James was homesick, so took them up on their offer to pardon him. He was then sent to Jefferson Barracks in St. Louis to swear his allegiance to the United States, and to sign an official oath of allegiance form. This form would make him a United States citizen again, giving him his voting rights back. After the Civil War, it would be required of all citizens in states that seceded from the union, or they couldn't vote in national elections.

"I just wanted to get back to my family," James said. "They put me on a train to Sedalia, but I didn't have a way get home from Sedalia, so I walked."

"What happened to your horse?" William asked.

"The Confederate Army took it and gave it to the cavalry," James said. "I asked if I could serve in the cavalry and keep my horse, but I was told that they were short of infantry soldiers, and that they had plenty of cavalry men, but not enough horses. That's why I was assigned to the infantry, and why they took my horse. The army was supposed to pay me for my horse, but they never did. They were always out of money. Lots of months we weren't paid for serving in the infantry."

"Where is Nathan buried?" Sarah asked, tears running down her cheeks.

"In a cemetery in Vicksburg," James said. "He and I were both in infantry companies in General Pemberton's army, and we were retreating from General Grant's Union Army toward Vicksburg when Nathan got shot in the arm. General Pemberton took over Vicksburg, and Nathan was taken to a hospital. From what I heard from other soldiers, it wasn't a fatal wound, but we were under siege for several months by General Grant's Army with nothing to eat, and no medicine. The word I got was that his arm got infected, gangrene set in and it went to his heart. They had nothing to treat him with because of the siege."

"Oh Lord," Sarah sobbed, "how he must have suffered."

"How did you survive the siege?" Martha asked.

"I just got hungry and wanted something to eat, so, after Nathan died, I sneaked out of Vicksburg and went south until I ran into a Confederate Unit and joined them."

"How did you get through the Union lines?" Ed asked.

"Well, like I said, I got sick of eating dogs, rats and anything else we could catch and skin so I decided to sneak out. It was on a Saturday night, and I went to the south part of the wall surrounding the town and just lay on the ground and listened to the Yankee soldiers on the other side celebrate. They had gotten hold of some whisky, probably moonshine, and were drinking it by the cup full. They were laughing and yelling and dancing and having a good old time. They were just out of rifle range from the wall, and they had a big bonfire going. I knew that since it was in the dark of the moon that they couldn't see very far out into the night.

I waited until about midnight when they were all good and drunk and climbed over the wall. I lay on the ground and watched as they changed guards at midnight. I could tell that the replacement guards were drunk, so I just crawled past them in the dark. They were still drinking whiskey from a tin cup, and not paying much attention to what was going on. I crawled past the guard furthest from the bonfire, and he didn't even glance my way. Once I got through their lines, I just stood up and sauntered on down the hill to the river. I went south along the river until I ran across some Confederate soldiers from a unit assigned to keep an eye on Grant's army. They challenged me, but when I told them I had climbed over the wall, they took me to their company commander. I joined their company, and was with them until I was captured and sent to Ohio."

Chapter 33

James took a much needed bath and dressed in some clean clothing that Martha got for him. Then, after he had shaved, she cut his hair. By then, Sarah had dinner on the table and they all sat down and ate. It was a joyful occasion, even with the bad news about Nathan.

By August 17th, 1863, the plan to go to St. Louis for John's birthday was complete. The train tickets had been purchased, and the Bull family notified. Sarah, Martha, and Ed would travel to St. Louis by train early on Saturday, August 22nd, to be met by William Bull in their Carriage at 11:20 A.M.

James had been invited to go, but he declined. He wanted to remember John as his older brother that he grew up with on the farm, not as a condemned prisoner to be hung in October. It made him sad just to think about John being hung. "Just give him a hug for me," he told his mother, "and tell him how much I love him. I'll stay home and help William with the chores around the farm."

Although one day shorter than the visit in May, their August visits on Saturday and Sunday afternoons were better in two ways. Number one was that John was in a much better mood. He seemed happier than in May, and there were fewer tears by John and his visitors. The Reverend Wilson Farrar, with permission from the Provost Marshall General, had given John a bible and had pointed out several verses that told him that if he would confess his sins, and accept Jesus as his personal savior, that he could go to heaven too, without a doubt. He told John to pray about it, and he would be comforted. John did pray about his salvation as the pastor told him, and he immediately started feeling better.

Number two was the news that James had been allowed to come home. John was saddened by the death of Nathan, but he had carried the thought with him for the past two years that since he hadn't heard anything from Nathan or James, that they were both dead. He knew that they had been through some heavy fighting, and he had barely escaped death on several occasions himself. He therefore had thought that the absence of any news meant bad news, so the news of James' safe homecoming had lifted his spirits a great deal.

Wednesday, December 26th, 2012, 9:00 a.m. Sedalia Public Library. By the time the big round clock on the wall showed 9:00 a.m., Johnny Clayton, Mary Schroeder, Brad Compton, and Jeanie Crabtree were assembled around their usual table by the front windows of the library, with their notes piled in front of them.

"I'd like to continue reading the rest of my notes about John Nichols, if you don't mind,"

Johnny Clayton said. "I want your opinion about what I have written so I can decide if I want to include it in my book."

"Please continue," Jeanie said, and Brad nodded in agreement.

"Yes," Mary said, "I may be able to use some of it in my term paper."

"Okay," Johnny said, "when I left off, , James had come home from the Confederate Army, and his mother, sister Martha, and Ed McNeal had gone to St. Louis to see John on his 22nd birthday.

Sarah, Martha, and Ed got to visit with John on Saturday afternoon August 22nd, and again on Sunday, August 23rd, 1863, which was actually his birthday, for two hours each day. They had to visit him at his cell and talk to him through the bars, because there was no officer on duty Saturday, or Sunday with authority enough to okay taking him from his cell.

Sarah left two changes of clothing, some writing paper, a pencil, and some stamps as a sort of birthday gift, so he could keep them informed. The guards in the cell block had been informed by higher authority not to let them give him anything else, such as a clipboard, or something hard that could be made into a weapon. The guards approved of the items Sarah had, and gave them to John after they left.

Plans had already been made for Sarah, Martha, Ed, and possibly James, if he could be persuaded, plus their pastor from Pettis County, to come back to St. Louis on the morning of Wednesday, October 28th for a final visit before the Sheriff of St. Louis County took him back to Jefferson City for his execution on the following Friday, October 30th.

The next two months went by very fast, or so it seemed to the Nichols clan. James, William and George, who was now

15, were able to get the corn crop in, and get enough wood cut to keep the fire palaces going all winter. Sarah, who was now 13, helped her mother and her sister Martha, get the fall canning done. They canned over 500 quarts of vegetables, berries, and fruits and stored then in the fruit cellar behind the house. Honey had to be gathered from the hives, strained and put up in small jars for the winter also.

With Wilson and John both gone from the farm, Ed came over with his two sons and butchered the two hogs that the Nichols' clan had fattened for the winter. The McNeal family had fattened two hogs also, so both of their smoke houses were now full of hams, sides of bacon, pork chops, ribs and loins that had been smoked and cured for winter. There were also jars of sausage patties that had been fried and packed in lard so they would keep most of the fall and winter. There were also some fresh pork ribs, chops and other cuts that that had to be eaten up right away, which were distributed between the Nichols and McNeal families.

Monday, October 26, 1863 was a busy day for the Nichols clan, getting ready for their final trip to St. Louis. In addition to packing what clothing they would need, Martha made some ham sandwiches with some of the newly smoked ham, and fresh baked bread in case they got hungry on the train. She put the sandwiches in a woven market basket that had handles for ease in carrying. She also put some newly made sweet cider with four small glasses into the basket so they would have something to drink. In addition to Ed McNeal, Reverend John O'Donnell, their pastor, was going with them this trip to give John the church's blessing, which accounted for the four glasses. A quart jar of Sarah's famous dill pickles completed the lunch. The left- over pickles she planned to give to the Bull family.

The train left the Sedalia station five minutes late Tuesday morning, but the conductor assured them that they would be back on time when they reached Jefferson City. The plan was for the four of them to stay with John as late as the Provost Marshall General would allow them, perhaps as late as 7:00 p.m., if they could, and then spend the night with the Bull family.

William Bull met the train in the family carriage and took them to his house to unload what few things they had brought. The basket Martha carried still contained the sandwiches, cider, and pickles, because they just didn't have the appetite to eat them on the train. Martha handed the basket to Mrs. Bull, who was delighted. "We'll just add this to our lunch she said," and she took the basket to the kitchen for the cook to add to the sandwiches she had already prepared. Sarah introduced Reverend O'Donnell, and Mrs. Bull seated them around the Bull dining room table for lunch.

They barely had time to eat lunch, before it was time to walk down to the prison entrance at one p.m.

William's father had persuaded Judge Harrison to accompany the five of them to the prison entrance so that he could intercede with the provost marshal general in case there was some objection to Sarah, Martha, Ed, William, and Reverend O'Donnell staying with John until about 7: p.m. At first, William had decided he wasn't going to go up to see John. He felt that he shouldn't get in the way so the rest, especially Sarah and Martha, would be able to spend as much time as possible with him, but a very special reason caused him to change his mind. He wanted every opportunity he could possibly have to be near Martha.

Twenty five year old William Bull, with his dark curly hair, handsome face, and manly build had dated several ladies since he graduated from high school, and could have dated many more, but most of them were too giddy and shallow to suit his taste. He was looking for a woman he could talk to on his level, who could be serious, and yet have a sense of humor. Martha was that woman, and he had fallen in love for the first time in his life. He liked the feeling.

As it turned out, Mr. Broadhead, the Provost Marshall General, was a very compassionate man. He understood that this would be the last opportunity for John to see his family before his execution, and he cooperated completely with their plan. Judge Harrison thanked him and walked back to his house alone, happy that his influence was not needed.

The only problem Mr. Broadhead had, was that he couldn't take John out of his cell for that length of time without showing a favoritism for him that would anger the other prisoners. He told Sarah that they could stay until seven, but they would have to see him at his cell on the third floor of the tower, instead of bringing him down to his office. He suggested they go up to see John now, which was a little after one p.m., and visit until five. "At that time," he said, "why don't you all go have dinner with the Bull family, I'm sure you'd be welcome, and when you come back at six you can bring some decent food for John to eat. Would that be alright with your family, William?" he asked.

"You can count on it," William said, "we'd be delighted to have everyone for dinner, you too Mr. Broadhead, if you'd care to come.

"No," he said, I can't make it tonight, but thanks for the offer."

CHAPTER 34

All five of them made their way up the steep stairs to the third floor without any problems. In fact the stair climbing had offered an opportunity and excuse for William to hold Martha's hand.

He went up the stairs first so he would have the chance to help the two ladies up the last step, which was a little higher than the others. He helped Sarah up first, and she thanked him. Then Martha offered him her hand, and when he took it his heart skipped a beat. Also, was it just his imagination, or did she give his hand a little squeeze just before letting go of it?

When they got to John's cell, he was standing at the door waiting for them. Sarah and Martha hugged and kissed him as best they could through the bars. John showed no emotion, except for the smile he gave them when they walked up. He seemed completely resolved to the fact that he would die on Friday afternoon, just two days hence. They had a good meeting with John despite the fact that he didn't talk very much. But then, all his short life, he had never been a big talker.

He had always been a man of action instead of a talker. He had written a note to both his mother and his sister, and sealed them in envelopes that Sarah had brought him on their last visit. He asked them not to open them until after his death.

At five, they temporarily bade John good-bye until they could get back at to his cell at six. They hurriedly walked back to the Bull house where the cook had a marvelous roast prepared.

Wednesday, December 26th, 2012, 8:50 a.m., Sedalia, Missouri Public Library.

Johnny Clayton was early for the first time since they had started having their meetings. He was early enough to find parking right in front of the library. It was a beautiful winter day, and he was feeling great, as he grabbed his briefcase from the seat beside him and got out of his car. He took the front steps of the library two at a time and swung the big door open.

He glanced into the reading room, and their favorite table was open, so he went over and tossed his briefcase on it. He pulled out a chair, removed his leather jacket (a Christmas gift from his sister), hung it over the back of the chair, and sat down.

Mary Schroeder was the next to arrive. She came through the front door carrying a stack of papers, and seeing Johnny in the reading room, came over and plopped her papers on the table.

"Been here long?" she asked.

He glanced up at the big clock on the wall and said, "No, sweetie, I just got here."

She pulled out the chair opposite of Johnny's, took off her gloves, stuffed them into the pockets of her quilted nylon ski jacket and hung it over the back of the chair. "Mom brought me to town," she said, "so when we are done here, you might have to take me home, is that okay?"

"No problem," he said.

Mary had just sat down, and Johnny had just opened his briefcase, when Brad Compton and Jeanie Crabtree walked up.

"Hi guys," Jeanie said, "sorry we're late. I couldn't get my hair to lay right, so blame it on me. Brad got to my house in plenty of time, but he had to wait about 15 minutes on me."

Johnny glance up at the clock, "It's only five after," he said, "that's not even late enough to mention. Sit down guys, so we can get started."

Johnny opened the meeting by offering the others a stick of chewing gum from a pack he had just opened. They all accepted, except Brad, who held up a ball of bubble gum that he was about to pop into his mouth.

"We're down to the week of John's execution," he said, "and most of the information I have today came from a diary that William Bull kept, plus some from Martha's journal."

Tuesday, October 27th, 1863, Gratiot Street Federal Prison, third floor of the tower.

It was 6:00 p.m. on the dot when Sarah, Martha, Ed and William got back to John's cell. Another prisoner in John's cell block at that time, a Captain Griffin Frost, who had been a newspaper editor before the war, and had kept a journal of his time spent in the Confederate Army. He was captured in battle, and temporally incarcerated in the Gratiot Street Prison until he could be sent to a more suitable facility for a man of his rank. His journal covered his stay in Gratiot which was October and November of 1863 (see the lead-in to chapter 1). Originally, he had been put in with less dangerous prisoners, until he had written an article that was not too complimentary to the prison. He had somehow smuggled it out to a local paper, who had published it. As punishment, he was put in with the murderers on the third floor of the tower, which wasn't really a punishment. The cells in the tower were not nearly as crowded as the other cells in the prison, and were a lot cleaner and more sanitary.

The Reverend O'Donnell gave John his blessing, and the Reverend Wilson Farrar, the local pastor from the Bulls' church was there to pray for John also. Martha reached through the bars, hugged John as best she could, and sobbed her heart out. William stood beside her, patting her on the back, his eyes glistening with tears. It was a very emotional hour, and it was hard for them to leave when the guard came to tell them it was time.

William's mother had hot tea and cookies waiting for them when they got back to the Bull house. The Reverend Farrar went on home, and the rest of them sat sipping the tea and ignoring the cookies. No one was the least bit hungry.

Their plan called for the four of them, Sarah, Martha, Ed, and Reverend O'Donnell to board the train for Sedalia in the morning, Wednesday, October 28th. All of them except Martha would get into Sedalia about 3:30 in the afternoon. Martha planned to get off at Jefferson City so she would be there when they hung her brother. She would spend two nights in a hotel close to the execution site so she could do whatever she was allowed to do to make John comfortable, and to let him know that she was there for him. She would buy a coffin for John's body, and have it shipped to Sedalia after the hanging. William and James would meet her at the train station with a wagon to take John's body to the Nichols' home for burial.

It was a task that she was dreading, but she knew that it had to be done. William offered to accompany her to Jefferson City, and stay with her until she left with John's body, but she shook her head.

"No," she said, "I might have to get tough with the sheriff's office, and I don't want you to see that side of me. I like you very much William, and I don't want to disappoint you in any way."

"It would be a pleasure if you would let me help you in any way I can," he said, thrilled that she had admitted that she liked him.

After much urging, Martha finally relented and allowed William to stay with her in Jefferson City. She did make it clear that she would pay for her hotel room for the two nights they would be there. She didn't have much experience with men, and she didn't want him to get the idea that she would even consider spending the night in the same room with him, even though they were good friends. William agreed that she was to pay for her room, he didn't want her to get the wrong idea about him either.

They all said their goodbyes on the station platform in Jefferson City, and Sara, Ed, and Reverend O'Donnell got back on the train to complete their journey to Sedalia. William watched his and Martha's bags while she went into the Railway Express Office in the depot to pay for the shipping of John's body to Sedalia. She got a receipt to show the agent on the train, to prove that the freight for John's coffin had been paid. Also, she still had the rest of her passenger ticket to Sedalia in her purse.

When she came out of the depot William picked up their bags, and they went looking for a cab to take them to a hotel. The cabbie suggested a nice hotel downtown, which happened to be just a block from the execution site. They registered, and a bellhop took them up to their rooms on the second floor. Their rooms were side-by-side, which was just what they wanted.

When they got back down to the lobby, William, who was getting hungry, suggested that they get a bite to eat in the hotel dining room. Martha agreed, so they each had a sandwich and a cup of coffee. She tried to pay for her lunch, but William insisted that he pick up the tab. "Please let me do this for you," he insisted until, she finally relented.

After lunch, they stopped at the front desk and William asked the room clerk where they could find a funeral home.

"Jefferson City is not a big town," the clerk said, "even though it's the state capitol, so there are only two funeral homes in town. I would suggest the one downtown," he said, "it's the most convenient to our hotel, and you might get to see some excitement near there tomorrow afternoon."

"What's going on tomorrow?" William asked without thinking.

"They're going to hang some bushwhacker right close to the funeral home tomorrow afternoon about 1:00 p.m.," he said. "I think his name is Nichols, you might want to watch it." Then he almost swallowed his tongue. He had just registered a Martha Nichols. "Oh, I'm sorry," he said.

The funeral home was just four blocks from the hotel, and it was such a pretty day that William and Martha decided to walk. They saw the sign hanging out over the sidewalk from a block away. It read, "Stephen McLaughlin and Son, Funeral Directors".

They walked in the front door, and were greeted by a pleasant, middle aged woman seated at a desk. She wore a black dress, and her dark hair was streaked with grey. "Hello," she said, getting up and offering her hand, may I help you?"

"Yes," William said, "we would like to purchase a coffin." He shook her hand, and pointing to Martha said, "it is for her brother, and he is quite tall."

The woman was taken aback, "W-will it be a c-church service, or will you want to use our chapel?" she stammered.

"Neither one," Martha said, "we just want to buy a coffin."

"I don't understand," she said, "our services are very nice, we furnish the music, and all transportation."

"We don't want a service," Martha said, doing her best to remain civil with the woman, "we just want a nice coffin to ship my brother home in, and to bury him in."

"Oh, I'm sorry," the lady said, "was there an accident?"

Martha had little patience with nosy people, "No, dammit," she said in a stern voice, "the powers that be in this state are going to hang him Friday afternoon for something he didn't do." She glanced at William, her face red in embarrassment for having used a swear word in front of him.

He put his arm around her for support. "May we look at some coffins, please?" he said.

"I'll go get the funeral director," she said, "he can help you." She disappeared through a door in the back of the office.

After about 10 minutes, a middle aged man in a black suit appeared, "I understand you are looking for a coffin," he said.

Martha and William both nodded.

"Come this way," he said, motioning for them to follow him. He took them through a side door that led to another space that had several coffins on display. "We're not in the coffin business," he said. "We're in the funeral business, so all of these coffins are priced to include a service plus a chapel, and transportation to the cemetery."

"Are you telling us that we can't just buy a coffin and take it with us?" William asked.

"That's what I'm saying, these coffins all include a service."

William took Martha's arm. "Come Martha," he said, "let's go talk to the other funeral director in town, he'll probably sell us a coffin rather than lose our business altogether." They started for the door.

"Wait," the man said, "please, we can probably work something out."

They paused and the funeral director pointed out the fanciest, and obviously the highest priced coffin he had. "This is the best mahogany coffin made," he said, "it's padded and silk lined, and as you can see, it's trimmed in polished brass. You told my receptionist that the deceased was over six feet tall, and this coffin would accommodate him. It's an expensive coffin, but I could let you have it for, let's say, $550.00."

"Are you charging us for a service that we don't want, and won't use?" Martha asked.

"Well, uh, yes," he said, otherwise, we would lose money.

"You're selling your coffins for below cost?" William asked, "That's ridiculous!"

"Well, that's just the way we price things in this business," he said.

"Let's go Martha, I don't trust this man," William said, a note of incredulity in his voice.

They started for the door.

"I could let you have it for $500.00 cash," the man said.

William looked at Martha, she shook her head no.

"Do you want to offer him $400 for it?" he whispered in her ear.

Not knowing what to expect, she had actually brought $600.00 with her in her purse, hoping to buy one under that amount. She gave William a slight nod.

"We'll go $400.00," he said to the funeral director, "not a penny more.

The man scratched his head for a couple of minutes. He was pretending to be mulling it over because he didn't want to appear too anxious. "Sold, he finally said, where shall we deliver it?"

"Deliver it tomorrow morning to the base of the scaffold across the street where they're going to hang my brother," she said, I'll be there to meet you."

"Fine," he said, holding out his hand, "that will be $400.00 cash please."

Martha fished in her handbag and pulled out a leather snap top purse that was stuffed full of paper money. William held out his hand, and she carefully counted out $400.00 in it. The undertaker reached for it, but William closed his hand and shoved it into his trouser pocket.

"Not yet," he said, "We'll give it to you when we see the coffin at the site, and it had better be the same one."

The man looked aghast, "Don't you trust me?" he asked, a note of astonishment in his voice.

"That's exactly why we won't give you the money upfront," William said, glancing over at Martha. She was nodding her head and a faint smile crossed her lips.

CHAPTER 35

William and Martha had eaten supper at the hotel and turned in early. They were both exhausted, so it was after eight Thursday morning when William tapped on Martha's door. She was ready. She was sitting by the window in her room, looking down at the river, and dreading what was to occur on Friday afternoon. They went down to the hotel dining room for breakfast.

It was a nice fall day, and all of the locations they wanted to visit were within a few blocks of the hotel, so decided to walk instead of hiring a cab. Their first stop on their itinerary was the jail where John was being held to see if there was anything that they could do to make him more comfortable. They also wanted to visit with him, if it was allowed. Their second stop would be at the Capitol Building where the deputy provost marshal's office was located. Martha had a lot of questions she wanted to ask him.

The County Jail wasn't hard to find, it was just down the street from the funeral home where they had bought the coffin to ship John's body home in. It was a stone building that had obviously been a hardware store at one time, because you could see the dim outlines of a sign across the front that had been painted over. Just above the door, a wooden sign hung out over the board sidewalk declaring it to be the jail.

William tried the door, and it opened into room with a wooden balustrade going the full width of the building, obviously put there to keep the public from going to the back where the cells were located. There was a deputy sheriff sitting behind an old wooden desk trimming his finger nails with his pocket knife. He was leaning back in his chair with his booted feet propped up on top of the desk.

He looked up and frowned. "What do you want?" he asked.

Martha walked to the balustrade and smiled, "We'd like to see my brother if we may," she said.

Without bothering to take his feet off of the desk, he asked, "Who is your brother?"

"John Nichols," she replied.

The deputy looked startled as he suddenly took his feet off of the desk and sat up straight. He hadn't expected the condemned man to have such a beautiful sister. He stood up, folded his knife, and dropped it into his front pocket. Without taking his eyes off of Martha, he strolled up to the balustrade for a better look.

"You don't look much like him," he said sarcastically, as he looked her over from head to foot, "you sure he's your brother?"

"I'm absolutely positive," she said, "may we see him?"

"Nope," he said, "they're hangin' him tomorrow, and he ain't supposed to see nobody, except that newspaper guy that's gonna talk to him in the mornin'."

Martha's eyes glistened with tears and she looked down at her shoes avoid the deputy's eyes.

William stepped forward.

"Do you have to be so rude?" he asked.

"Aw, did I hurt the little lady's feelings?" he asked.

William leaned over the rail so he could get right into the deputy's face, raised his voice and said, "Yes!" and it was very rude of you!"

They stood face-to-face for a minute staring at each other when the door to the back flew open. A big, clean shaven man in a plaid flannel shirt and woolen trousers stepped through it.

"Any trouble, deputy?" he asked.

"Naw, we was just talkin', the deputy said, in a much lower voice.

"Yes there is, Sheriff," William said, assuming that the man was the sheriff. "Your deputy has been very rude to Miss Nichols and me." He pointed at Martha, whose tears were now running down her cheeks.

"Is that true, deputy?" the sheriff asked.

"Naw," the deputy said, "we was just talkin, and this feller got kinda smart with me, and I might have yelled back at him. We didn't mean nothin' by it."

The sheriff pointed to the door he had just come through, and said, "Go to the back and wait for me, I'll deal with you later."

With his head down, the deputy shuffled through the door and closed it behind him.

The sheriff glanced, first at Martha, and then over to William. "What happened?" he asked.

William told him exactly what had occurred. Martha took a hankie from her purse and was dabbing at her eyes while the sheriff looked on.

"Is all this true?" he asked Martha.

She nodded.

"My apologies to both of you, and especially to you Miss Nichols," the Sheriff said in a humble tone. "Jake is our assistant jailer, and he comes from a very rough family. I've been working with him to no avail, and I have been looking for an excuse to fire him. I'll take care of him, he'll be gone before the day is over."

"I don't want to cost him his job," Martha sniffed.

"I do," William said.

"Miss Nichols," the sheriff said, turning to Martha, "I'm sorry, but I am under strict orders from the deputy provost marshal not to let anyone in to see John today. I don't agree with him, but he is my boss, and I have to do what he tells me to do. I do know that he's not the nicest man in Missouri." There was a momentary silence and the Sheriff said, "Why don't you come back tomorrow morning at, say, about 10:00. Maybe I can get you in to see him then. They have six men guarding him around the clock, but they are going to let him talk to a reporter from the Missouri State Times to tell his story to the press tomorrow morning. Maybe you can be with him while the reporter takes his statement down, would that help?"

"Yes," Martha sniffed.

"We'll be here tomorrow morning, sheriff," William said, "and thank you very much." He put his arm around Martha's shoulders as they turned to go out the door.

"Shall we go see the infamous deputy provost marshal?" William asked as they stepped out of the door into a balmy fall day.

"Yes, let's do," Martha said, regaining her composure.

"Let me think," William said, "The clerk at the hotel said to go North on Madison, which is this street, to East Capitol Street, and turn left for two blocks to the capitol. That's five blocks in all, do you think you can make it?"

"Oh yes," she said, "this is a grand day for a walk."

Fifteen minutes later, they were walking up the wide front steps of a Classical Revival building in the center of a circle that was formed as East Capitol Street split to encircle it and reform on the other side as West Main Street. They were told by the guard at the door that the deputy provost marshal's office was on the second door.

They had no trouble finding the office they were looking for, but when William tried to turn the knob, it was locked. He knocked, and a female voice from inside said, "Who is it?"

"William Bull from St. Louis, and I need to talk to the deputy provost marshal on an urgent matter," was William's reply.

"He's indisposed right now, could you come back at another time?" the voice said.

"No," William said, "it's urgent, and I have come a long way to see him."

"I'm sorry, but you can't see him right now."

William wanted her to open the door so he could peek into the room, so he said, "I'm sorry, but I didn't understand what you said."

She repeated herself, only louder.

"I'm sorry," he said, "would you repeat that?"

The door was suddenly yanked open, and a rather obese woman in her forties put her hands on her hips and sarcastically repeated her statement one word at a time, "I-said-he-was-indisposed-and–you can't-see-him-now!"

While she was talking William peeked around the door, and he could see an office beyond the reception area. There was a man in a black suit sitting in a chair with a top hat (sometimes called a stovepipe hat that was popular in 1860s) on the desk in front of him. His highly polished boots were propped up on a corner the desk top, and he appeared to be sleeping.

William jerked his thumb in the direction of the man, "How about the gentleman sleeping in his office back there, may we see him?"

She tried to slam the door, but William's foot prevented it. "I'm a good friend of the Provost Marshall General in St. Louis, Mr. James Broadhead, have you heard of him?" he asked.

She said she hadn't, as she kept trying to close the door. The ruckus they were making apparently wakened the sleeping man in the next office, because he came out of the room rubbing his eyes with one hand, with the top hat in the other hand.

"What's going on out here?" he asked.

"I told this man that you weren't to be disturbed hon… uh sir," she said.

"Did she just start to call him honey?" William said to himself, then he muttered under his breath, "there must be some hanky-panky going on in here."

"Oh," the man said, "well, what she says, goes, in this office, so you'll have to go."

William stiffened his back as he looked over at Martha. She had an astonished look on her face, as she straightened her back also, and stuck her chin out.

"Are you the Deputy Provost Marshall in this district?" William asked.

"Yes I am," he said, "and you are out of order!"

"How am I out of order?" William demanded. He had told himself on the way to the capitol that he was going to control his temper when he talked to the man who had condemned John Nichols to death, so as not to upset him, thinking that he might be able to get some kind of concession from of him. He had discussed it with Martha, and she felt the same way. Now all of that was out the window, William had already lost his composure and was red faced as he talked to this obstinate man.

"Because you were told not to disturb me, and you didn't leave." He put his hands on his hips and scowled at William and Martha.

"Oh," William said, "I talked to the Provost Marshall General in St. Louis, and his office is open to the public. I was led to believe that yours was too. All we want to do, is to ask you some questions about a hearing you held last May so that I may be clear on some procedures that were followed during it."

"What hearing are you talking about, whose hearing?" he demanded.

"John Nichols' hearing last may," William said, "we don't think it was a fair hearing, and neither did Provost Marshall General, James Broadhead in St. Louis."

The man took his stovepipe hat off and threw it on the floor. His sandy hair had receded back to the crown of his head, and the bald skin was fiery red. "Dammit," he yelled, "James Broadhead does not run this office, I do! John Nichols' sentence will be carried out tomorrow afternoon at one, and you can count on it! Now get the hell out of my office!" He made a shooing motion with his hands as he spoke.

His yelling was starting to draw a crowd, and there were five people standing out in the hall straining to see what was going on.

William offered his arm to Martha, and she took it. As they walked out, in a rather loud stage voice, William said, "I'm sorry we disturbed your little tryst, Deputy Marshall, we'll go now, so you and your lady friend can get back to the little game you were playing. Bam! Went the door behind them as they left, slamming so hard that it splintered a piece of the jamb.

Chapter 36

Thursday had not been a very fruitful day for Martha and William, and they were both tired when they got back to their hotel at 5:15 that afternoon. They stopped at the coffee shop long enough to eat a bowl of their rich chicken and noodle soup and a grilled cheese sandwich.

Martha had a cup of tea with hers, and William drank a glass of tomato juice.

After stopping at the front desk long enough to check for messages, and for William to buy a copy of The Missouri Times, they went up to their separate rooms on the second floor. They both had bathed, and were in their beds sound asleep by 8:30 p.m.

In spite of the fact that Friday, October 30th was the big day, both Martha and William, mainly because of their fatigue from Thursday's activities, had slept until seven a.m. They were dressed, and in the Coffee Shop having breakfast by 8:30. William showed Martha the front page of newspaper he had bought the night before.

She gasped when she saw the picture of John under the headline...**Bushwhacker to Die at One Tomorrow!** Instead of having the paper's photographer take a decent picture of John for their front page, the paper had used the one that the sheriff had taken after his recapture in May. It was the one with John sitting in a chair with leg irons on and a heavy chain leading to an iron ball on the table beside him. His pant leg had been ripped open so they could dress his leg wound where they had shot him. All in all, not a very flattering picture.

Martha was distressed at the picture. She thought it would give people the wrong impression of John. She was so embarrassed by it that she wanted to get out of the hotel as soon as they could. It would soon be ten o'clock and she couldn't wait to get down to the jail to see if they could get in to see her beloved brother before they hung him.

William looked at his pocket watch, it read 9:15. He showed it to Martha and said, "We need to go," as he got up from his chair. William insisted on paying their breakfast tap, and by 9:20 they were out on the sidewalk headed for the jail.

The reporter from the Missouri Times was standing in front of the jail talking to the sheriff when they got there. "You're just in time," the sheriff said, doffing his hat to Martha.

She nodded, then turning to the reporter she scolded him for using the old picture of John on the front page of yesterday's paper. He told her that that was not his doing, that one of the editors at the newspaper had worked it up, and it was printed before he even knew it existed. He apologized to Martha for the picture, and assured her that he was not going to use a picture for his article today, he was just going to print what John told him.

"We had better go inside and get started," the sheriff said as he opened the door for them.

"Are we going to be allowed to be with him while he gives his story to the reporter?" Martha asked, pointing herself and William.

"Well," the sheriff said, "I asked around to see if anyone objected to you two being in there with him while he talked to the reporter, and I didn't get an answer from anyone, so I'm going to allow it. I thought that surely the Deputy Provost Marshall would object, but I haven't heard a word from him.

"I think he's probably occupied with taking a nap," William said.

"Could be," the sheriff said with a chuckle, "Come on back to his cell", he motioned for them to follow him.

John was sitting on his bunk going over some notes he had written, and he got up quickly when he spotted Martha. "Hi sis," he said, "I'm glad you came."

The sheriff noticed that the only furniture in the cell was one chair and a bunk. "I'll go get some more chairs," he said, disappearing around the corner.

"Let me help," William said, following the sheriff. They were soon back, each carrying a chair, which the sheriff placed in the cell. It was a little crowded in the cell when the three of them were seated facing John, but no one seemed to mind. The reporter opened his notebook and took out a hand full of sharpened pencils. He nodded at John and said, "I'm ready when you are. Just talk normally, but not too fast, and I think I can keep up with you."

John was calm and started out with a statement that rather surprised the reporter. He wasn't used to hearing prisoners speak as well as John, not knowing that John had received a good education at home from his mother, and from the wealth of good books that the Nichols family had in their home library. It seems that everyone from the Confederate army to the Federal court system including their staff at the Gratiot Street Prison, had underestimated John, just from his appearance. But when he began to talk, they soon changed their minds. Such was the case of the newspaper reporter when John opened his story with the following statement.

"I, John S. Nichols, make the following statement of facts in my history for the past two years, the truth of which I solemnly affirm before God in whose presence and at whose bar I am soon to appear, declared guilty by that court which I have been tried and condemned to suffer the severest penalty of the law."

He went on to tell his history, when and where he was born, and the year that they moved to Missouri from Kentucky. Then he fast forwarded to May 18th, 1861, when he enlisted in the Missouri State Guard under General Price. He told of several battles he fought in with General Price's Army, culminating in the Battle of Pea Ridge, March 6-7-8, 1862.

Between the Battle of Pea Ridge and May 14th, 1863 when he was captured by the Federal Army in Morgan County, Missouri, he had spent several months recruiting men for the Confederate Army. He raised three companies of men in that time and served as Captain of Company E (one of the companies he had recruited) under General Thompson until May 4th of 1863, when he left Company E to go back to Missouri to recruit another company. That was when he was captured and eventually taken to Jefferson City for his trial as a bushwhacker.

December 26th, 2012, Sedalia Public Library, 11:45 a.m.

"Wow!" Mary said when Johnny Clayton put his paper down to get the others' reaction. "John Nichols must have been pretty good at getting men to follow him. In a little over a year, he recruited three companies of men for the Confederate Army, and this for a man barely 20 years old."

"From what I read about him," Johnny said, "he was very mature for his age, and with the education he had he was able to get older men to look up to him, and follow him, a rare talent in any time.

"Do you have a description of his hanging, and what happened after that?" Mary asked.

"Yes," Johnny said, from William Bull's diary and Martha's journal, shall I read it?"

"Yes," Jeanie said, "I want to hear more. It looks like Martha's got a boyfriend too, and I want to hear more about this William Bull."

"Me too," Mary said, "he sounds pretty yummy to me, sorry about that Johnny."

"No problem," Johnny said, "I kind of like him too." He continued.

October 30th, 1863, Jefferson City, Missouri, Cole County Jail.

John Nichols finished his statement and look up at the reporter from the Missouri Times,

"What time is it?" he asked.

"It's a quarter to twelve," the sheriff standing behind Martha said, "and you folks will have to leave. It's time for John's last meal."

"Oh," Martha said, placing her hand over her mouth to keep from saying something she shouldn't. She managed to control her emotions, and looking back at the sheriff, said "May I kiss him goodbye?"

"Yes," he said, "but make it quick."

John stood, and the six deputies standing outside of his cell closed in, pistols drawn. The sheriff waved them back, and Martha stood up, put her arms around her brother and kissed him hard on the cheek, "Goodbye John, I'll see you in Heaven," she said.

John kissed her back, "Good bye Martha, I love you," he said.

The sheriff herded the three of them out of the cell and escorted them to the front door of the jail. A chef from a nearby hotel was sitting in the foyer with a tray of food on a table beside him. It smelled delicious to Martha and William as they walked past him to the door. It was John Nichols' last meal.

Chapter 37

They stepped out on the sidewalk into a beautiful fall day. It was ten minutes to noon, and already Madison Street was teeming with people wanting to see the hanging. The scaffold holding the noose was just across the street from the jail, but Martha and William had to elbow their way through the crowd get to where the hearse from the funeral parlor was parked. It was right in front of the scaffold, and the rear door was open showing the coffin that Martha had purchased to ship John's body home in.

The funeral director spotted them coming through the crowd and waved them over. "Here is the coffin as promised," he said, holding out his hand, "that will be $400.00 cash."

Martha nodded to William, who had the money in his coat pocket. He walked over to the hearse and looked the coffin over to make sure it was the one that they had ordered. When he was certain that it was, he counted the money out into the undertaker's hand. He tucked the money into a pocket of the vest he was wearing, grinning from ear to ear. "I'll need some help taking the coffin out of the hearse and setting it down on the street," he said, looking at William, "it will take four men to do the job."

William spotted one of the sheriff's deputies nearby and took him by the sleeve, "Will you lend a hand with the coffin please?" he asked.

With William and the deputy on one side, and the undertaker and his assistant on the other, they managed to lift the bulky coffin down to the street. It weighed almost 200 pounds, and it was magnificent. Martha was well pleased. The undertaker opened the lid and she ran her hand along the satin lining. This would be her brother's final resting place, and tears ran down her cheeks as that thought hit her. William put his arm around her, struggling to keep his own emotions in check.

The undertaker indicated some folding chairs that he had placed in a row beside the hearse. A hand printed sign tied to one of them read "Seating, 5 cents per chair."

"Nobody is going to make money out of this side show," Martha said, as she tore the sign off of the chair and stuffed it into her purse. She and William sat down on two of them to wait until the sheriff brought John over from the jail.

"Hey," the undertaker yelled after a few minutes, "where's my sign?" He ran over and stood in front of Martha and held out his hand, "That will be ten cents please."

Martha and William both jumped up at that demand.

"I tore it off, you mercenary Ogre," Martha said, "get out of my sight before I shoot you."

He looked at William for help, "I've never seen her like this before," William said, "you'd better do what she says."

"Huh," the undertaker sniffed at the angry Martha. When she stood her ground, he cowered back to his hearse to lick his wounds.

Martha and William sat back down and waited. With the sign gone, the other five chairs were soon filled.

The crowd started murmuring when the door to the jail opened and the sheriff walked out. He was followed by two deputies with their guns drawn. Next came John Nichols with his hands tied behind him, his body straight and his chin held high. He was closely followed by two more deputies, also with guns drawn.

The crowd parted to let them pass, and they walked straight to foot of the steps to the gallows. William looked at his pocket watch, it was 12:50 p.m. He leaned over and whispered in Martha's ear, "Ten minutes to one."

Martha nodded and a tear dripped off of her chin as she sat with both hands clutching the purse resting in her lap.

John started up the stairs with the sheriff close behind, hanging on his belt to steady him.

John's hands were still tied behind him, which made it hard for him to climb the steps without falling. One of the deputies followed them to platform at the top of the gallows. The other three deputies went over and stood at the front of the gallows. Obviously, they would be the ones to take John's body down after he was dead. There was also a man in a suit and a stethoscope dangling around his neck.

When William pointed him out to Martha, she asked, "What's that hanging around his neck?"

"I think it's one of those new bi-aural stethoscopes," William said, "it has only been out about ten years."

"What's it for?" she asked.

"To listen to a person's heart," he replied, "the old ones only had one earpiece. That one is much more advanced."

"Will he be the one to pronounce John's death?"

"Yes, I think that's what he's here for," he said.

Martha sniffed and looked in her purse for her hanky.

The hangman and a priest had already climbed up to the platform and were waiting for John to arrive. When John got to the top of the stairs, the sheriff guided him over the trap door that would drop to send John down to the end of the rope. The noose was hanging just over John's head. Martha and William stood to get a better look as the priest said a prayer for John. When he had finished, the hangman placed the noose around John's neck, and the sheriff asked him if he had any last words.

John stood tall with his chin up and a calm look on his face, showing no emotion at all. "I will show them how a Confederate Soldier can die," he said.

"Oh," Martha said, holding her hands over her eyes as the hangman pulled the lever that sprung the trap door. In less than a second, John's body was dangling at the end of the rope, his feet about three feet off of the ground. His legs jerked a little, but he did not utter a sound. The drop had broken his neck, and the noose crushed his wind pipe. He soon died of asphyxiation.

The hangman and the sheriff lowered John's body down to the street where the doctor could listen for a heartbeat. He listened for a couple of minutes, then he stood and nodded to the sheriff's deputies. The funeral director had instructed them the place John's body in the casket at the rear of the hearse, so the three deputies lifted the body, carried it to the end of the hearse and gently placed it in the satin lined casket. The funeral director arranged John's arms over his chest and turned to Martha, who was standing right behind him. "I have just one thing left to do, then I'll turn the body over to you," he said.

"What's that?" she asked.

"We're going to prop the casket up so that the head will be resting on the back of the hearse."

"Why?" the irritated Martha asked.

"So we can take his picture," he said, motioning to the man setting up a camera at the foot of the casket.

Martha flew into a rage, her face reddened and she pushed the funeral director back from the casket. "Oh no you're not!" she said at the top of her voice, "no one is going to take a picture of my dead brother!"

"B-but it was in our agreement when you bought the casket," the astonished man said, "I have a right to take his picture."

"I had no such agreement with you!" Martha said firmly, "there'll be no picture."

"But it's in our contract," the Director said, just as firmly. He motioned to the deputies and his assistant to lift the end of the casket.

Before they could act, Martha ran here hand into her purse and pulled out a small, two shot, 45 caliber Derringer Colt pistol.

This was certainly a side of Martha that William had never seen, and he was taken aback by it.

"You've got a gun!" the funeral director gasped.

"Yes, I have," Martha said calmly, "and I know how to use it, so you had better step back."

"Sheriff," he said, turning to one of the deputies, "are you going to let her intimidate me with a gun? Isn't it illegal?"

The deputy reached for the gun in Martha's hand, but she blocked his hand with her elbow. "It's legal for me to carry a gun in Missouri," she said, "you should be familiar with the gun laws in Missouri."

He blushed as he withdrew his hand, it was apparent that he didn't know the law.

"This gun is legal," she repeated, "and I know how to use it." She turned it again on the funeral director and said "You don't have any agreement with me about taking John's picture, so move your hearse out of the way so I can take his coffin to the train station."

"But-but I," the funeral director stammered.

William intervened, "do what the lady said," he told the man very firmly as he took him by the sleeve and pulled him away. "You'd better get your camera out of the way," Martha said to the surprised photographer, and he immediately began taking his camera down and boxing it up for removal.

A dray wagon came up the street, and Martha heard it passing in front of the hearse. Once again she did something that showed the other side of her personality to William and it surprised him immensely. She walked to the side of the hearse, put two fingers of her right hand into her mouth and emitted a loud, shrill whistle that startled everyone within a block of her.

William's mouth flew open in astonishment, but the whistle had gotten the job done. The drayman heard it above the noise of the crowd and pulled his team to a halt. He looked over and saw Martha waving her hand.

"Are you for hire?" she shouted. He nodded and she motioned for him to follow her.

He wrapped his reins around the brake lever, jumped down to the street, and followed Martha to the casket. When the funeral director saw that Martha meant business, he motioned to his assistant, and they both climbed into the hearse. They left for the funeral home in a hurry.

Pointing to her brother's casket, Martha said, "I want this casket taken to the train station, can you do it?"

"Is it empty?" The drayman asked.

"No," Martha said, "it has my brother's body in it."

The drayman glanced over at the sheriff and his deputies who were standing nearby. He was looking for some guidance in the matter of moving a dead body without the undertaker's permission.

CHAPTER 38

December 26th, 2012, Sedalia Public Library, 12:15 p.m.

"I wondered about that too," Mary Schroeder said, "if it was legal for her to take charge of her brother's body without the undertaker's permission?"

"That was 1863," Johnny Clayton reminded her, "there weren't a lot of laws regarding the handling of dead bodies then like there are now. Things were much simpler then."

"I kind of figured that," Mary said, "but that Martha is something else."

"She sure is," Johnny said, "but if you'll think back, we knew that she was a very good shot with a rifle, and an expert horseman." He glanced up at the clock on the wall. "Hey guys, it's 12:15," he said, "my mother will be waiting lunch on us, let's take a break and go eat some leftover turkey."

They gathered their papers up and headed for the door.

October 30th, 1863, Jefferson City, Mo, 1:25 p.m.

The sheriff nodded, "As far as I know, there's no law against her taking charge of her brother's body."

The drayman backed his wagon up as near to the casket as he could get, and solicited the aid of four of the sheriff's deputies to help William and himself lift the heavy casket into the back of the wagon.

"You got a ride to the station Miss?" the drayman asked Martha.

"No," she said, "may I ride with you?"

"Yes," he replied, and he helped her up onto the passenger side of the wagon seat. He climbed up beside her and took the reins. William jumped up beside the casket, held on to the side of the wagon and rode with them. Very carefully, the drayman got the team moving up Monroe toward Capitol Street.

After Capitol Street, Monroe went downhill for three blocks to the railroad tracks and the train station. Standing in front of the station was a five car train waiting to be loaded so it could make its run to Sedalia. Behind the engine was a baggage car, a dining car and three passenger coaches.

At Martha's instructions, the drayman pulled his wagon in as close as he could to the open door of the baggage car. William jumped off and helped Martha down from her seat. A Railway Express employee came to the open door of the baggage car, and seeing the casket, jumped to the ground and introduced himself.

"Hi," he said to William, "I'm Jeff Kindred, and I'll help you load the casket into the car, we've been expecting you."

"Hi," William said, my name is William Bull, and this is Martha Nichols. She will be escorting her brother home."

"May I see your receipt for the freight on the casket?" Jeff asked. Martha took the receipt from her purse and handed it to him. He looked it over, nodded his head in approval, tore it in half at the perforation and handed Martha her half. "Thank you ma-am," he said, "here's your receipt, you'll need to keep it until you retrieve the casket in Sedalia."

She thanked him and put it in her purse.

Just then, the conductor walked up. He's the man who keeps the train running on time, punches the passenger's tickets, and looks after everything in general.

"Is everything alright?" he asked Jeff

"Everything's in order," he said, "now all we have to do is get the casket into the baggage car, and we can be on our way."

The conductor nodded, and turning to Martha said, "Is this your casket?"

"Yes sir," she said, as she took out her receipt to show him.

He shook his head, "I don't need that," he said, "save it to show to the Railway Express man in Sedalia."

A thought suddenly crossed William's mind, he and Martha had left their bags at the front desk in the hotel, and they hadn't retrieved them.

He turned to the conductor, "When is this train leaving," he asked.

The conductor checked his watch, "In 16 minutes," he said.

William explained his dilemma to the conductor. "I think I can make it to the hotel and back in that time," he said, "but what if I can't make it, Martha will have to leave without her luggage?"

"Then, I guess I'll just have to hold the train up until you get back," the conductor said with a sly smile on his mustachioed face. "Run quickly."

"Can you get us some help to load this casket into the car?" Jeff asked, "It'll take about six men, and there are only two of us here. He pointed to the drayman and himself.

"I think I can," the conductor said, and he walked up the track looking for strong backs to help lift the heavy casket. He soon returned with three switchmen who were working the switches in the rail yard nearby. With the conductor helping, the six of them slid the heavy casket out of the wagon and hoisted it into the baggage car. Turning to Martha, the conductor said, "Ma-am, may I see your ticket?"

Martha retrieved her ticket from her purse and handed it to him. He looked it over, punched a hole in it with the punch he carried with him for that purpose, and handed it back to her.

"Come with me" he said, "and I'll show you to your seat in one of the coaches." He motioned for her to follow him.

"Sir," she said, "I want to ride in the baggage car with the casket," if you don't mind."

The conductor's eyebrows went up as he looked up at the Railway Express man standing in the door of the car. The Express man shrugged his shoulders, "It's alright with me if it's alright with you," he said.

"What will she sit on?" the conductor asked.

"Can't you borrow a chair from the dining car?"

"I suppose I can," the conductor said, peeking into the baggage car to see if a chair would fit between the piles of boxes and the casket, "I'll go get one if you'll help this lady into the car."

"What about my luggage?" Martha asked, "it should be here soon."

The conductor looked up Madison Street and saw William running as fast as he could toward the station while swinging a suitcase in each hand. He paused for a minute until William reached the car where they were standing, panting as hard as he could to recover his breath.

Martha was delighted, not just to get her suitcase back, but to have a chance to invite William to Sedalia to spend Thanksgiving with her and her family. It was only three weeks hence, so she was worried that it wouldn't give him enough time to make arrangements.

William handed Martha her suitcase, and she grabbed his hand, "Please hand this up to the man in the car," she said.

William handed the Express man the bag, and the conductor went looking for a chair. This left Martha alone with him for a couple of minutes. She took one of his hands and looking into his eyes said, "Can you come to my house for Thanksgiving? You don't have to stay long, but we would love to have you for as long as you can spare."

This was what William was wanting to hear from her, so he didn't hesitate, "I think so," he said, "but I'll have to check with my family to see what plans they have made. I will send you a wire to the Sedalia station as soon as I get home and check with Mother. I hate to disappoint her, but I'm sure she'll understand, she likes you very much, you know."

The conductor returned with a chair borrowed from the dining car and handed it up to the Express man who placed it by the casket. Martha gave William a big hug, which surprised him so much that he stood dumbfounded as the conductor led Martha to the steps at the rear of the baggage car, and helped her climb up and seat herself in the chair by John's casket. The Express man jumped down from the car, slammed the sliding door shut, and locked it with a padlock that took a key that was common to all Railway Express agents. The conductor waved at the engineer, who waved back and then pushed the throttle forward. With a big puff of smoke and steam, the engine lurched forward. There was a loud clanging as the moving engine took up what little slack there was in the couplings between the cars, and the train started down the track toward Sedalia. The conductor jumped aboard the last car as it passed and William stood waving goodbye, although he knew that Martha could not see him. Finally, he turned and walked into the station to confirm his ticket to St. Louis on the next east bound train.

Chapter 39

Martha's train rolled to a stop at the Sedalia station. This was as far as the train could go, it was literally the end of the line. Martha got off with the help of the conductor, and spotted

William and James sitting in the Nichols' wagon on the other side on the platform, waiting to take John's body home. She waved, and James jumped down from the seat and ran to meet her while William sat holding the reins to keep the horses still.

She was about to ask them if they had brought any one with them to help load the casket when she spotted Ed's Surry across the street. The Railway Express agent came out of the station and unlocked the baggage car door. Martha ran over to him and pointing to James and

William in the wagon said, "I have three men to help unload the casket, but I think we'll need three more, it's very heavy."

The Express agent smiled, "Do you have your receipt from the Jefferson City agent?" he asked.

Martha produced the pink receipt she had in her purse and handed it to him. He copied a number from it on a pad he had in his pocket, and handed it back.

"Keep this for a while," he said, "just in case there are any problems." He got one of the high wheeled wagons on the platform and pulled it over to the door of the baggage car. Purposely, the bed of the wagon matched the exact height of the baggage car.

"I'll get a couple of men from the station, and if you will get your men ready, we can move the casket from the car onto the wagon, and wheel it over to your dray wagon. I'll be right back," he said as he went into the station.

Martha, still holding her little suitcase and her purse went over to tell her men what to do. Ed had walked over to the Nichols' wagon to wait for instructions and when he saw the bag Martha was carrying, he took it from her, "Let me put this in the surrey where it will be safe," he said, "you'll be riding with me on the way home." By the time Ed got back from the surrey, there were three men waiting for them at the baggage car door. Ed, James and William walked over to the car and introduced themselves. The Express man had them all get up into the baggage car with him and they slid the casket out of the car and onto the wagon. Then they rolled the wagon across the station platform to the dray wagon. It was a struggle, but the six of them managed to lift the casket down from the wagon and slide it into the dray wagon. William closed the tailgate and locked it in place. He and James climbed up on the seat of the wagon, and William picked up the reins.

"We'll see you at home," he said as the horses slowly pulled the wagon away from the platform and into the street.

"We'll be right behind you," Ed yelled, as he and Martha got into the surrey and pulled out into the street to follow the dray wagon for the 12 miles to the Nichols' farm.

It was a slow cumbersome trip to the farm. William didn't want to drive very fast. He wanted the casket to be jostled as little as possible with its precious cargo. The 12 mile trip took two hours, and it was nearly dark by the time the little caravan got to the farm. William parked the wagon beside the house next to the kitchen door, wrapped the reins around the brake handle, and with James, jumped down into the yard.

ED pulled his surrey up next to the wagon and helped Martha down to the ground. He helped her retrieve her suitcase and purse, and turning to William said, "Do you have a tarp big enough to cover the wagon?"

"I think so," he said, "what for?"

"To cover the casket in case of rain."

Sarah was coming out of the kitchen door at that time, and heard the conversation between the two men. "Can't we at least set it on the porch out of the weather?" she asked.

"No, Ed replied, for two reasons. One, it weighs nearly 400 pounds, and it would be very difficult for us to get it up those steps and onto the porch, and two, it needs to be out here in the open tonight where the cold wind can swirl around it to keep John's body as cold as possible. It will also save time in the morning when we get ready to go to the cemetery.

"I see what you mean," Sarah said, walking over to the wagon, "William, go get the tarp," she said in a commanding voice.

William started out to the barn with James right after him. "That tarp is too heavy for just one man," he said, as he fell in step with him.

Martha set her bag and purse on the steps to the kitchen. She walked over to her mother and put her arms around her. "Do you want to view his body, mother?" she asked softly.

Sarah shook her head, "No," she said, "I want to remember him the way he looked when he was alive and here with us."

William and James spread the tarp over the casket, and tied it down to the bed of the wagon, and they all went into the kitchen for the supper that Sarah and 13 year old little Sarah had prepared.

December 26th, 2012, Sedalia Public Library, 1:30 p.m.

After a big lunch at Johnny Clayton's house, the four researchers settled down at their usual table to button up their history of John S. Nichols.

Mary was going through her stack of papers, when she said, "As a woman, I find it heart rending just to think about how hard it must have been for Sarah and her daughter Martha to deal with the death of three members of their immediate family in just three years. Her husband, and now, a second son, I don't think I could have stood up under all that pain."

"You'd be surprised what you can take when the time comes," Johnny said, "but remember, this was at a time when there were no miracle drugs, and the practice of medicine wasn't nearly advanced as it is today. A death in the family was always near at hand."

"I suppose so," Mary said, "but it's still hard to comprehend."

"I know," Johnny said, "and that's why I am so grateful to be living in these times when we can take so many of our advantages for granted. I have a few more pages from Martha's journal that is so connected to our story of John Nichols that I have included it in the manuscript of my book. Would you like to hear them?"

"Oh, yes," Mary said, "I sure would," as she scooted her chair closer to the table, and picked up her pencil.

Johnny looked around the table to see that Brad and Jeanie had done the same, so he started to read from his manuscript.

October 31st, 1863, Hickory Point cemetery near Green Ridge, MO, 10 a.m.

John Nichols' funeral service was short and purposeful. It had been restricted to family only, but family included Ed McNeal and his clan because they were so close to the Nichols'. The Reverend John O'Donnell and his wife were there, of course, because he presided over the brief service. When some of the church's members had asked the reverend what they could do to help, he suggested that they take food to the Nichols' home and leave it. "It would be very nice," he had said, "for them to have food ready when they get home from the service." They had readily agreed.

Reverend O'Donnell read the 23rd Psalm, which was standard with his funerals, said some nice things about John, and the Nichols' family. Then he nodded at Ed O'Neal for him to give the eulogy.

The big man strode to the head of the grave, looked down at the casket and said in his usual strong voice, "John Nichols was like another son to me. I first saw him when he was just a baby in Sarah's arms. He was a good man, he was not the mad-man that the infamous Deputy Provost Marshall in Jefferson City portrayed him to be. He was a good soldier, not the depraved bushwhacker that the Deputy Provost

Marshall said he was. It's the Deputy Provost Marshall who's the mad-man, and it's a pity that he's not the one we're burying today. John was the best horse rider that I've ever known, and the best rifle shot in the entire state. We'll all miss him very much. That's all I'm gonna say," he said as he stepped back and nodded to Reverend O'Donnell.

There was no closing hymn, just a brief prayer for the soul of John Nichols as Ed McNeal, James, William, and George Nichols, plus Ed's two sons, Gabe and Harold, lowered the casket into the grave, and started shoveling dirt into it.

CHAPTER 40

The next three weeks went by swiftly at the Nichols' farm. True to his word, William Bull had sent a telegram to the Sedalia railroad station on Wednesday, November 4th. It was picked up by Ed O'Neal that afternoon during one of his frequent shopping trips to Sedalia. He rode back to the Nichols' farm as fast as his big red stallion could take him, knowing how anxious Martha was to hear from William, and handed the message to her as she was feeding the chickens.

The message read...*Mom & Dad happy for me to spend Thanksgiving with you. I arrive Wed 25, 3:15 train, leave Sat 28. Meet me at station William Bull.* Martha was delighted, she thanked Ed and ran into the house to show her mother. Sarah was happy to have the chance to reciprocate with the

Bulls' for all of the kindnesses they had shown to her, Martha and Ed.

"We must sit down and plan our menu," she said.

Ed, who had followed Martha to the house, was standing in the doorway. "Let me furnish the turkey," he said.

"It will probably take two with the number of people we'll have," she said.

"I'll get two middle sized ones," Ed replied, that would be better than one great big one. They would be tenderer, and wouldn't take as long to cook.

"That would be wonderful," Sarah said, "but I only have one oven, how could we cook both turkeys so they would be ready to eat at the same time."

"That's easy," he said, "I'll bring the oven over from my house, I won't be using it. I'll bring some bricks and build a fire pit to heat it on, and cook one of them out in the yard."

"Do you think that would work?"

"Sure, why not?" he said.

As it turned out, it did work well, and the turkeys were both delicious.

William arrived at the Sedalia train station on the 25th of November, and was met by Ed and Martha in Ed's surrey.

He was in the Nichol's living room being greeted the whole clan by 5:15 that afternoon. After a supper of fried chicken with green beans and baked potatoes, they all adjourned to the living room again, to just visit. At bedtime, William (as he had expected) slept in the bunkroom with Ed and the male members of the Nichol's clan. With the death of Nathan and John, there were two extra bunks, which were just enough.

Ed was in charge of cooking the second turkey, so he was up at 6:00 a.m., building a fire in the pit he had made in the backyard. It was a cold, but sunny day, and he huddled over the oven all morning, adding more wood to the fire as needed to keep it at a constant temperature, coming into the kitchen only to warm up and report on the progress of the turkey.

At 1:05 p.m., the call went out to everyone in the house that dinner was on the table. All of the males with the exception of William, who was sitting with Martha on the couch in the living room, and Ed who was helping Sarah and little Sarah with the dinner, were up in the bunkroom playing cards. Martha had helped with the dinner earlier, but about 11:00 a.m., Sarah shooed her out of the kitchen so she could spend some time with William who was not interested in playing cards, and was sitting in the living room reading a book.

At 1:15 p.m., they were all seated at the dining room table, except the four youngest Nichols children who were seated at the kitchen table. Ed asked the blessing on the food, which could be heard all over the house because of his booming voice, and the eating began. By 1:45 all of the first turkey was gone, and some of the second one. Also, a big pan of candied yams, two bowls of mashed potatoes, a large bowl of giblet gravy, and two bowls of green beans cooked with bacon bits, had all but disappeared.

The men, all except James who was helping Sarah and little Sarah clean up the kitchen, and William, who had gone for a walk with Martha, were in the bunk room upstairs napping. Also, little Mary was in her crib in Martha's room taking a nap.

By 2:00 p.m., the outside temperature had risen to the mid-fifties without much wind, so Martha and William had donned their coats and had gone for a stroll. It was a good chance for them to discuss some things that needed to be talked about.

"Do you love me enough to marry me?" William asked as they turned down the lane to the road leading to Sedalia.

Martha didn't hesitate, she had truly fallen in love with William, "Yes," she said firmly.

William took her by the arm and stopped. She turned to face him and he looked into her eyes.

"I love you so very much, Martha," he said, "that I do want to marry you as soon as it can be arranged."

"How about a June wedding?" she asked, "that's seven months away, would that be time enough for you?"

"I think so," he said, "let's plan on it."

"Okay," she said, as they turned to continue walking.

They discussed children. Both of them had come from large families, so they agreed that they wanted children, perhaps three or four. They decided that the wedding should held in the Nichols' living room, or outdoors, if the weather was nice. Neither wanted a large wedding with lots of guests, just immediate families, plus a few special guests such as Ed O'Neal and any of his family that might want to come. They were both Presbyterians, so religion wasn't a factor in their plans. They would invite the Rev. John O'Donnell to perform the ceremony.

After they had worked out most of the details, they turned and walked back to the house to break the news to Sarah and the rest of the clan, and Ed O'Neal, of course.

Sarah was delighted for Martha. She had had her eye on William, as a possible husband for Martha, ever since she had met him in St. Louis. The phrase, "Martha's getting married," rang out through the Nichols' home, and they all gathered around the couple to offer their congratulations.. Sarah suggested that William come back to visit them, at Easter, so they could put the final touches on their wedding plans.

"We can do most of that tomorrow," Martha suggested, "William doesn't go back home until Saturday."

"I would like to come back for Easter too," William said, "if that's alright with everyone."

They all agreed that that would be a very good idea, so it was set. William would come visit again at Easter.

Martha, Sarah, and William spent most of Friday ironing out as many details of the impending wedding as they could. They worked out the wording for the invitations so William could have them printed in St. Louis and bring them back with him at Easter. There was no local printer that could print wedding invitations, so that was a necessity.

Sarah had managed to save her own wedding dress all these years, but the material was stained and smelled of moth balls. It did fit Martha, however, so Sarah could use it for a pattern to make her a new one. After William went back to St. Louis, she took the dress apart and made a paper pattern from it. From the pattern she calculated the amount of material and other things needed for the job. Martha then wired the amount of yardage and type of material, plus what ribbons and other accessories Sarah needed, to William. He bought the yards and yards of white satin and taffeta, plus satin ribbon and white tulle at a St. Louis store to take with him when he came up at Easter. After Easter, Sarah and Martha could busy themselves cutting out and sewing Martha's wedding gown.

The days flew by at the Nichols farm after Thanksgiving. There were still a few acres of corn that needed picking, there was also some mending of winter coats for Sarah and Martha to do before the weather got real cold, and there were school classes for the younger children to be scheduled so they could keep up with their education. Then there was always the wedding to looming in the background and getting closer by the day.

Christmas was on them before they knew it. There was no time for putting up decorations, but William and James went out into the woods and found a nice fir tree, which they all helped decorate with popcorn strings and red bows made of ribbon left over from last year. To save time and expense the family drew names for presents and Sarah set a limit of ten cents to spend on each present. That would be about $8.00 in today's dollars.

Christmas came on Friday so the Nichols Clan opened their presents at eight that morning, and had their dinner at noon. Then they all went to a Christmas service at their church at six that evening. James had drawn William Bull's name, and then traded it to Martha for little Mary's name. He bought Mary a set of pretty ribbons to wear in her hair, and also made her a nice rag doll out of a one of Wilson's old Rockford socks. Sara had skeins and skeins of yarn that she had used through the years knitting caps and scarfs for the family, and Martha borrowed some of the prettier colors from her. She then sat up nights on the end of her bed and knitted a beautiful scarf for William. It turned out to be a pretty nice Christmas after all. The nicest part was having James home for the holidays. His presence took some of the edge off of having to bury John in October.

Ed came over after his family's Christmas. He was there when the Nichols family got home from church. He had brought some candy for the small children, and since he had drawn James' name, he brought him a brand new pair of fur lined leather gloves. They had been given to him last Christmas, but they were too small for his big hands so he had kept them for just such an occasion as this. Sarah had traded for ED's name, and had knitted him a beautiful scarf with cap to match. Ed had brought his guitar, and they all gathered around him and sang Christmas carols until bedtime.

Yes, it turned out to be a pretty nice Christmas after all.

Chapter 41

December 31st was spent just catching up on chores for the Nichols clan. They were not big on New Year's Eve celebrations, so it was to be a quiet evening and normal bedtime. By half past noon, everyone had eaten lunch and Sarah and Martha were finished cleaning up the kitchen, when Sarah turned to Martha and said, "I'd like to visit John's and Wilson's grave, do you want to go with me?"

"Yes," Martha said, "the sun's shining, and it's not too cold out, I think a buggy ride to the cemetery would be nice."

Martha went outside and saw William coming up from the barn. She walked toward him and when she was within speaking distance said "William, will you hitch the little mare up to the buggy and bring it up to the house? Mother and I want to take a ride over to the cemetery."

He nodded and headed back to the barn. In a few minutes he returned leading feisty little mare, that Martha preferred, hitched to the buggy. Sarah and Martha were waiting, and were soon on their way to the cemetery. The mare William had chosen was prone to run, rather than walk, and that's why Martha preferred her. They were at the cemetery in 10 minutes rather than the 15 minutes that it would normally take. They got down from the buggy, and Martha removed the stub of a stick that was stuck in the hasp to hold the gate closed, and they walked back to the Nichols' grave site. Sarah's husband Wilson's grave was on their left, and her son John's was beside it on their right.

The two of them stood for a few minutes with their hands clasped in front of them, just looking down at the graves. John's grave was only two months old, and there no grass growing over it at this point. Sarah was the first to speak.

"It's so quiet and peaceful here," she said.

Martha took her mother's hand in hers, "Yes," she said, "we must come here more often."

They stood for a moment longer before Martha spoke again, "Don't you still have one of those curses that the old Indian Chief gave you?" she asked.

"Yes, I do," she said, "are you thinking what I'm thinking right now?"

"I'm thinking about how mean that Deputy Provost Marshall in Jefferson City was to condemn John to death as a Bushwhacker, without even checking to see if he was a Confederate soldier."

"Yes," Sarah said, "and the old Chief told me to use the curses to protect us from our enemies.

I keep thinking about how many more young Confederate soldiers he might condemn, and how we might protect them."

"You still have the one curse," Martha reminded her.

Without a word, Sarah dropped Martha's hand, and raised both of her arms above her head.

She looked up at the sky and chanted the three syllables in Cherokee that the old Chief had taught her. Then she lowered her arms so that her open hands were at eye level, palms up. She pronounced the man's name and his rank of Deputy Provost Marshall, and after a pause, said, "December, 31st, 1863 at three in the afternoon. She finished her rite by lowering her hands to her sides, looking down at the two graves in front of her, and chanting three other syllables in Cherokee that the old chief had given her.

Martha opened her coat and looked down at the watch she always kept pinned to her dress.

"That's less than two hours from now," she said.

"Yes," Sarah said, "we must be getting back to the house." She turned and started to the gate.

Martha followed her and closed the gate as they left, jamming the stub back into the hasp to keep it closed. They climbed into the buggy and started home. The little filly ran most of the way home, and they got back to the house by 1:25 p.m. William heard them coming up the lane, and met them at the back door of the kitchen. He held the horse's bridle while Martha and her mother got out, then he led her back to the barn, un-hitched the buggy, and turned her out into the corral with the other mares.

Martha and Sarah hung their coats and bonnets in the big closet off of the kitchen, and started making supper. At 2:30 Martha ran upstairs to check on Mary who was napping in her own little bed in Martha's bedroom.

Sarah heard horses coming up the lane. She parted the curtains and peeked out to see who it might be. She had been expecting Ed for supper. He had spent the day with his family at the O'Neal farm, but always slept in the bunkroom with the Nichols men at night. She was surprised to see two strange men on horseback riding across the yard toward the kitchen door and the hitching rail there. She yelled up the stairs at Martha, but she didn't answer. Just as she was turning around, there was a loud rap on the door.

She went to the door and opened it a few inches to peek out. Seeing the door open, the men shoved their way into the kitchen, almost knocking Sarah down.

"Are you Sarah Nichols?" the tallest of the men demanded.

"I am," she said, "what right do you have forcing your way into my home?"

The tall one was about six feet tall with tufts of black hair sticking out from under his broad brimmed felt hat. His face was scruffy with a short unkempt beard, and squinted dark eyes peered from under the hat brim. Under his denim coat, he had on a plaid shirt and a pair of tan pants that were wrinkled and dirty. The only thing outstanding about him were a pair of fancy silver spurs that stood out against his worn, dirty, leather boots.

The shorter of the two men was hatless and had blond hair and a clean shaven face. He looked to be in his late twenties, much younger than the taller man. His heavy woolen coat had a wide collar which was turned up around his neck and face.

"Did you put a curse on me?" the tall man demanded, punching the index finger of his right hand toward her to emphasize his words.

Sarah stepped back to avoid his finger and glanced over at the kitchen table to make sure Martha's purse was still laying on it. She knew that Martha kept her little two shot Derringer in it, and she might need it. "I don't know, what's your name?" she asked.

"I'm Henry Heimsoth, and this here's Bobby Brownly," he said pointing to the shorter man.

Sarah walked over to the kitchen cabinet and pulled out a drawer. She took a sheet of paper from it and went down the list of names on it with her finger. The last two names on the list were Henry Heimsoth and Robert Brownly.

She turned to the two men and said, "Yes, you're the last two on my list."

The tall man walked over, and before she could avoid it, snatched the paper from her hand, and glanced down the list.

"You bitch," he screamed, those were all friends of mine, and now they're all dead on account of you."

"No!" Sarah said defiantly, "It was because of what you did. Your gang shot my husband in cold blood. Shooting an unarmed man, for no reason, calls for drastic action, don't you think? Especially when one of them is the county sheriff."

The grandfather clock in the hall struck, **Bong**, the man reached for Sarah, she stepped back. It struck again, **Bong**, the man clutched his chest and his knees buckled. Sarah looked at the other man, he was going down to his knees also. The clock struck a third time, **Bong**, both men were on the floor writhing with pain. Suddenly, all was quiet, the men were dead.

Martha came down the stairs holding her Henry rifle at the ready. "I've been watching the proceedings from the stairway," she said, "just in case you needed me."

"I figured that," Sarah said, "when did you notice them?"

"Oh, I saw them ride up the lane," she said. I was checking on Mary to see if she was still asleep, when I heard them coming. I watched them out of my bedroom window, and they didn't look like anyone I knew, so I got my rifle out and tiptoed down the stairs." Martha reached down and picked the list up from where the man had dropped it. She laid it on the table and took a stub of a pencil out of her purse. Carefully, she drew a line through each of the last two names on the list. That's that," she said.

"Yes, that's that," Sarah said.

CHAPTER 42

They heard a team of horses coming up the lane.

"That must be Ed," Sarah said, "he will help us get rid of the men's bodies."

They heard Ed say, "whoa," and the team pulling his surrey stopped at the hitching rack.

They heard his heavy boots hit the wooden steps of the back porch, and soon the back door swung open. Ed was startled to see two dead men lying on the kitchen floor.

What's this all about?" he asked.

Sarah told him what had happened just before he arrived. Ed stooped down and felt for their pulses, and soon stood up shaking his head. "That old Chief sure knew what he was talking about when he said you would need those curses to protect you from your enemies."

"Amen to that," Sarah said.

William heard Ed drive up the lane, and came up from the barn to see if he wanted him to unhitch his team and put the surrey away. He stuck his head in the kitchen door and stopped in his tracks when he saw the two men on the floor. Ed motioned for him to come on into the kitchen, and his mother explained to him what had happened.

"I need you to help me load these bums into the back of the surrey," he said, "so I can take them into town and turn them over to our new sheriff."

"Do you want me to go get James and Charles?" William asked.

"No," Ed replied, "I think you and I can drag them out to the surrey and lift them into the back."

"I can help," Martha said, standing her rifle at the end of the cabinet and walking toward the taller man, Henry Heimsoth, lying on the floor. "William, you take one leg and I'll take the other," she said, "and Ed, if you'll grab him under his arms, I think we can lift him into the surrey."

Doing as Martha suggested, they managed to drag him out the back door and down the steps. It took all of the strength they could muster, but they did get him into the back seat of the surrey. They laid him on his back on the seat with his legs dangling over the end.

Sarah, who had followed them out to the surrey, spied the shiny silver spurs on his boots.

"Wilson made those spurs for him as a gift when he bought one of our horses," she said, pointing to his boots. "I think he forfeited them when his gang killed Wilson. Take them off for me, will you?" she asked looking up at Ed.

Ed unfastened the spurs and handed them to Sarah. "They're yours to keep," he said, "he won't need them any longer."

They had to stuff Robert Brownly's body onto the floorboard of the back seat, but they did get them into the surrey well enough so they wouldn't fall out during the trip to town.

Ed took his watch out and checked the time, it was 3:20 p.m. "It'll be nearly eight when I get back from town," he said, "I'll get a bite of supper at the café."

Sarah put her arms around him, and standing on her tiptoes, kissed him on the cheek. You're always such a big help to me," she said, "I don't know what I'd do without you."

"Oh, you'd manage," he said as he climbed into the driver's seat of the surrey, smiling from ear to ear.

It was 4:30 that afternoon when Ed pulled up in front of the Pettis County Courthouse in his surrey with the two dead men stuffed into the rear seat and on the floorboard. Needless to say, he had attracted a lot of attention from pedestrians along Sedalia's streets on his way to see the sheriff. In fact, his arrival in town had already reached the sheriff's office. A deputy had spotted him as soon as he reached the Sedalia city limits, and had hurried on ahead of him to the courthouse to tell the sheriff what he had seen. They were both waiting for Ed when he pulled up.

The sheriff recognized Ed. "What's this all about?" he asked as the surrey came to a stop in front of him. Ed told him about how these two men had forced their way into the Nichols home, intent on punishing Sarah for the death of 10 members of their gang. The sheriff was familiar with the story of his predecessor heading up the gang that had killed Sarah's husband, Wilson, and about how Sarah had supposedly placed a curse on all of them for their murderous crime.

He turned to his deputy and said, "Go get the undertaker down the street and have him bring his hearse up here pronto. The deputy dashed off down Ohio Street to do the sheriff's bidding, and in about five minutes the hearse pulled in behind Ed's surrey.

Phil McBride, the undertaker, was also the county coroner, and he kept two teams of horses in a barn behind his business. He kept one team hitched up to his hearse/ambulance all of the time in case of emergencies. He jumped down from the hearse's seat, and glancing at the surrey, walked over to the sheriff.

"Where'd the bodies come from?" he asked.

The sheriff introduced him to Ed O'Neal, and between the two of them they managed to fill the coroner in on what had happened.

"Help me get them into my hearse," the coroner said, "I need to get them embalmed before they start to decompose."

The four men had no trouble taking the two bodies out of the surrey and transferring them into the hearse.

"I know those two men," the coroner said, "and they used to run with the sheriff before you in that gang of his, just like you said. They were supposed to be a secret gang of some sort, but everybody in town knew who they were. The big guy is Henry Heimsoth, and the other one is Robert Brownley."

The sheriff was a little suspicious of Ed, so he said to the coroner, "See if you can tell how they died," he said. "I know Ed pretty well, but his story sounds a little fishy. You know, they walk into Sarah's kitchen and both of them drop dead within a minute of each other."

"Haven't you heard about Sarah's curse?" the coroner asked.

"I have," the sheriff said, "but I don't believe in that hocus-pocus stuff. I want you to look them over carefully for any puncture marks, bruises, or any signs of violence. I'm ordering you to do an autopsy on both of them, and pay particular attention to the contents of their stomachs, do you understand me?"

"Is the county gonna pay for the autopsies, embalming, coffins and all of that stuff?" the coroner asked.

"I'll find out who their next of kin are," the sheriff said, "and they will be responsible for all of that."

Ed pointed to his surrey and said, "I'm going home now, if you need me for anything, you know where I live."

"I heard you were living with Sarah Nichols now," the sheriff remarked as Ed got into his surrey.

"I'm sleeping in the bunk room with the boys, if you're inferring that I'm sleeping with Sarah, but I don't know what difference it would make to you, Sheriff, we're both single, and over the age of consent."

"No need to get huffy about it," the sheriff said, "I'd sleep with her too if I had the opportunity, she's a handsome lady."

"Mind your own damn business," an angry Ed said as he drove off.

Ed was still seething at the sheriff when he got home from town. He drove out to the barn, unhitched his team and hung the harness up, and when he walked into the kitchen there was a lighted candle on the table, and a note from Sarah. It read, "Good night and sweet dreams, tell me about your trip in the morning, Sarah.

He smiled and tucked the note into his shirt pocket. He wanted to go upstairs to her bedroom and hug her, but he didn't want to wake her. He went back to the bunkroom, kicked his boots off, hung his clothes on the end of his bunk and went to bed. He was so tired that he was asleep almost as soon as his head hit the pillow.

On Monday, January 4th, 1864, Ed rode into town to check on the two bodies he had left with the sheriff. Out of curiosity, he rode down to the train station and checked with the telegraph operator for any news from Jefferson City.

"There's big news," the operator said, "the Deputy Provost Marshall dropped dead last Thursday of a heart attack."

"Are you sure it was a heart attack?" Ed asked.

"They're pretty sure that's what it was, he hadn't been sick or nothing. It was the last day of the year, and he was hearing another one of them bushwhacker cases. You know, a young feller claimed he was a rebel soldier, and the Provost Marshall said he was a bushwhacker. He was just gittin' ready to sentence him to hang, about three in the afternoon, when he grabbed his chest and fell down dead."

"What are they going to do about the fellow he was trying at the time?"

"They're talkin' about turning him loose, since he'd been tried but not sentenced. Don't look like he'll ever be sentenced now, so the sheriff wants to just turn him loose. I hope he does."

"Me too," Ed replied. He got on his horse and road up to the courthouse. When he cornered the sheriff, he found out that the two bodies had been claimed by next of kin, and were to be buried the next day.

Satisfied that Sarah would be happy to know that she had saved at least one young Confederate soldier's life, he rode home to tell her.

He found her in the dining room with Martha working on wedding plans. When he told her how her curse had saved a young soldier's life, she was ecstatic. She jumped up from the table, gave Ed a big hug, and kissed him on the mouth.

Chapter 43

December 26th, 2012, Sedalia Public Library, 4:45 p.m.

Johnny Clayton looked up at the three students with him at the table where they sat. He put the papers he was reading from aside, and said, "That was all very interesting, don't you think?"

"Yes," Mary Schroeder said, "that should be enough to finish my term paper for my history class. It tells how John Nichols died, and where he's buried, and it also tells how Sarah used her last curse."

"And it will make a good ending for my book," Johnny said.

"Do you believe in all that stuff about the curses?" Brad Compton asked, "I think it's a lot of hooey."

"How else do you explain how all of those men died, and all of them in a three year period?" Johnny asked.

"And what about the Deputy Provost Marshall dying?" Jeanie Crabtree asked, "was that just another coincidence too?"

"All four of us have seen John's ghost, two times," Mary said, "was that a lot of hooey too?"

"I'll tell you what we should do," Johnny said.

"What?" Brad asked.

"I think we should all go out to his grave Saturday night, have a cook-out, and pay our respects to John Nichols one more time before we have to go back to school. What do you think?"

"Great idea," Mary said, "are you guys game?" she turned to Jeanie.

Jeanie nodded, "Okay by me," she said.

Brad nodded his head signifying his approval.

"Great," Johnny said getting up from his chair and pointing at the clock, "it's almost five, and I have to go. I'll get the van lined up for Saturday night, and pick you guys up at Mary's house at six.

By seven p.m. Saturday night, the Clayton van was parked at the Hickory Point Cemetery. Johnny had the grill out, and a charcoal fire was glowing, ready to grill some hamburgers. It was a clear night, but a cold wind was blowing from the northwest, so the four of them were bundled up in their jackets and huddled around the grill to keep warm.

They ate their hamburgers in the van with the motor running and the heater on. Johnny had one of his mother's CDs playing, and everything considered, they were quite comfortable. For desert, Johnny's mother had baked some brownies, and had made a thermos full of hot chocolate to warm them up.

"She's so thoughtful," Mary remarked as they ate brownies and drank the hot chocolate at 11:00 p.m., after stuffing themselves with hamburgers and chips.

"I know," Johnny said, "she has me spoiled according to my father."

Johnny put what was left of the fire out, packed the grill in the van, and they made small talk until Johnny pointed at the electric clock in the dash. It read 11:45. "Our ghost should be arriving soon," he said.

All four of them sat up in their seats and looked out the windows of the van, straining to see the horse and rider arrive. Johnny had the defroster blowing, so the windows were clear.

They sat, hardly breathing, tensely awaiting for their apparition to appear.

At mid-night, there was a soft glowing from the area of his grave, but no ghost. At 12:15 a.m., Johnny spoke up, "Looks like our ghost isn't going to show up," he said.

"I wonder why?" Mary asked.

"I have a theory about that," Johnny said.

"What is it?" she asked.

"I think that all of these years, John Nichols just wanted his side of his story told. He wanted people to know that he was not a bushwhacker, but a Confederate soldier, just doing his duty. History has recorded it the other way around, but now that I have written a term paper telling his side, and I'm working on a book to be published this spring telling the same story, and with your paper, Mary, I think he's satisfied that his story has now been told. His spirit has moved on to better things."

"Sounds good to me," Mary said. She looked around at Brad and Jeanie. They were both nodding their approval.

Johnny put the van in gear, and drove them home.

AUTHOR'S NOTES.

I visited Hickory Point Cemetery back in 2002 when I was doing research for my book. I easily found the graves of Wilson and John S. Nichols. John's gravestone was upright and in good shape. Wilson's gravestone was lying flat on the grave, but was whole and I could read the inscriptions on both of the stones easily. There were a number of other gravestones from the same era, i.e. the 1860s and 1870s that were also in good shape. I went back there on the 25th of March this year and was horrified to see that virtually all of the old tombstones from the 1800s were gone. The few that had survived were broken into small pieces. I couldn't find either the John S. Nichols, or the Wilson Nichols headstones. They were gone completely. I don't know whether, over the past 14 years, through carelessness, the person, or persons who have mowed the grass, have demolished them with their tractors and mowing machines, or if vandals have knocked over the head stones, and purposely demolished them. It is terrible that such a wonderful, old historical, cemetery could be so completely desecrated.

The obverse side of that story is that the old Confederate Cemetery at Higginsville, Missouri, just 55 miles northwest of Hickory Point, has been restored and has been made into a beautiful park. James, John's younger brother, lived out his years at the Confederate barracks which stood near the cemetery, and is buried there in a well-kept grave. The barracks were torn down after the last Confederate soldier living there died, but their church and some other buildings still stand.

My understanding is that the United Daughters of the Confederacy were the group that restored the old cemetery and pay for its upkeep. They even had Nathanial (Nathan) Nichols' body exhumed at Vicksburg and moved to Higginsville where it is buried beside his brother James' body under one large headstone.

It would be nice if The United Daughters of the Confederacy would take an interest in Hickory Point Cemetery, and restore it. It could easily become a tourist attraction for Sedalia and Pettis County. After all, one of their Confederate heroes, John S. Nichols, who fought at the battles of Lexington, Wilson's Creek, and Pea Ridge (also known as Elkhorn Tavern) is buried there. He's the same John S. Nichols who was mistakenly hung as a bushwhacker during that terrible time when Missouri was ruled by General Order Number 10, which was spitefully enforced by Deputy Provost Marshalls.

I couldn't locate where Sarah Nichols is buried, but I'm still looking. Sarah and Wilson Nichols were my maternal great-grand parents, and John S. Nichols was a great uncle of mine. His younger brother, Charles, was my grandfather.

Johnny Clayton and his friends Mary, Brad, and Jeanie, are fictional. They were simply used as a vehicle to carry the story along.

—Wayne Hancock,

Author.